WALRUS TALES

Edited by
Kevin L. Donihe

Eraserhead Press
Portland, OR

ERASERHEAD PRESS
205 NE BRYANT
Portland, OR 97211

WWW. ERASERHEADPRESS.COM

ISBN:1-936383-54-3

TABLE OF CONTENTS

WALRUS TALES

INTRODUCTION

Welcome to *Walrus Tales*—the only anthology of walrusian fiction on the planet. Herein, find tales of all stripes: horrific, satiric, comedic, tragic, erotic and a bunch of other "-ic" and "non-ic" words, like "Lovecraftian" and "Bizarro."

Why devote an entire anthology to walruses? Perhaps I admire their large ivory tusks and wish I had a set of my own. Perhaps I sense something vaguely mystical about them and wonder if they're privy to ancient secrets. Perhaps a walrus saved my grandfather from drowning off the coast of Greenland. In the end, it doesn't matter. *Walrus Tales* is here, so stop asking questions and let it into your soul. Let it fill the pinniped-shaped void for walrus-centric fiction you never knew you had.

NOTE: Some stories use the word "walri" rather than "walruses." While I'm aware that the plural of "walrus" is "walruses," I prefer the latter, as it sounds more distinctive, clannish even. And, really, shouldn't it be "walri?" (*Octopus/octopi. Cactus/cacti.*) Also, I want to mention that I too have written a walrus tale, but it's not in this book. If you want to read it, you'll have to pick up a copy of *Space Walrus.*

But I'm digressing when I should fly off and let you start filling that aforementioned void...

—Kevin L. Donihe, Editor
June 27, 2012

THE ILLUMIWALRI
Greg Beatty

This manuscript is a construct, but it is not, I believe, a falsehood. The distinction between these two terms is essential to understanding The Illumiwalri, *and perhaps to the salvation of the human race.*

A falsehood is just that, false, something that is not true. If I were to write "My head does not throb," that would be a falsehood.

A construct is something else: it is constructed, but out of materials that are really there, and in this case, not just convincing but shocking. This manuscript is a construct.

The shock was not in the first discovery. Many walrus tusks have been cut, carved, adorned, or used as a canvas for scrimshaw. These renderings are usually pictorial, but some pictures are signed, especially since the Inuit culture has been pervaded with external concepts like that of individual ownership of art. Therefore, a tusk completely covered with written script is rare, but not unprecedented. What is so new, and, again, so shocking, is first that the script is hitherto unknown. It was not English, Cyrillic, or any variation on these most likely alphabets; the characters were independent of any known system, but were eventually shown to be a syllabic language. So, the script itself was unexpected, and remained untranslated until the second tusk was found.

Finding the first tusk buried deep in the Arctic ice was the second untoward element; it was not part of any regional culture to drive tusks into the frozen surface of the world. It is simply too hard to do so without shattering them, and too hard to retrieve them, if and when. It was finding the second tusk—in the Northern Territory of Australia, approximately 75 miles from Alice Springs—that provided the greatest early shock. What was a walrus tusk doing so far inland? And what was it doing covered with an unknown script? It was at first taken for an element of Aboriginal dream time, a marker of the song lines followed by local visionaries, and close to a decade passed before bloggers concerned with the esoteric matched images of the script.

This was soon followed by an anonymously posted image of a third tusk spiraled with script, and a map of the site in Africa where it had been found, and left by suspicious poachers, then by a fourth, and a fifth, and so on.

Each of the tusks was found some great distance from one another. Each was buried deep in the local firmament: ice, tundra, earth, rock, etc. The burial sites formed a pattern, though the final shape of that pattern was the subject of great debate until the tusks were clearly dated. Once the order of composition was determined, great circles could be traced from one to the next, until the final shape was conclusively determined as a great if irregular star. This was confirmed when the shape was used to locate the penultimate tusk, which had heretofore gone undiscovered in the concrete and asphalt of Manhattan. (Regarding the ultimate tusk, more below.)

Once a sufficient number of tusks was discovered, deciphering what became known as the Walrus Codex proceeded apace; the project flamed the imaginations of scholars around the world, and indeed, as a linguist who is also an ideological narratologist (ask the CIA, or rather, don't, as they will not answer), I can speak directly to the passion of those early days.

Those days are past. While the script yielded readily to analysis, an academic civil war erupted over the meaning of the resulting text. All publication on the topic was forbidden, and the many references to the topic were expunged from the blogosphere. (Feel free to check; Google and Blogger both cooperate with traditional authorities in times of genuine need.)

For a time, I abided by this decision, keeping the results of my long study secret, even maintaining silence during my stay at the hospital. However, given the recent developments in Kobe, in my own health, and at the site of the final tusk, I must break silence and share this manuscript with the world. You will see what we must do. I must believe that.

I have arranged the contents of the tusks in chronological order, but have identified what sections of the manuscript came from what tusk, so that future scholars may check my work, if there are any future scholars. The translation itself was a shared endeavor, but the composition of this construct is my own. It is an attempt to capture the sense and cadences of a collective story, a myth, if you will.

I.

Once upon a time, the fight was fair, and the pinnipeds were happy. Oh yes, humans killed walri, hurling spears through the frosty air to thunk, quivering, into their sides, then slicing them open for their meat, their fat, their hide and their tusks whenever they could, and when they did, walri mourned, thrashed to and fro upon the cold, cold ice and plotted a black revenge that involved hot blood and crushed humans.

But a leading bull walrus weighs as much as 20 ringed seals (*2000 pounds—ed.*), and wields great tusks that are as long as a human's forelimb. Walri are fast upon the ice and fast in the water, where humans are slow, and so the walri fared well against human hunters. A few walri died—the slow, the old, the weak and the flatulent *(There was much debate over this term. Some insisted on a more extended translation: those that disperse noxious gasses—ed.)*—and a lot of humans died.

Those that remained on both sides were stronger, and everyone ate well. The humans immortalized walri on their tusks, carving artwork into them, and the walri sung and danced their private dances of the few brave human intruders who passed. It was a deadly rivalry, but a balanced one.

II.

It was a lethal rivalry, but a fair one. Then things changed. At first, the pinnipeds thought the change might be for the better. The new humans who came close to them showed no understanding of how well a walrus could move, and so even though their boats were larger, and driven by wind rather than paddle, more humans died.

However, if the ship was not capsized quickly enough, a fierce noise like an ice floe cracking might be heard, and a walrus would die, without spear, without sign and without potential to reach his attacker. What's worse, it was no longer the weak who were killed.

III.

Sadly, it was no longer the inferior who were dispatched. In earlier clashes, those who could not fight or flee were the most vulnerable, because their incapacities left flanks exposed to spearflight.

In the new wars, things were different. The high and majestic bulls rose above the herd, and were therefore most visible to the new humans. They were the greatest targets for the guns of the cowards. It was the great who died, time and time again.

What is more, the great were not treated with song-filled respect, as the pinnipeds treat brave humans, and as true humans treat the pinnipeds defeated. They were treated as products. This was a great insult, for justice and dignity are great matters among the walri.

IV.

Justice and dignity are great matters among the walri. Justice and dignity are great matters among the walri. Justice and dignity are great matters among the walri. Justice and dignity are great matters among the walri. (*This too was disputed. Other tusks echoed one another; this repeated, twisting down the length of a small and malformed tusk. Ed.*) Justice and dignity are great matters among the walri, so something must be done to create balance.

V.

When something must be judged fair or not fair, the pinnipeds have an advantage over all the mammals of the sea. A walrus loves the sun and the flat, and knows the ice. A walrus loves to dive deep, and knows the water. What's most important, a true walrus floats.

Humans lack hollow places in their hearts. Humans have only their own solidity. This means they know not justice.

Walri have hollow places in their hearts. This means walri can draw in air and float, suspended between air and water, on the level of the ice but not on it, able to see, sing, and resonate with all, but not snared or snagged by any of it. Pinnipeds can float and sing, so pinnipeds know justice better.

VI.

Floating, singing, but clumsy upon dry land, the walri decided to bring justice to those who lacked it, to bring justice to humans. It took many walri, positioned around the dry places, to sing a new justice into being. The flatulent sang a song of simple poison. (*Here again we see the reason for the dispute over a term; what culture gives special titles to the gassy?—ed.*) The cows argued for simple revenge; the cows always want to defend the herd.

The bulls—the few bulls remaining—positioned themselves equidistant from all singers, and floated until a harmony emerged from these dissonant songs. The bulls decided to bring men into the herd of justice—but to show them what treating the worthy as product did to all involved.

VII.

(*The site that should have housed the seventh tusk was Bikini Atoll. Only a few radioactive shards remained.*)

VIII.

And so the plan was implemented. Resonant with small swimmers, their chest cavities full of justice to share, the great bulls swam to the place where the waters swirl, to the place where cold waters run to the magnetic, to the place where all humans fear to go, even in loud boats, to the place that is never still, where even pinnipeds fear. (*A rough map of the sea floor fills much of the remainder of this tusk, suggesting that this contingent of walri found their way to the British Isles. My minority contention, based upon the internal evidence contained in these descriptive passages, is that the walri found their way to the Corryvreckan, the infamous whirlpool off the coast of Western Scotland.*)

There the great bulls lost their balance and lost control of their limbs, surrendering to the whirling waters until they were torn apart, and the rising waters deposited their corpses on the grassy land, far from the mourning herd. In dying, they sowed the seeds for justice.

IX.

The death of the starred bulls sparked justice, for as their great brains lay upon the grass, they were eaten. They were eaten not by fish, but by the winged and the furred and the horned of the land. This last were their targets, for the walrus wanted to be eaten by herd beasts—by beasts that were in fact food products for the human. These starred bulls gave up their flesh to the cow, that there might be justice.

X.

Bobbing off the coast of England, bobbing off the coast of Japan, bobbing off the coast of America, the walri wait. Bobbing, pinnipeds sing no longer, but instead listen for the sounds of justice being restored.

Two things destroyed the fatal balance between man and walri: guns, which allowed humans to kill at distance, and the attitude which treated walri as product, not worthy partner in the bobbing dance of life. The walri waited for both to dissolve as their stars moved through the land. (*Some scholars insist the mark rendered here as "stars" should be read as "seeds"—ed.*)

XI.

Bobbing walri wait for their stars to move through the cattle, and they do. Cattle, though not graceful as walri, had heretofore walked steadily to the field and from the field, to the barn and from the barn, to the knacker and their deaths.

Now, though, their hoofs betrayed them. No longer was the land stable beneath their feet, but rather, they walked like walri upon the land. Their legs became as flippers, and the grass like ice. They flailed and stumbled, and rose, and flailed and stumbled again, frothing and biting, unable to control their limbs. And great hollows opened in their brains, hollows that resonate to a song heretofore unheard.

XII.

Flailing, but listening, the cattle died. And the humans ate them, as humans eat all. And time passes, as time eats all. In time, the humans began to hear a song heretofore unheard resonating in the star-shaped hollows of their brains. Some humans ran mad, ran into the sea, mistaking madness for the call of the waves.

They ran without their guns, and the walri rejoiceth.

Some humans grew wan and still. They did not think of using their guns, except upon themselves, and they regretted treating cattle as product, though they did not sing of walri. They did not even think of walri.

Other humans began to slip and stumble. Their movements were sudden and random, like walri shot from a distance. Their hands became like flippers and they could no longer use their guns. The humans looked upon their tainted meats, and they knew fear.

The humans knew fear, and the walri knew justice. And the walri sang of that which was to come, the new world of balance and fairness.

XIII.

There is no thirteenth tusk. There is only a hole in the ground where the tusk is to be. It makes my hands hurt and my head tremble, or rather, my head hurt and my hands tremble, when I think of the implications of this tale constructed from these tusks, and when I think ahead to what may come next. Am I wrong to find this mythic tale resonant with the symptoms of mad cow disease? And if I am wrong, why did the UN have all mention of The Illumiwalri expunged from human records? And if I'm wrong, why does my head hurt so, and what is that distant song I hear echoing in its hollow places? Is it the distant song of the walrus, calling for justice?

WE ARE ALL TOGETHER
Bentley Little

I first heard about The Walrus after Kate's death. Like the others, she'd been slaughtered, gutted and left for dead. Unlike the others, she was not a hooker but a waitress over at Monty's steakhouse in Tempe.

And I'd been dating her.

It wasn't anything hot and heavy, and, truth be told, whatever we had was probably on its last legs anyway. But her murder shook me to the core, and when I got a call from her brother Kevin, telling me what had happened, I actually had to sit down. Time was when such news would barely have fazed me. But ever since I'd been back in Phoenix, I seemed to have gone soft. I wasn't sure why that was, but I didn't like it, and I knew there'd come a time when it would start to affect my work. So far, I'd taken things easy. My clients had been husbands worried that their wives were cheating, wives worried that their husbands were cheating, parents looking for runaway kids, shit like that. I'd stayed away from the hard stuff.

But that was about to change.

I was going to find out who'd killed Kate.

It wasn't that I didn't trust the cops. Hell, with Armstrong gone, I'd even gotten to like a few of them. But police were creatures of habit, always imposing patterns where none existed, and I knew they'd automatically mark Kate down as a pro and not take her death as seriously as they should. She'd be number four in a series, no more, no less.

I couldn't let that happen.

I owed her that much.

So I went with her brother to the morgue and took a look at the body, feeling sick to my stomach as I saw her lying nude on the slab, skin peeled from her chin and neck, a hole ripped into her empty chest cavity, twin gashes splitting apart the flesh of each leg. Kevin, next to me, started crying. "That's Kate," he confirmed through his sobs. "That's my sister." There was very little blood, I noticed, and although ordinarily that would not have set off any alarm bells—bodies were always cleaned up before being shown to family members—I'd read that not only had all of the recent victims lost a lot of blood but that their bodies had been scrubbed prior to being dumped.

I didn't want to bring it up in front of Kate's brother, but I had a chance to get the coroner alone while Kevin was putting his signature to something, and the man told me that, yes, her body had lost an impossible amount of blood and had come in unusually unsoiled. I asked if he had any theories as to how or why it had happened, but either he didn't or he was unwilling to share with a civilian.

On the way home, Kevin, still distraught but angry now as well, asked me to find out who had killed his sister. He didn't trust the cops and he and the rest of the family *needed* to know who had done this. Anticipating rejection, he said he was willing to pay my going rate, no discounts, but I wanted to work this my own way, without anyone looking over my shoulder, so I lied and told him that I'd already made some calls and the police were close to nabbing the psycho who'd murdered Kate and the others. He seemed relieved, and though I probably should have felt guilty for deceiving him, I didn't.

The minute he dropped me off, I got to work.

It was Rudolfo who clued me in about The Walrus. I'd gone to him first, just to get the lay of the land, and he said word on the street was that The Walrus was getting into the Phoenix flesh trade, looking not just to join the fray but to take it over, all of it, and he was making a statement with these killings, letting everyone know that he was playing for keeps and that if anyone got in his way the consequences would be swift and certain.

"Who is this 'Walrus?'" I asked.

"I forgot. You been gone awhile."

"Awhile," I agreed.

"He come in about three or four year ago. No one know nothing about him, but all of a sudden he is there. Everyone start talking about him. Everyone *afraid* of him. One of the Gringo's men disappear? Everyone say it's The Walrus. Litvac's street taken away right under his nose? The Walrus. He have his hand in everything but no one know how it happen. Now he stepping it up."

"Kate wasn't a working girl," I said.

Rudolfo shrugged. "Sometime The Walrus make mistake. But he not apologize. Ever."

In my mind, I saw Kate as she'd looked on the table. It was the last image I had of her and the only one that would remain. Someone had to pay for that.

"Where's his base?" I asked. "Where's he operate out of?"

Rudolfo shook his head to indicate that he didn't know, but the expression on his face was one of fear, not ignorance, and that shook me. I'd never known Rudolfo to be afraid of anything.

I switched gears. "You know anyone who can tell me more?"

"No one going to talk about The Walrus." He lowered his voice. "People who talk about The Walrus disappear."

"But you're talking to me."

His face clouded over. "Not no more."

I left Rudolfo with a Jackson. He declined at first, but times were tough for everyone, and it didn't take much to change his tune. On my way back, I tried to think of someone who might have more information. *And* who'd be willing to talk. Rudolfo was about the toughest hombre I knew, and if *he* was taking the fifth I doubted there were many others who'd spill. Especially to me. As Rudolfo said, I'd been gone awhile.

At the end of the block was a junkyard, and as I sat in my car at the crosswalk and waited for an old lady to hobble across the intersection, I glanced over to my right. Next to me, leaning against the inside of the rusted iron fence that surrounded the junkyard, was a lifesized statue of a fat happy bum wearing a frayed black coat, one of the figures that had stood outside Hobo Joe's coffee shops in the 1970s. The blissful hobo had a slightly stoned look on his face, and that reminded me of someone.

I suddenly had an idea.

I decided to talk to Teddy Boy Phillips.

Teddy Boy lived in a duplex in the bad part of town, behind the blackened remains of a meth lab that had blown up sometime in the 1990s and had never been rebuilt. Before he'd lost his sight, before his ex-wife had fired the bullet into his head that had severed his optic nerve, Teddy Boy had been the go-to guy for off-the-record info for both police and private detectives. A former cop who'd turned in his two-week notice with a hard right to the captain's jaw, he'd made a subsistence living on the buying and selling of information, which drove the captain crazy because his own men were Teddy Boy's biggest customers. He was still more plugged

in to the street than anyone I knew, and he owed me a favor that
I'd never cashed in, something I was hoping he'd remember.

He did.

He'd lost weight since the 'nineties and no longer resembled Hobo
Joe, but the change was not a positive one. He wasn't one of those
guys who looked good thin. His formerly ruddy cheeks were gaunt
and sallow, his sparse hair was gray, and even someone who didn't
know him would say he looked sick. *Cancer* was my first thought
when I looked at him, but I kept the diagnosis to myself and didn't
pry. I told him about Kate, repeated what Rudolfo had told me and
asked him what he knew about The Walrus.

Teddy Boy was facing my direction, and though his eyes had no
sight and remained hidden behind dark glasses, I would have sworn
he was looking at me. "The Walrus," he repeated. "That's not a name
that's spoken aloud too often."

"Well, I'm speaking it."

"He's a bad dude."

"So I've heard."

"You don't want to tangle with him."

"Tell me what you know," I prompted.

The Walrus, he said, had built up quite an operation in the last few
years, forcing the Dominicans out of drug distribution, even frightening
away the Russians—who did not scare easily. The part of the Family
that remained in Arizona was now working for him.

"Why do they call him The Walrus?" I asked.

"No one knows." Teddy Boy leaned forward, dark shades focused
on me as though he could still see. "But the rumor is that he's a *walrus.*"

I frowned. "I don't understand," I said. "You mean a walrus like...
the animal?"

Teddy Boy nodded, and I could see the fear on his face. "Jimmy
G. told me that he and Tonto saw him once and that he was giving
orders from some sort of stage. They were there delivering a message,
and they said his men were all bowing down before him, like he was a
god. He was huge, they said, eight feet long and a thousand pounds, at
least. He had enormous tusks."

"But that doesn't make any sense."

"No. But that doesn't mean it isn't true."

He was right. I knew that better than anyone.

"He was talking English?"

"Yeah."

"So where was this?"

"Somewhere off Southern, although Jimmy G. had the impression that the place was temporary, not his real base." Teddy Boy paused. "Jimmy G. disappeared after he told me this. I mean *disappeared.* I don't know if he was silenced or if he lit out for another state, but there's been no trace of him anywhere for over a year, and that's pretty damn hard to do. I don't know who or what this Walrus really is, but my suggestion for you is to drop this right now, tell no one we had this conversation and get on with your life."

I thanked him for his suggestion, though I had no intention of following it. The best idea, I'd already decided, was to stake out an area where the working girls walked. They might know more than they were telling the cops, or there might be rumors floating around I could pick up on. I could even end up catching something as it went down. Leaving Teddy Boy, I grabbed a slice at a pizza place where mine was the only white face for miles and where the crowd was so rough that the Stones song I played on the jukebox sounded like Donny fucking Osmond.

In the old days, the pros used to walk Van Buren, but redevelopment over the past two decades had driven them out, and now there was no specific street or neighborhood in which they consistently plied their trade. But I made a few phone calls and talked to a few cops who told me that south Central after dark was still a good bet. That was also where two of the victims had been found. Kate had been killed in Tempe, near the university, and Rhonda DuPar, the first woman, had been dumped in an alley behind a Circle K in Sunnyslope. But the other two had been discovered off Central, and if this sicko's thing was hookers, South Phoenix was apparently the place to be.

By the time I finished eating, it was already night. All of the killings had occurred between nine and midnight, according to the coroner, so I still had some time, and I drove around, scoping out the area until I found a series of streetcorners along a mile stretch that all seemed to be occupied. It's a funny thing: the ones who worked the street were always the skankiest—fat, ugly, dumb—and it was an irony of the business that men would pay to have sex with women they'd turn down for a date. I parked my car in the empty lot of a condemned produce market, made sure the doors were all locked, then went out to the sidewalk, where I stood next to an overturned bus stop.

From the nearest corner, a seriously overweight black woman shoved into a sparkly red halter top and short-shorts two sizes too small came strolling over alongside a skinny white chick with crooked buck teeth and severe acne that covered not just her face but her exposed shoulders. They were both vying for my attention, but before they could start their spiel, I told them I was a private detective staking out—

"Fuck you!" the fat one yelled angrily, and both of them turned away before I could explain that I was after the person who'd been killing and gutting women on the street.

I didn't have any better luck with the others I approached, and several blocks down, after my fourth go-round, I decided to just hang out, watch and wait.

There was an old Sonic drive-thru that had been renamed "Son's" and whose half-lit sign featured a stick-figure Jesus fish. A Christian burger joint, I assumed. I ordered a large black coffee from the lone Korean guy manning the window and sat down at one of the cracked plastic tables under the awning where car hops had once brought food to waiting customers. I could see four hookers from here, and the area was dark and empty enough that it was conceivable something could go down.

From the shadows, a man walked up wearing a ratty suit jacket over mismatched shirt and pants. He was holding an old worn Bible, and the eyes above his stubbled cheeks and runny nose were focused and far too intense. On the lapel of his jacket was a brightly colored pin: a yellow cross within a red sun. I hadn't seen one of those since the 1980s, but I recognized it instantly. It was from Jacob's Ministry, a low-rent self-help church that had, until its founder's arrest for tax evasion, catered to alcoholics and drug users. The pins signified that their wearer had been sober for a specified period of time. I had no idea whether Jacob's Ministry was still around, but I had no problem believing that the burnout in front of me had substance abuse problems.

I turned away, sipped my coffee.

"I know who is killing those harlots," the man said to me.

I turned slowly back. How could he know that I was here investigating those murders? Maybe he'd talked to one of the girls, I thought. I decided to say nothing, let him go on.

"It is the will of the Lord." His eyes burned feverishly into mine. *"He* has sanctioned their removal."

"I doubt that," I said.

"What know you of the Apostle Paul?" the man asked.

"Not much," I admitted.

"He is here," the man whispered, and there was reverence in his voice, reverence and also fear.

"Here on earth?" I said, not understanding. My biblical scholarship was more than a bit rusty.

"Here in Phoenix," the man said. "He is clearing the way for The Return, wiping out the unrighteous, cleansing the world of those who are unworthy in His eyes."

"Okay," I said. I stood, starting to move away, but the guy followed me.

"The Apostle Paul, formerly Saul, was a persecutor of Christians converted by Christ on the road to Damascus. He traveled throughout the known world, preaching the gospel and establishing churches. There are those who thought he died. But he did not die. He continued on. And now he is here, preparing the way."

"Thanks for the lecture," I told him. "But I think it's time for you to push off now." I started walking back down the cracked sidewalk toward the parking lot where I left my car.

"He knows you!" the man called after me. "He knows you!"

Two Mexican whores, one with a missing tooth, laughed at me as I passed by them, and I figured they were the ones who'd sicced the loony on me.

I got home sometime after two, frustrated and tired, and crashed.

In my dream, Kate was alive, and we were eating at Monty's, and the other waitresses were gathered around our table singing "Happy Birthday." I awoke feeling sad and empty. I spent a long time in the shower, letting hot water hit my inexplicably aching back, then made some coffee, turned on the TV and watched the local morning news, afraid I'd hear about the murder of another woman. But the only fatality of the previous night had been a drunk driver in an accident on Black Canyon Highway, and for that I was grateful.

I was trying to decide whether to toast the two pieces of crust in my refrigerator for breakfast or whether to eat the last half of a Subway sandwich from a couple days back when there was a knock at my door. I went to answer it. Two men were standing outside my apartment, two shabbily dressed men with unshaven faces—wearing pins featuring a yellow cross within a red sun. I barely had time to register surprise when the taller one said, "You're coming with us." He held a gun in his hand.

The guy was shaky and inexperienced, a punk ass, and I could have easily taken the weapon from him, but I wanted to see where this would lead. Playing pansy, I said nothing but closed and locked my door and went out sandwiched between them to a waiting car, a black Nissan that I knew neither of these twitchers owned.

The short guy drove, and Punk Ass sat in the back with me, keeping the gun trained on my midsection. They were obviously working for The Walrus, and I wondered how they'd found me. I thought of Rudolfo's and Teddy Boy's warnings, and realized that I hadn't taken The Walrus as seriously as I should have. I believed he'd killed Kate and those other women, but I hadn't bought into the whole omniscient thing that had spooked Rudolfo and Teddy Boy and probably most of Phoenix's criminal underclass.

I would have to be on my toes here.

The car headed downtown. I stared out the window. Something that crazy guy last night had said reminded me of Teddy Boy's story, though I couldn't immediately connect the two. It had been nagging me ever since, but I hadn't been able to put my finger on it. Still couldn't.

We hit the buildings, headed south.

"Where're we going?" I asked.

"To see *Him*," Punk Ass said, and there was a reverence in his voice that made me think of the way that religious loon had referred to his "Apostle Paul." I thought of something Jimmy G. had told Teddy Boy, that The Walrus' men had been worshipping him like a god. I didn't like where this was going.

In the old days, Jacob's Ministry had been based in a storefront on skid row, and it was still there, though the windows had been fortified with wrought iron over the blacked-out glass.

No graffiti marked the door, walls or sidewalk, and in this neighborhood that spoke volumes.

"We're here," the driver said, pulling to a stop in front of the building, and Punk Ass added, *"He's* waiting for you."

The driver got out and came around to open the back door. The second I emerged from the car, I kicked him hard in the crotch, then wheeled around and punched Punk Ass' throat with my fist. He went down, dropping his gun, and I grabbed it, slamming the butt against the head of the driver, who was already starting to get up. He went down again, and I quickly made sure they were both out of commission before turning to face the unblemished white door of Jacob's Ministry.

I felt nervous. The Walrus was in there, with his men, or his followers—

like a god

—and I was all alone with nothing to protect me other than a gun that might or might not work. The smart thing for me to do would be to leave immediately and inform the police. But I thought of Kate's body lying open and empty on that table in the morgue, and I checked the gun's magazine to make sure there was ammunition.

There was.

I let myself in.

I was in a small, darkened room, an antechamber. Beyond, through another doorway, was a bigger room, more well-lit, and I moved slightly to my left in order to see a wider view of it.

Most storefront ministries were little more than meeting rooms, with folding chairs and Formica floors. But this looked like a church, and Jimmy G.'s description had been on the money. There was indeed a raised stage in front of the rows of wooden-benched pews. On the side of the stage was the man I'd met last night, the one who'd told me about the Apostle Paul. He'd been crucified, and his naked bloody body hung impaled from a cross next to those of two other men I did not recognize.

At the front of the stage sat The Walrus.

He was indeed an animal, and he was gigantic. Twice, maybe three times the size of a man. He was fat and sated with blood, his huge rolls of blubber waterfalling down to the wooden floor of the stage. From where I stood, I saw no eyes in the brown folds of the face, but I did see the whiskers and the tusks bright with crimson. A massive flipper was holding down the remains of a man? A woman? I couldn't tell, but it had been a person and The Walrus had been feasting on it. Bones were scattered about him, bloody ribs and skulls with hair still affixed to the scalps. The remains of other people, other meals.

His worshippers were bent before him, dozens of them, and though many looked like derelicts, I saw a few well-dressed men amidst the crowd, a couple of others wearing gang colors. There were no females, I noticed, and I remembered from somewhere that women had not been allowed to join the early Christian church.

"Bring to me the woman," The Walrus intoned, and his voice,

though deep and gravelly, was recognizably human. There was, in it, an offhanded arrogance, a sense that it was used to being obeyed.

The Walrus was Paul.

It was a teasing line from the song *Glass Onion*, John Lennon making fun of all those Beatle freaks who read import into every image on every album cover and who thought the Fab Four were leaving them secret clues that Paul McCartney was dead. But in this case it was true. The Walrus *was* the Apostle Paul, and my mind began running through the words to *I Am the Walrus*.

I am he as you are he...

A chill passed through me, and I suddenly wondered if The Walrus had spent the 1960s in London.

No. It was a coincidence. It had to be. But it was still creepy as hell, and I ducked back into the darkness, flattening myself against the wall, trying to think.

How had this happened?

He had changed from Saul to Paul to The Walrus, and though that last metamorphosis had happened over a period of some two thousand years, it was still incredible and made no logical sense. This guy was one of the authors of The Bible, for Christ's sake. To Catholics, he was a saint. How could he have ended up the head of a criminal organization in Phoenix, Arizona?

Who knew? Who the hell cared? Things happened. That was the way of the world. If there was one thing I'd learned after all these years, it was to just roll with it. Whatever it was.

I moved forward again, so I could see. A sacrifice had been brought forth, a young woman who stood on the stage while a tough-looking character used a knife to cut off her t-shirt, her shorts, her underpants. He backed away, moved off the stage. The woman stood there naked, wobbling slightly. She seemed dazed, drugged.

Before I could do anything, before I even knew what was happening, The Walrus had lurched forward, his massive tusks rending the woman's body, sinking deep into her flesh and tearing open her abdomen. She fell to the boards, screaming for the few seconds she remained alive. Blood was everywhere, and The Walrus began lapping it up with a thick disgusting tongue that made me think of a pinkish gray boa constrictor.

He had what he wanted, and he looked up angrily, bloody flesh clinging to the stained ivory of his tusks. "Get out!" he thundered.

As though this was the expected end of a well-rehearsed ritual or the formal conclusion of a church service, the rows of worshippers stood. My muscles tensed, and I raised the pistol, intending to back out of the building, hoping I wouldn't have to shoot anyone, hoping no one would shoot me. But as the first row started to leave, I saw that The Walrus' followers were not heading back toward my direction but were exiting through another door to the side of the seats. Of course. There was no room for all of their cars on the street. Their vehicles were in a parking lot in the back. I breathed a sigh of relief but did not lower the gun until the last of them had left and I could hear the sounds of engines starting up.

I remained in the darkness of the vestibule for several more minutes, until the engine sounds were gone and everything was quiet.

Quiet.

Except for the sickening slurping sound of The Walrus eating the woman.

There were two half-consumed humans on the stage next to him now, and he was grunting to himself with pleasure. Still in the darkness, I moved slowly forward until I was standing in the doorway between the two rooms. The Walrus did not see me. He was obviously full, but greed could not keep him from licking up the fresh blood around the dead woman's open midsection.

I thought for a moment, then walked into the main room of the ministry, gun extended.

The Walrus looked at me. "You," he said.

I didn't know what that meant. I didn't know if he was clairvoyant and had seen this in a vision, or if he had simply been expecting my presence because he had sent those two jokers out to bring me in. I didn't care. I just kept walking forward, up the main aisle toward him, gun hand in front of me.

He watched me, saying nothing.

Did he like what he had become? I wondered. I didn't think so. It looked to me as though he wanted someone to put him out of his misery. He had lived for this long and Jesus had not returned for him, God had not called him home, and he sat there in this abandoned ministry, a bloated animal, bloodthirsty and mad.

"You killed a friend of mine," I said, and my voice sounded louder than I'd intended.

He did not answer, licked blood off his whiskers, grunted.

"She wasn't a hooker, she was a waitress."

I reached the edge of the stage and moved to the right, away from the center, climbing up the raised platform next to the crucified man who had told me of the Apostle Paul. The Walrus shifted his enormous weight to face me, but he said nothing, did not try to talk to me, did not try to get away, did not try to attack me, did not call for help. I strode forward, looking into the animal's eyes, trying to see in there any sign of humanity.

There was none.

"Her name was Kate," I said.

And shot a bullet into his brain.

He'd been alive for so long that I was afraid he was immortal, afraid that he could not be killed. But the great bulk sagged and fell forward, and I emptied the rest of the bullets into the back of his scarred brown head, and then he was dead.

I stood there for a moment. I half-expected The Walrus' minions to come barreling back in from the doorway through which they'd exited, but no one returned, and I put the gun in the waistband of my pants, pulled my shirt over it, hopped off the stage and walked up the aisle the way I'd come. I strode through the vestibule and outside, where the two men I'd knocked out remained unmoving on the sidewalk.

From down the street came the peeling bells of St. Catherine's cathedral, marking the hour. I started walking in that direction, and a few minutes later I reached the church. It wasn't Sunday, was Wednesday, but there were probably people in there. I had just finished killing one of their saints, and his grotesque body lay dead and cooling less than a block and a half away. I should have felt bad about it, but I didn't, and as I looked up at the sky, at twin jets speeding southeast over the city toward Williams Air Force Base, I knew I'd done the right thing.

I realized I was hungry, and I kept walking, past the church, past a thrift store, past a massage parlor, to a dingy diner, where I ordered a cup of coffee, scrambled eggs, hash browns, sausage and a side of toast.

Afterward, I used a pay phone to call Kate's brother.

I told him the story as he drove me home.

NIGHT OF THE LONG TUSK
Paul A. Toth

MONDAY

He stumbles towards the water and sees, as his mind registers it, *chunk.*
Chunk of something big, something good to eat. The world's biggest
clam. His mother watches. Always watching, that one. But for once,
she lets him go all the way to the water's edge. His brain feels warm at
the thought. The whole world warms over. The world is clam. Life
will be easy. Cold but easy. Still, he has to kill the thing somehow.
Then, he will be anointed. They will lift him by their tusks, a net of
ivory. Never will he walk again, forever lofted above the herds, king
of the walri. Let him be blessed. He is blessed. Let his reign last a
thousand years. It will. It shall. They will strip the skin from the recently
dead and wrap him in coats one hundred miles thick. With each new
coat, his body will extend until it embraces the entire planet.

Except that when he bends to attack the chunk/clam, spearing it,
his left tusk plunges so fast and deep that he cannot extract himself,
nor can he lift his new appendage. He writhes in frustration, attempting
to beat the ground with the block, but it will not crack open. His mother
runs towards him in the first gear of all her biological care, but she
cannot yell for him to stop except for that grunt which he has not yet
learned to interpret. Before she arrives, he manages to lift the ice half
an inch into the air. When he drops it, his tusk breaks in two. His
mother stops running.

It is at that moment his paranoia plants its first flag. Soon, it will
extend its empire over the whole of my friend's mind.

Six months now I've been in Greenland. Perhaps one day a
university will finance my research. Until then, my father can foot the
bill. It will give him a place besides my ass to put that foot. But such
memories only help me understand my friend's predicament all the
more, for now his mother gazes with embarrassment at what from a
distance must look like her son's bizarre new mustache, cut in two by ice.

TUESDAY

Morning. He is still at the site of the incident. His mother keeps her distance. Suddenly, she is the mother of a one-tusk walrus, and she makes no effort to conceal her disappointment. Perhaps if she had simply lent a fin, or curled up beside him, his fate might have been different. Instead, he already seems to have spiraled into self-doubt. He toys with the tusk, occasionally nipping at it. Now it is not a tusk but a broken sword. The blame, he must by now realize, could be placed on his maker, himself, his mother, the ice, the world, anything and everything. This is paranoia at work, drawing him into infinite suspicion.

At noon, he manages to find a few clams, but the food falls out of his mouth before he manages to ingest it. Then, he gums the tusk and leans backward, as if trying to reattach it. The tusk instead falls into his mouth. He tries to wail, but he emits no sound. There is only choke and gurgle until he finally somehow forces the tusk out of his throat. Then he looks back towards his mother and tries to grunt, but now he cannot even make the choking sound. He has silenced himself. His paranoia wins another victory. He is unlikely to mate now, since no female will hear his silent call. In less than 24 hours, he has rendered himself useless to males and females alike.

I start to move towards him, hoping I can somehow offer comfort. Then I realize it is better to let him rest. I have a new theory in thinking about all of this: What if a walrus—or any other animal, for that matter—found itself bereft of all its evolutionary assets. Might it not, in desperation, creep towards consciousness? With nothing better to do, and mental illness threatening in its ghostly fashion, would not such an animal—such a walrus—begin to consider its problem? Yes, it would begin to ponder solutions. It might even philosophize, or at least rhapsodize about the past it had lost and the future it would never experience. Yes, it seems all too reasonable. But no one wants to know about such matters. Why else would I have to perform this research without the slightest assistance?

But it's late, and the fire makes shapes on the tent that resemble letters of the alphabet, which when exhausted I interpret as words. I am not hallucinating. But there are messages.

WEDNESDAY

The little bugger has taught himself well and has regained appetite for the clams he traps. It is clear he now understands I am watching him. Occasionally he looks over at my shelter. He has not yet ventured near. He has become adaptively antisocial. He has no choice, since the others now completely exclude him. They won't even run and play near him, and his mother is spending more and more time in the water, looking for someone new with whom to copulate. Right in front of her son, I might mention. I make no judgments. But still.

Sometimes my friend watches the birds crisscross the sky. He flaps his fins. But he is a grounded bomber in a sky of ultralights.

Meanwhile, the symbols are coming clearer, and, although I cannot read the entire text, they seem to be forming a walrus alphabet. I am making notations about the various grunts I hear. My friend has not regained his voice, but he has achieved a kind of raspy whisper. I fall asleep with a new language forming its rules and regulations in my mind. Such structure is unavoidable but necessary. I try to remember that.

THURSDAY

Today he wanders right up to my shelter. I have not yet learned to speak his language, but he whispers to me. I write down the words, however unintelligible. He may well be schizophrenic, but I believe, whether human or animal, a schizophrenic's words can be interpreted. It's just that the language is so individual. I make a note to one day invent a deciphering machine. I shall invent the software that will form the brain of this machine. This time, I will be the one imposing rules and regulations. By sifting through the various permutations of schizophrenic speech, my machine will regurgitate plain-spoken English. There can be little doubt my father will be impressed, at last, by this remarkable achievement.

FRIDAY

For the first time, we speak. Earlier, he crept inside my shelter and sat beside my feet. For a long time, we just looked at each other.

Then he whispers hello, and I say hello to him. It is a poetic moment, if I, a scientist, can pretend to know about such lofty sentiments. "Here we are," we seem to both say, "just the two of us."

He falls asleep at my side. I try to stay awake in case he has anything to say while dreaming, but the added warmth he imparts makes me sleepy, too. Work will have to wait.

SATURDAY

This morning we progressed so quickly that we now speak of astronomy and geology. We look wistfully at the Big Dipper and wish to take a warm drink from its bowl. My friend indicates he would like some coffee, but I unfortunately cannot tolerate caffeine. We make the best of our situation but both agree there must be more than that to this life. Still, we are becoming a little more realistic, and I suppose in that way he helps me as much as I help him. How could I have thought that he was schizophrenic? He is the sanest creature I know, and under his sway I find all doubt about myself eradicated.

Later, we drag in several carcasses. I remove the skin and make for my friend a cloak. I find his broken tusk and set the scepter at his feet. There will be much slaughtering in the days to follow. We require lebenstraum, and it is time for outsiders to go.

THE RHINOCEROS AND THE WALRUS
Dave Fischer

Distractedly tapping my water glass with my fork, I wonder again if I'm wasting the afternoon trying to meet my mysterious source.

"Oh yes," I have to remind myself with a grin. "Free lunch even if he doesn't show. Thank you, business account."

As a journalist for a relatively large left-of-center newspaper in a major metropolitan area, I am frequently bombarded by offers of top-secret earth-shattering revelations of one insane variety or another. Sometimes the stories never even materialize; other times I am inundated by words but not by meaning. Most of the time I get a story that is at least self-consistent. That's a polite way of describing it.

Insane conspiracy theories seem to cluster around just about every person, place and historic period known to man. It's a surprise to see a theory in an entirely new genre. Which explains why I'm waiting for the kook-of-the-day to meet me here for lunch at a little secluded cafe.

"Ionesco revealed too much when he wrote *Rhinoceros!*" the voice had informed me over the crackling phone line. "That's why he had to be killed in '68!" The voice rose to a crescendo.

The idea of someone actually thinking that there was some kind of government cover-up involving Ionesco's absurdist play *Rhinoceros* was a new one to me. The fact that Ionesco had simply not died in 1968 actually made me more interested for some reason.

Your typical conspiracy theorist grovels over the puzzle pieces that he has decided go together, and he will eventually find an incredibly clean and elegant scenario that ties up all the loose ends. It won't have much connection to the real world, but all of the facts he has chosen to use will fit perfectly.That's why the Ionesco thing intrigues me. I've never met a conspiracy theorist that would propose such a fundamentally flawed theory.

I notice him a block away even though he hadn't given me a description. The trench coat and wide-brimmed hat are clichés of kookdom, but it's his body language that really screams "paranoid schizophrenic." I don't understand how someone can do something as simple as walk down the street, and make it seem so uncomfortable.

He recognizes me as quickly as I did him and rushes over to sit at my table. He thanks me repeatedly for coming here to meet him and begins the standard ramble about how everything will be okay now, once I expose the evil-doers to the bright light of day.

"So...you think Ionesco revealed important information about some major conspiracy when he wrote *Rhinoceros?*"

"He spoke in code, of course!"

Of course.

"The play isn't really about the rhinoceros! It's about the walrus!"

Eh?

"The Walrus? Is that the code name for some Pentagon project or something?"

"No, no! Walrus! The arctic marine mammal!"

Eh?

"And the walrus, rather than the rhinoceros is...in....umm. The rhinoceroses in the Ionesco play are...well, people turn into rhinoceroses. What does that have to do with the walrus?"

"My God, can't you see!?! Can't you see what's happening all around you!?! Could Ionesco's warning have been any more clear!?!"

"Well...perhaps..."

Suddenly, his look of scorn flickers for an instant into suspicion, then blazes into sheer terror as he reels back, knocking over his chair and stumbling into the street.

"You're one of them! You're one of them! Noooooooooo!"

His scream of protest ends abruptly as he turns to run and finds himself being ground under the wheel of a speeding tractor-trailer.

"He probably would have thought that was deliberate. Nutjob," I mutter to myself as I remove my mask and absent-mindedly pick at my tusk with a toothpick.

Guess I'm not getting a story today. I hope the sandwich I ordered is less disappointing.

MEET THE TUSKERSONS
James Chambers

Someone once said show business is about second chances, but that's a lot of nonsense. Just ask Ernie McCabe. Remember him? That wiry, bobble-headed comedian from years back, had that corny catchphrase, "I got a million of 'em." Laughed like a St. Bernard with the flu. Second-rate stand up until he hit it big with that routine about the cheerleaders in the chewing gum factory. That's what landed him his top gig ever, starring on that old television show. Used to be on Thursday nights, and they did that Christmas special their first season. The one with the walrus family that lived in a Los Angeles bungalow: the Tuskersons.

Remember? Those happy, whiskered faces were everywhere back then. You could have been living in a cave at the bottom of the ocean with a metal box bolted on your head, and you still would have known about the Tuskersons.

Kids from coast to coast wore Tuskersons pajamas, played with Tuskersons action figures, and used Tuskersons breakfast bowls to eat Tuskersons breakfast cereal (corn pops mixed with walrus-shaped marshmallows). You could buy Tuskersons wrapping paper, greeting cards, and party favors; Tuskersons iron-ons and Underoos; Tuskersons three-wheelers (with plastic brake levers that let you spin out and handlebars that looked like tusks); Tuskersons Colorforms and Tuskersons coloring books; Tuskersons pens, folders, and notebooks; Tuskersons lunch boxes (with a Thermos!); and of course, Tuskersons board games. The Tuskersons even hit the recording studio for a few albums of pop songs and Christmas standards. If they could slap a picture of a walrus on it, they made it into Tuskersons merchandise.

No doubt about it, those Tuskersons were a talented bunch of sea mammals, and everyone loved them.

You remember, now, right?

Then you must remember Ernie McCabe. He played the Tuskersons' madcap next-door neighbor, that guy always popping in uninvited, looking for Mr. Tuskerson's advice. McCabe worshipped the wisdom of the walri on everything from romance to stock tips, but in the end he always wound up right back where he started. Like that episode when Mr. Tuskerson told him he should serenade his dream girl, the cute local librarian he'd only admired from afar. So, the whole show, while the Tuskersons are carrying on like the Cleavers (only they're 600, 800 pounds apiece, all with whiskers and a healthy hankering for sushi before it was fashionable), McCabe is running around, sheet music flying in his wake as he ducks in and out of the back door and practices his "do, re, mi"s and his "mi,mi,mi"s, while plucking at the nape of his throat. Then at the end of the show, he gets down on one knee, lets out the shrillest, most hair-curling yodeling since Slim Whitman, only to discover that his designated sweetheart is stone deaf.

That was Ernie McCabe, all right, in more ways than one.

Ask Ernie about show business and second chances, he'll tell you what it's all about and none of it has much to do with redemption, not unless your self-resurrection can raise the dead presidents, too. Because it all comes down to cold hard cash and big fat bank accounts. Satisfy their greed and they'll beat a path to your doorstep. But comebacks don't come easy and they don't come to folks who have already spent the whole of their talent and creativity. They don't come to worn-out comedians with new jokes that sound like old jokes the first time they're told.

Like the old saying goes, "Comedy is hard, death is easy," and Ernie McCabe wasn't much of a survivor.

That time when he could placate the network gods of avarice passed much too fast. A few more years on top and he might have been set for life. But it all turned sour one day and then the only knock that came on Ernie's door was the county sheriff there to escort his sorry bankrupt soul out of a lovely seaside house that had become the property of a faceless bank. Ernie took his clothes and whatever else he could stuff into his Mercedes and left the rest behind. He didn't need the furniture and the decorations; he didn't want them.

They reminded him too much of Rita.

His faithless ex-wife wasn't a complex girl, but she had three things going for her: her looks, her sense of humor, and her razor-sharp instinct for self-preservation. Number one made sure she was never alone. Number three kept her comfortable in the style in which she had established herself when she was a punk kid (she preferred "ingénue," of course) straight out of some backwater, Midwest cow-town hell-bent on making her way in the City of Angels. Number two persuaded most people to forgive her for one and three.

Ernie never did, though.

He understood her, sure. He'd known from the day they met what kind of girl she was, but still he never forgave her for abandoning him. Three months after they cancelled Ernie's big show, the afternoon he came home from his fourth failed pitch for a new series, Rita kissed him hard on the lips, said goodbye, and then drove off in her Jaguar, her bags packed in back.

If she had only stayed a little longer, Ernie often told himself, his luck might have turned. If Rita had been there to love and support him through that first desperate year, he might just have found the inspiration he needed to land on his feet, but instead he sank, deep and fast, into obscurity, and in Tinseltown that meant he ceased to exist.

So, how do I know so much about some washed-up has-been like Ernie McCabe? Well, I'm the last person who saw Ernie alive the night before he disappeared forever from the real world and not just Hollywood.

"I loved them big, goofy walruses," said Ernie McCabe. "How could I not? They were like giant, wet teddy bears. Working with them day and night, training them to pull off the gags, watching them learn—it was great! Those guys had some sharp timing, let me tell you. Natural comedians. Hit a beat like Gene Krupa. They weren't just dumb animals. They understood! Not the whole television thing, no way, but they knew they were part of something, and once they saw where you were going they met you halfway. They loved it when the crew laughed, because then they knew they had done good, and, of course, then they got to chow down on a few fish. Best straight men I ever worked with. Cute as ribbons when they poured on the charm.

"So, yeah, I didn't mind sharing the limelight with the Tuskersons. Technically, I was the star of the show—that's what it said in the credits, that's what it said in my contract. My name was the only one that came up before the title. But the Tuskersons made people feel good. They made *me* feel good. Best damn years of my life working on that show. Only time I ever truly *loved* what I was doing.

"Who knew walruses could be so affectionate, so friendly, so *funny?*

"There was this one bit of business, let me tell you, this one routine, see, where Mr. Tuskerson and I snuck off to go fishing on the sly from Mrs. Tuskerson and the kids. So we're out on this dock on a lake, both of us decked out in fishing vests and caps pegged with lures, and I'm hauling around the poles and tackle. So, the gag is that when I put one foot in the rowboat, Mr. Tuskerson knocks the mooring rope loose and next thing you know I'm making like a cheerleader—doing a split and flapping my arms. Mr. Tuskerson is supposed to knock off his fishing hat, dive into the water, and push the boat back. Except—except it turns out a school of fish is going by and he swims off after them, leaving me hanging until—splash!—into the drink."

Ernie chuckled at the memory, and when his laughter faded to a dry crackle, he sipped some water from the glass beside his chair to soothe his tired voice. He straightened his shirt collar, primped his thinning hair, and winked broadly at the camera opposite him. "I look okay? Huh? You fellows be honest. I know it's been a few years, and I don't want to look like a slob for this. You sure you got film in that thing? It's awful small. What? All digital these days? Well, that's okay, I suppose, as long as the next word isn't 'exam,' heh-heh, right? Right.

"So, we figured we'd shoot the scene all the way through a few times and edit the best takes together later. SOB, right? Standard order of business. Know what happened? Soon as we run through the first part, Mr. Tuskerson sees me flapping my arms as the boat drifts loose, and he knocks his cap off and dives in right on cue, but he doesn't come up!

"Stays down a good thirty seconds, while my thighs are getting homesick for each other, and then—surprise! He's back! And remember all of this is unrehearsed. This is a *walrus* ad libbing! Well, Tuskerson jumps out of the water right beneath me, and I take one look at those pointy tusks of his heading for my own private Idaho and you can guess what kind of look flashed across my face. But Mr. Tuskerson—he comes up soft as a pillow, lifts and balances me until he can nudge me back onto the dock. Then he swims out and pushes the boat back.

"Heh-heh, yeah, there you go," said Ernie. "Still good for a laugh today. Left me howling on the dock, the crew cracking up all over the place, and Mr. Tuskerson backstroking through the water like a champ who'd won the title in three rounds. The director loved it. Said we never could have staged something like that, so they wrapped it, rescripted the dubbing, and voila, a classic television moment was born.

"Oh, yeah," said McCabe. "Yeah, I got a million of 'em."

This wasn't too long ago.

I wandered into that little corner place down the block on a rainy Monday night. A high-class dive that place was, but I knew it would be warm and quiet but not empty and depressing, and that was what I needed. I'd been struggling all day with an article for one of the trade rags, trying to mold an interview with Miss Vapidity 2004 who had somehow convinced a bunch of producers that she was movie star material (and having seen those collagen-enhanced lips of hers, I could just guess how she'd pulled off that neat trick), and I had gotten tired of banging my head against the keyboard trying to make this woman sound fully brain functional.

So I sipped a whiskey, soaked in the gentle buzz of the place, and let the frustration melt away. The bartender, Tuba (and don't ask about the name because it is not a pretty tale), liked to keep the televisions mounted at either end of the bar on mute. That suited me fine. I watched images flicker by and made up dialogue that was, no question, far more entertaining than the real words. And the heat of the whiskey, the mellow mood of the bar, and its dusky atmosphere were working. I had just about figured out how to make next year's rehab-bound celebrity crash-and-burn case (no one was born as marvelously dense as this young lady; she had to be abusing some serious chemicals to achieve that) sound like a philosopher naïf when the door slammed open and in walked this big-headed, gangly guy.

"Oh, no," Tuba growled the moment he saw him. "You heard me last time, funny guy. You know the rules. Now get your butt out of my bar before I get physical with you."

"Sheesh," said the skinny man. "Keep your shirt on, Tuba, and your pants, too, while you're at it, and do us all a favor. Here. Look what I got. Okay?"

The thin guy raised a crumpled fifty over his head and snapped it tight between his hands. Tuba squinted hard like he thought it might be funny money, held the glare for a long few seconds, then went back to washing glasses.

"Keep it where I can see it," he said.

"Sure, sure. Got a million of 'em," the man said under his breath. "Don't I wish."

I knew right then who it was, but the years had not been kind to Ernie McCabe. The truth is that they had been brutal. Picture Father Time as a mob of baseball bat-wielding punks in steel-toed boots working out their "issues" on Ernie McCabe in a dark alley and that'll get you halfway there. And he kind of smelled, too. He didn't stink. He wasn't dirty, but the air around him had a strange tang to it, kind of like very old, dry paper.

But his voice—man, it was still clear and full as ever, and that's what gave him away. That voice rocketed me back twenty-five years and all of a sudden I was a little kid in *Star Wars* pajamas sitting Indian-style in front of the television, laughing hard and listening to my parents laugh behind me, waiting for that famous line that, as clichéd as it was, somehow delivered the weight of all humor when Ernie McCabe said it just so.

"Got a million of 'em," I said. "I can't believe it—you're Ernie McCabe!"

Ernie raised an eyebrow and scrutinized me. "Huh, a fan," he said. "Well, I ain't who you think I am, so you just go on abusing your liver and leave me the heck alone, chucklehead."

He took a seat at the opposite end of the bar, putting his back to me so he could see the television. He dropped his fifty on the bar and waited for Tuba.

"Hey, put that money away, Mr. McCabe," I said, walking down next to him. "I'd like to buy you a drink."

He turned halfway around, made a "shoo-shoo" gesture with his hand, and gave me a loud, wet raspberry.

"No, really, I remember your show and you were great," I told him. "How often does a guy get a chance to buy a round for his childhood idol?"

McCabe twisted back around. "Idol?" he asked.

Now I'll admit that I was a big fan of Ernie's when I was a kid, but he never really had been my idol. That honor went to baseball players and writers, but I wanted to get his attention—it surprised me how badly I wanted it, how eager I was to talk awhile with old Ernie McCabe. Why? Partly for the novelty of it, I suppose, and partly because it let me put off tackling "little miss reality-challenged and her inarticulate road show" for just a while longer, but mainly because I sensed that there might be a story in Ernie McCabe, one too good to pass up.

"Who are you?" Ernie asked me, his brow knit with suspicion.

I introduced myself, leaving out that I was a writer, and told him to put his money back in his pocket. This time he shrugged and did it, so I called Tuba, and when the burly man had filled our drink orders I parked myself on the bar stool beside Ernie's.

"You really mean what you said?" he asked. "You idolized me when you were a kid?"

"Sure," I said. "Watched your show every week. My whole family looked forward to it. Great stuff. Funny stuff. Not like all this 'ultra-hip' sex stuff they show nowadays, all that melodramatic soap opera crap, and those whining comedians who just bitch and moan. Your show had class, Mr. McCabe. It had style. It had a heart."

Ernie nodded, taken aback by my sincerity, but I could see doubts still lingered. "Yeah, right, I'll bet you don't even remember the name of the show, smart guy."

My mouth hinged open; I drew a blank.

It was one of those rare but insurmountable failures of the recall system.

I knew the title of Ernie's show. It was on the tip of my tongue, but somehow I just couldn't bring it past my lips. I had watched that show every week, even the Christmas special, listened to the records, badgered my parents into buying most of the junk that went with it. The theme music, the sets, even the first names of each of the Tuskersons—all that was clear in my memory—but I just could not summon the exact name, and I could see in Ernie's eyes that I was losing him.

That's when I was saved by television: On the silent screen above the bar, a new program rolled, one of those entertainment insider nostalgia shows that dish up all the stale, behind-the-scenes gossip on popular old programs. It just happened that tonight's episode was about Ernie's old series, and with the corner of my eye I caught the bright-colored title logo from the opening sequence playing in a window above the narrator's right shoulder.

I leaned toward Ernie and said, "*Meet the Tuskersons.*"

Ernie's face beamed. "Yeah, that was it all right. Wow, you really do remember."

I pointed at the television. "Look, it's on right now."

Ernie bounced around in his seat, glanced at the screen then lunged across the bar and shouted for Tuba. "Turn it up!" he cried. "C'mon, Tuba, buddy, please, turn it up, pal, okay? I really need to see this. Been waiting three months! I came in tonight just to watch it. C'mon and do a guy a favor, will ya? This is important!"

Tuba shrugged and obliged, more to shut Ernie up than to accommodate him, I'm sure, but he aimed the remote, and then the narrator's baritone voice filled the bar and familiar theme music that I hadn't heard in years played in the background.

"...also starring Ernie McCabe, this oddball family of five captured the hearts of America for three seasons on *Meet the Tuskersons*. Tonight on *Hollywood Back Lots*, the behind-the-scenes story of how five wacky walri and one funny man turned a short-lived sitcom into an American legend."

The narrator faded out as the show cut to commercial.

"Oh, boy, this is it," Ernie said. "Finally! Ernie McCabe is going to be back on the map, baby!"

Ernie squirmed on his barstool and propped himself up in line with the television. He sipped his drink once and then seemed to forget it was there. His eyes stayed glued to the set, his lips twitched with impatience at the commercials, and when the show returned, an eager smile sprawled across his weathered face.

"So, right around the middle of the second season, we knew we had something special. We barely squeaked by for renewal after our first season, but now our audience was going up 20 percent every week. We were doing the best work of our careers then—me, the directors, the writers, even the Tuskersons. It was fabulous. It was unexpected. And people loved it!

"I was feeling so good, I popped the question to Rita at our favorite restaurant, and faster than she could say 'Yes' we were on our way to Vegas for one of the happiest nights of my life. We even hit the jackpot on a one-arm bandit on our way out of the Chapel of Eternal Union. That was a night to remember, let me tell you."

Ernie's excitement faded. He settled back into his chair, and a serious look swept his face as he drifted loose among his memories.

"Of course, it couldn't have lasted. I should have known all along, should have been ready for it, you know? But, hey, some shows go on for years and years, right? Look at *M*A*S*H* or *Leave it to Beaver.* Those aired for more than a decade, and I figured, why not us? Still can't say exactly why we were canceled in our third season, and just ten shows shy of a syndication package, too. I couldn't figure it out, then, and I don't understand it, now, but I know this: once we were on top, things got ugly. Maybe that was the reason. People just got too greedy, forgot that our jobs were to make people laugh, not figure out new ways to screw another buck out of everyone else.

"I've never been very good with money, but I had dedication back then. I'd have done anything to keep our little show going. I ran ragged doing promotional appearances, putting in sixteen-hour shooting days, doing interviews, rehearsals, guest-shots, you name it, I did it. But I didn't mind! It was everything I had ever wanted from my career. And when I wasn't working I took care of Rita, took her out on the town shopping and went for weekend getaways. It was hard work to keep up with a young woman like Rita, but I held my own.

"And I never fell back on drugs to help me, like the rest of them did. They were everywhere, too, but I never touched them. Hardly even drank during the shooting season. Made me look Amish compared to everyone else. Coke, heroin, pot, booze, you name it, someone was taking it, and usually on the set. Hell, after a while, the producers were practically giving the stuff away like candy to keep people working without raises, but I always steered clear. I liked to keep my mind sharp for the show.

"It got worse toward the end of the season. One of the production assistants and a cameraman died in a car crash, both of them high as kites. Then the producers had a falling out that nobody could understand. Rumor was a woman came between them, but not one of their wives. They stopped talking to each other for more than a month. One day they trashed each other's cars in the parking lot—scratched them up, smashed the windshields. Crazy, crazy stuff. And then they fired our top director and two of our best writers when they pressed for better deals in mid-season.

"It wasn't fun and games, anymore, but it was still good. I was doing what I did best: being funny! I was living the dream that had kept me going through a couple of decades of stand-up, working the clubs and variety shows. All that stuff going on around me? It just didn't seem important, at least, not until Rita got into it, too. See, once I was famous, we could walk into any place in town and get a tab e without waiting. People came up to us looking for everything from an autograph to a loan to a part on the show. I was flattered. I tried to be nice, but Rita could be a real snob sometimes, really nasty. And I knew she was out there doing stuff I didn't like while I was working, doing stuff she shouldn't have been doing with people she shouldn't have been doing it with.

"Let me tell you, I never had any illusions about that girl, but, well, sometimes you have faith in a person even when you know you shouldn't, and you hope maybe they'll do a little better by you than they do by everyone else.

"That's the real joke, isn't it? Hope?

"Yeah, I guess it is, but no one's laughing."

McCabe paused for a moment as he gathered his thoughts.

"That's when I started hiding out on the set and spending time with the Tuskersons. The producers had built them a custom habitat

next to the studio. It's still there today. Heard they converted it into a
monkey house when that chimp craze hit, but back when the Tuskersons
lived there, their manager, Corinna Dobbs, used to let me in whenever
I wanted. Dobbs told me the walruses loved me like one of their own,
but then Dobbs could charm the skin off a snake, so I didn't pay much
attention. Still, I liked hanging out there, and a lot of nights, me and
Dobbs sat on the rocks while the Tuskersons swam around their pool
or basked under their sun lamps.

"And the Tuskersons were the same at home as they were on the
set: relaxed, playful, friendly. I felt good being around them, and Dobbs
loved all my old material. Made me go through it over and over again,
and laughed every time. Real laughter, not just going along with me. I
mean, I must have done cheerleaders in the chewing gum factory thirty
times for that gal, but every time she slapped her knee like she was
hearing it new all over again.

"I missed that in those days. There were millions of people cracking
up at home every week when I came on the tube, but I couldn't see
them, couldn't hear them. And not even Rita laughed like Dobbs did.
That gal was a genuine fan. Made me nostalgic for my club days when
I was a nobody and all that mattered was getting a good guffaw out of
the crowd. Not that I wanted to go back to that. I had too much to lose
then, and I could feel how slippery my grip was. I was 'in,' but I
wasn't 'in,' if you know what I mean. Sure people loved old Ernie
McCabe, but one hit show isn't enough to make them remember you
when you're down and out. The distance between where I was and where
I had been was pretty slim, and I never wanted to be an outsider again.

"But that's life, right? Gives you hopes, fulfills them, and then
takes it all away, and leaves you with…well, memories, I guess, only
memories."

Hollywood Back Lots had done their research.

Mostly.

They covered all three seasons of the show and they spun all the
old rumors in what felt like a new direction. The "documentary" started
with the Tuskersons: five walri from nobody knew precisely where.

Well, that's not quite right.

Corinna Dobbs, their agent/trainer, had known, but she never told.
Dobbs was a cagey, old school showgirl from Cockeysville, and she
knew better than to miss a chance to tease the public.

Dobbs claimed she found the Tuskersons in the far northern reaches

Chambers
43

of the Canadian wilderness where she had gone for solitude after a
string of busted deals and lost clients. Out there in the frozen wilds,
alone, destitute, desperate, Dobbs had thrown herself into an ice hole,
and there she found her fortune. She hadn't planned on coming back
up, but five walri that broke through the frosty crust had other ideas.
They dragged her out of the Arctic water, fed her fish, and kept her
warm by sleeping around her. It was her bulky, gray down coat, soaked
with water, Dobbs claimed, that attracted her saviors. The coat made
her look like a sickly walrus.

More than a few scientists poked some fairly slackjawed holes
into Dobbs' account, but in show business, the story is mightier than
the fact. It was all about the mystique, and Dobbs' tale was more
dramatic than admitting that the Tuskersons were castoffs from some
second-rate Seaworld that couldn't afford to keep five trained walri
anymore, which was probably much closer to the truth.

No one lost any sleep over it.

The Tuskersons were America's mascots, and no one wanted to
spoil the parade.

Whatever Dobbs' eccentricities, she was one hell of a
businesswoman. Got the Tuskersons booked on *Good Morning
America*, Letterman, *The Tonight Show*, Donahue—you name it, the
Tuskersons did it. They had cameos in summer blockbusters and guest
roles on ailing sitcoms. By the third season (before anyone knew it
would be the last) the walri craze broke the stratosphere. Happy
Tuskersons fans could go on "The Walrus Diet" ("Fish fat: the secret
to longevity!"), take walrus safari cruises, or unlock the secrets of
human potential via the wisdom of walrus psychology ("Make your
psychic blubber work for you!").

The entire viewing public was too busy appreciating the Tuskersons
to care about whether any of it made a lick of sense. And watching
those old behind-the-scenes clips of the Tuskersons waddling and
frolicking in their on-set habitat, I could see where the crux of their
success lay.

The Tuskersons, you see, were the perfect family—*the* perfect
family. More perfect than any plastic television family unit, more
together than any phony gaggle of smiling, attention-starved child actors
bound for convenience store robberies, and their drug-addled, ego-
tripping, grinning-like-fools parents. The Tuskersons loved and cared
about each other in a simplistic but powerful, primal way. The
Tuskersons lacked all guile.

The old clips rolled and soon I was sitting, head propped on my hands, leaning forward, rapt, just like Ernie. On screen the Tuskersons shambled their remarkable girths across a standard sitcom set with all the comic grace they could muster. When they talked, their mouths flapped and smacked, a bit out of sync with their dubbed voices, but still firmly convincing. They delivered lines in a way no human actor could, with placid expressions devoid of presumption, their faces like happy masks, but real. It was enthralling, the special effect compelling in its crudeness, defined by some element, some quirk of editing or sound design that lent the Tuskersons a touch of extra credibility that set them squarely apart from their anthropomorphized animal star counterparts like Mr. Ed, Flipper, and Babe the Pig.

Funny, but I had never noticed that before, had never even given it a thought.

Hollywood Back Lots said Corinna Dobbs had trained the walri to flap their gums on command, but she had never revealed the secret of how.

A procession of talking heads went by, the voice actors who lent the Tuskersons speech, the writers and directors, the producers, the supporting actors, and each one reminisced about their days on the show, all the time they'd spent laughing, and how innocent the whole thing had been compared to today's sophisticated programming. They called it a magical time, and flashed cosmetically sublime smiles honed to feckless perfection as they oozed well-rehearsed zaniness and pretended they just might burst into a hearty knee-slap at their great memories. None of them could hide the dollar signs flashing behind their eyes when they mentioned the upcoming DVD boxed-set release of *Meet the Tuskersons: Season One*.

The narrator cut in with teasers for the rest of the show, and then the self-congratulatory sound bites gave way to more commercials.

Ernie looked at me and asked, "How long is this show?"

"An hour, I think," I told him.

"Huh. I must be on toward the end, then."

"They interviewed you for this?"

Ernie nodded vigorously. "Oh, yeah. About three months ago. They put me up in a fancy hotel for a weekend, sat me down in front of the cameras, and roll, baby, let it roll. Told them all about my days on the show, even snuck in some new material. Had 'em rolling on the carpet! Cameraman had to stop shooting while they got themselves together. Even got paid, except that fifty is all I got left. But I figure this is going to put me back in the game, get old Ernie McCabe's name on people's lips again, and then we'll see who takes my calls and who thinks I'm a washed-up has-been when America remembers how much they love me."

"Back on television after all these years," I said and slapped him on the back. "Must feel great, Mr. McCabe."

"You betchum," he cracked. "And this is just the start. I feel it in my bones, y'know, the way it feels when it's gonna click, when this rocket is about to take off—" Ernie swept his flattened hand across the space between us and thrust it over his head, "—and shoot the moon, baby! I tell you, my new material is gold. Been working on it for ten years. It has to be good. Just you wait and see if you don't fall off that stool laughing when you hear it. And, you know, I got a million of 'em."

When he said it that time, desperation creaking into his voice and raw hope pooling in his lachrymose eyes, a sudden cold premonition filled my gut and then rolled and spun like a weather map hurricane. The narrator's slick face filled the screen. Ernie swiveled about, once more front row center, and I turned slowly, reluctantly, with him.

"Weirdest thing that ever happened to me on the Tuskersons happened one night after we wrapped for the day. This was around the start of the third season. I took a nap in my dressing room to rest up for Rita, but I was so tired I wound up sleeping past midnight. So, I'm passing by the set on my way out, and I realize how different the Tuskersons' living room looks without the studio lights blazing and the Tuskersons wobbling around. When we were shooting it felt like a real home, but not at night in the dark and the quiet. So, I decide to stop by and see the walruses. I figured I'd be on my own, but while I'm crossing the parking lot, I see Dobbs walk into the habitat door ahead of me, and I think, 'Hey, great, it'll be good to talk to someone sane for a while.'

"But then I open the door, walk onto the landing, and there's Dobbs, thirty feet below standing buck-naked up to her waist in the water with the Tuskersons splashing around. I should have said something, let her know I was there, but I was too shocked to speak, and next thing I know, Dobbs dove under the water, and the Tuskersons followed her. Their shapes swam out and when they came up on the rocks on the far side of the pool, there were six walruses! Six! Not five, not five and woman, but six.

"Dobbs was really a walrus in disguise! At least, that's what I thought at first.

"Then I thought I was seeing things, but I was sure Dobbs hadn't resurfaced, and that meant either she was drowned at the bottom of the pool or she had become a walrus. Neither option particularly appealed to me.

"So, I climbed down the stairs to the pool level and took a seat on the rocks where Dobbs and I usually hung out. An hour goes by. Nothing happens. The Tuskersons are all off out of sight in the back of their habitat. I nodded off again, and when I woke up there were six walruses standing by the edge of the water, tusks shining, whiskers dripping, rolls of blubber floating. One of them waddles up onto the rocks, and I must have blinked or something, because one moment it was a walrus and the next it was Corinna Dobbs, drying herself and putting her clothes on, and looking unbelievably casual about the whole darn thing.

"'How's it going, Ernie?' she asked me.

"I told her it was going alright.

"She buttoned her shirt and kind of combed her gray hair back with her fingers. Then she said, 'I can tell how much you love the Tuskersons, Ernie. They're special animals, all right. Simple, uncomplicated, peaceful. They're pretty fond of you, too, you know. They think you're pretty damn funny.'

"'Dobbs,' I said. 'Either I'm still dreaming or you're a walrus pretending to be a woman. Now, which is it?'

"'Neither,' Dobbs said. 'You're awake and I'm a woman, but I'll admit, I'm thinking about becoming a walrus. It's a fine life, Ernie.'

"So I explained to Dobbs that unless the laws of nature had just been repealed and I hadn't gotten the memo, she couldn't just decide to become a walrus.

"So she tells me, 'I know how it sounds, but it's true. The Tuskersons make it possible. Heck, you just saw me turn into a walrus and then back again, and you still doubt it?'

"I doubted it all right. I'd just seen it, but I was afraid to believe it. Maybe the stress was getting to me, making me hallucinate. Maybe I'd picked up someone else's Dr. Pepper by mistake and gotten a little surprise dose of something.

"Then Dobbs says, 'You get used to it after a few times, Ernie, and then you find yourself not wanting to change back. There's the water sliding by when you swim. There's peace and quiet. No one clamoring for a pound of your flesh or dragging you into screwed up headgames and power struggles. No biting your nails waiting for the ratings to come in. No worries about money or sex or how best to live your life. When you're a walrus, you just know how to do it. The hardest choice you make is which fish to eat, which rock to sleep on, and there are always others around you, your family, close-knit, always looking out for each other. It's the best, Ernie, no doubt about it. And I can see in your eyes that it appeals to you.'

"'Dobbs, you're crazy,' I told her. She just laughed.

"But, yeah, it appealed to me, I admit. Especially right then when I was running so ragged, and I was already losing Rita. I think some part of me deep down knew the end was coming. We were still high in the ratings, then, but the show was splitting apart at the seams. People were at each other's throats, and I should have known that it couldn't last, but I didn't want to admit it, and I sure wasn't going to say all that to Dobbs.

"'Consider it, Ernie. That's all I'm saying,' Dobbs said. 'Things change, and one day, you may be looking for a way out. And you could still make people laugh. You could still do your job. Just promise me you won't tell anyone about this. The Tuskersons are kind of particular, you understand? They took me in when I was in pain. They see the same in you, and sooner or later, you will, too. Maybe tomorrow, maybe not for a long time, but you will and the offer will always be on the table. Just keep a lid on it, okay? Our contract is up for renewal next season, after all, and this getting out could complicate it.'

"I promised Dobbs to keep her secret, and then we left. We split up outside the door, and by the time I got home, I had myself convinced that I'd imagined it all, that Dobbs was just some weirdo who liked to pretend she was a walrus. And when things started to crash and burn, I forgot all about it, tucked it away in a mental junk drawer, until a year after the show was canceled and the Tuskersons moved into their permanent habitat.

"Dobbs had arranged for their earnings to pay for a private area at a local zoo, but she had disappeared by then, and no one knew where she had gone. I had an idea when I saw the pictures in the news and there were six walruses in the Tuskersons' new home. The papers said the sixth had been an understudy, but we'd never had any understudy. I thought of that night at the studio and I knew it was Dobbs. She'd finally become a walrus for good and wouldn't ever be changing back.

"Wait. Why are you stopping the camera? You don't believe me, do you? Can't say I blame you, but there's no other explanation, and trust me, I've spent years trying to think of one."

Hollywood Back Lots ended half-an-hour later. Ernie turned to me with bloodshot eyes brimming with tears and said, "Well, goddamn it."

He clutched the drink he had been ignoring and knocked it all back in one gulp, then wheezed and slammed his glass down. He threw his crumpled fifty on the bar and hollered for a refill.

The *Hollywood Back Lots* theme played over the closing credits. There had been no sign of Ernie's interview, his contributions acknowledged with a montage of his best moments and the explanation that he had been too ill to make an appearance. Twice, other former cast members referred to him in the past tense, and then quickly corrected themselves. Ernie was in no prize shape, but I believed what he had told me about being interviewed for the show. He had been the only human star of *Meet the Tuskersons*. It was almost inconceivable that he might be excluded, but he had been.

Ernie stared out from beneath his drooping eyelids and looked so sad that Tuba spotted him his next drink.

I did not know what to say. My thoughts clashed as I looked for the right words, but before I could speak, Ernie reached out and put one of his knobby, shaking hands on my shoulder, and squeezed it.

"Don't sweat the noggin muscles, kid," he said. "You'll never guess. I got along fine with all of them, and I wasn't lying when I said I had a blast at the interview. The crew loved me. They all loved me. At least, that's what I thought back then, but maybe...maybe..." he said, and then fell silent.

Ernie's shoulders sagged even further. "You think, maybe," he whispered, "they all resented me? Because I was the star? Because I didn't go in for all the partying like they did? I never gave anyone a hard time about it. It just wasn't important to me. The show was important to me!"

His breathing turned deep and then he lifted his head and looked me in the eye. "Dammit, I knew I never should have told them about that time Dobbs turned into a walrus!" he said. "They cut me out because they think I'm loony-tunes."

I opened my mouth in time for my speechlessness to catch its second wind. This was part of the story *Hollywood Back Lots* would never touch.

Ernie told me the whole thing, just the way he had told it on camera for an interview that would rot on the back shelf of an archive somewhere if the producers hadn't already erased it. He couldn't explain exactly what the Tuskersons were or how they could help Dobbs turn into a walrus, but he was certain they had. He knew how it sounded, and except for having seen Dobbs change that one night, Ernie wouldn't have believed a shred of it. And it was hard not to believe the old comedian when I heard the conviction in his voice. To him this was all real, and I wondered how long his mind had been so addled. Maybe as far back as when the show went off the air.

"They cut me out tonight, because they know," he said when he was done. "That must be it. They know Dobbs told me her secret, and they know the Tuskersons would never have any of *them*. So, they cut me! Ernie McCabe? Poof! Gone. Who's that? Who needs him? Maybe, if I hadn't talked about it, maybe if I had said things like those other people instead of the truth, instead of being honest, they would have let me back in, but after all these years, all the doors they've closed in my face, all the rejections, and the snickering behind my back—that has to be it! They're jealous because the Tuskersons chose me and not them!"

"Sure, Mr. McCabe," I said. "That must be it."

He nodded his head, and said, "Yes, yes, that's it."

"Mr. McCabe," I said, an idea blooming, "why don't we get your story out to the world? Look, I'm a writer. I get published all the time in all the big trade rags. We could meet tomorrow, go over the facts, get it all straight, and then I'll make sure everyone knows exactly what happened to good, old Ernie McCabe, the straight dope."

His eyes burned with the prospect. "Yes, yes," he said. "We should tell everyone. Get my name back out there. Maybe we can work in some of my new material. It isn't fair what they've done to me. Not fair, at all, how they've locked me out for all these years. I was a star!"

"That's right. A star. And stars deserve better than being tossed out like garbage. Let the public decide who's right and who's crazy," I said.

"The public always loved me," Ernie said. "And you believe me, right? You do, don't you?"

It could have been the half-second pause before I answered or maybe my eyes diverted for an instant—I'll never know but something told him the truth when I said that I believed him, and he knew I was lying. He was coming out of the haze of his disappointment, and he sensed that all I was after was a hot story about a crazy old comedian and that maybe the folks at *Hollywood Back Lots* had done him a favor by not embarrassing him. I can admit it now—maybe what he saw were the dollar signs flashing in my eyes at the prospect of painting a washed up lunatic as a crazy outsider poised for a big comeback that would never materialize.

Who can say what was really going through Ernie McCabe's mind that night? I didn't much wonder until he missed our meeting the next morning.

I spent a week trying to find him before I gave up. Got as far as a cheap motel in a bad part of town, where he had stayed before the show aired. The manager hit me up for a hundred bucks, Ernie's outstanding bill.

After that I let it go. The story wasn't worth chasing, and I was feeling a little guilty about what I might have done to an old man who once made me and my family laugh, long ago, back in the days when we could still do that together.

I'd done some research that week, though, getting ready and boning up on *Meet the Tuskersons*, and a big chunk of Ernie's story held up. Corinna Dobbs had disappeared after the show was canceled, and six walri, not five, had moved into the permanent habitat at the Barrymore Zoo, a small, private facility north of the city that had been built in the thirties by a rich movie producer. The drugs and the show's collapse were common knowledge, and Ernie had been right about the Tuskerson's old studio living quarters—they had been converted into a monkey house for about eight years before the whole thing had been torn down to build a new soundstage.

Not long after I gave up looking for Ernie, I saw an article in the paper about a new arrival at the Barrymore Zoo—you guessed it, a walrus, a new resident in the Tuskerson's private pavilion. Of the six original walri, four still lived, though they were improbably old by walrus standards, and that included the one that had supposedly been the understudy. The new addition was a guest that Corinna Dobbs had made provisions for back when she was still managing the walri, an addition the zoo had been waiting a long time to receive, and once more there were five walri, and in a strange way, the Tuskersons were complete again, the perfect family they had been years ago, the perfect family they would always be.

I considered driving out to the Barrymore Zoo, thought about seeing for myself if maybe Ernie McCabe hadn't been crazy after all, if maybe he'd finally found his next big role, but I knew it was impossible, knew it couldn't be true. Right? And you know what? Even if it was true, so what? Who wants to hear about some second-rate has-been getting the best of the world in the end? I mean, where's the story in that?

NAMING DAY
John Sunseri

Hrutu woke alone. His mate was already up, already making clattering noises in the other room as she prepared breakfast, and Hrutu remained motionless for several minutes, listening, thinking about the upcoming hours. The cold air of the sleeping room felt freighted with some unseen menace, some inchoate sense of foreboding, and Hrutu lay as if paralyzed, looking up at the carved ice of the ceiling as if he could read the future in its smooth whorls and spirals. Finally, though, he shook off his lethargy and rolled out of bed onto the snowy floor.

"Are you finally up?" came Nikat's voice from the other room, and then she was in the doorway. Hrutu knew that some of the other Walri in the labs had silently questioned his choice of mate when he had made it, but he had never once regretted picking Nikat—the cow was small, true, at only six feet or so, and she came off as abrasive sometimes, an uncomfortable thing to be in a society that demanded harmony among its members...but these little disadvantages were far outweighed by Nikat's plusses. She was fiercely bright, completely dedicated to her work, and she kept a fine, comfortable home. She was also a strong, passionate lover, and Hrutu and Nikat sometimes (though it was frowned upon by society) spent their scarce free hours mating, even when it wasn't the season for it.

"I am, mate," said Hrutu, putting happiness into his voice though he didn't feel it. "I was just thinking of you."

"I see that," said the cow, her eyes moist with amusement as she looked down at the result of his thoughts. "And if it wasn't such an important day, I might be tempted to come over there and take care of that for you, but..."

"I know," grunted Hrutu, feeling the swelling begin to subside and drawing himself up onto his flippers so that he stood. "Naming Day is already upon us."

"It is," she said, her voice changing slightly. "Come on then, sleepyhead. I have food ready, and I've already dropped the children off in the common room, so they'll be tired with play when we come for them."

"Are they..." began Hrutu, and then he stopped. What was he going to ask her? The children would be as they always were—loving, eager, stupid, like lumps of rubbery affection waiting for a cuddle or a friendly cuff on the flanks. A wave of fierce possessiveness swept through him then, and his body shook with it. Nikat, who had halted in the doorway when he had begun to formulate his half-question, now tossed her head to the side and did not look at him.

"They're playing," she said quietly. "They're with the other kids of the crèche."

"Yes," he said. "Yes. Of course. I'll be right there, my love."

She nodded, and after one more silent second she heaved her bulk through the doorway. Hrutu was still shaky, but he moved to the hole in the corner of the floor and slipped into it. The freezing salt water engulfed him like a living fist, squeezing him with its frigid fire, but he adapted quickly. He bathed for five minutes or so, swooping through the dark water in gleeful flips and turns, able to switch off his mind for a few blessed moments while he let his instincts take control of his body. He felt, as he sometimes did, like a god—a god of the sub-zero waters, free in his chosen element, dancing through the liquid like it was air and he a flying thing. But it could not last long, this feeling of omnipotence, and soon he was squeezing himself through the other hole in the apartment, the one in the food room.

Nikat had arranged the dead herring, clams and sea cucumbers on the eating floor, a sizable pile of meat, and she had also somehow collected a bunch of seaweed into a rare salad. Hrutu snorted when he saw it.

"Where on earth did you find the greens, my love?" he asked.

"After my shift at the lab yesterday, I was feeling antsy. So I took a swim up to the Masking Grounds."

"You did," said Hrutu, his tone suddenly flat.

"It's permitted," said Nikat, defiance in her voice. Well, that was what he got for mating with a firebrand; he would never get meek or apologetic from her. "I broke none of the rules."

"I know you didn't, Nikat," he said, "but there are good reasons why we don't go up there."

"We may be making the trip again today," she said, annoyed. "I wanted to get a look at it, that's all."

"It's not good for you to see such things, my love," said Hrutu. "Your emotions, your feelings—it would be easier if—"

"If I hid them, like you do?" she asked, her voice sharper than her tusks. "If I put all concerns, all feelings out of my mind until it comes down to Naming Day, and then have to deal with a flood of them, all at once? Should we both be as reticent and meek as you, then?"

"Nikat..."

"No, mate!" she said, eyes blazing at him. "I will have my say!"

Hrutu moved to her quickly, rage overcoming him. She saw him advance, could have avoided his rush, but she stood defiantly, waiting for his attack. He clubbed her with one of his powerful flippers, and her small frame instantly crashed to the icy floor, scattering snow and dead herring in a cloud, and then Hrutu was on her, pummeling her with his flippers, landing on her with his bulk, all ten feet of him. He growled incoherently as he flailed at her, and she whimpered in pain as she took his blows.

And then the anger was gone, and he rolled off of her. He lay beside his mate and closed his eyes so that the tears would not flow from them.

"Feel better?" she asked, and there was tenderness in her voice. He kept his eyes shut. Naming Day, the projects they were working on, the image of his small, stupid children playing with their crèche-mates, all these things had brought him to the verge of crying. But it was the concern of Nikat—the love of his wife, his mate—that pushed him over. He felt tears welling in his eyes, and knew that Nikat could see them rolling down through the fur of his face.

"I know you are not as cold or analytical as the others say you are," she crooned. "I know that, no matter how much man-science you work on, how many of their machines you study, you are a warm, compassionate, feeling walrus. I know you, my love, and I know your heart. Let the emotion come."

And he did. He opened his eyes to look at Nikat, and now the tears flowed like cataracts off a spring glacier. She was crying, too, and he could feel his heart beating in tandem with hers, two fleshes joined, two minds linked.

Together, they wept.

"Ah, Doctors Hrutu and Nikat," said the young walrus at the computer. "Welcome."

"We thank you for your welcome," said Hrutu, staring straight ahead at the young scientist so as not to see the rest of the chamber. Nikat was silent.

"And you've brought all four of your brood? Ah, yes, I see they've been checked in already."

"All four are in the chambers," said Nikat, fire in her voice. "Almu, Dasan, Hrogar and Yellum."

"You've named them?" asked the young technician, a frown creasing itself around his tusks. "You know that—"

"We know," said Hrutu, taking over the conversation before Nikat could expostulate further. "My mate is a cow of deep feeling. I allowed it."

"That's your choice, of course, Doctor," said the young walrus, his tone expressing all the disdain and disgust his words could not. "But for the purposes of Naming Day, you will be asked to rename the ones that—"

"For the sake of the God," hissed Nikat, "we *know* all this. Now get your blood samples and DNA swabs, and let us wait in peace!"

"Of course," said the tech, his voice now cold and flat, like the sheet ice on the ocean surface far above them. "If you'll step this way, the nurses have the needles all ready."

Minutes later, ensconced in the examination room, Hrutu turned to his mate, exasperated.

"You're not making this easy, you know," he said.

"They didn't make it easy on me a year ago," she said. "All the fertility drugs I had to take, the poking and prodding, the operations…"

"You understand why. It was necessary."

"Necessary or no, the God made us Walri cows to bear one pup at a time. Now we're producing litters of three, four, five—and it hurts, knowing that the scientists will soon decide how fruitful our labors have been."

"You believe in your God," said Hrutu, a whirl of emotions in his heart. "Perhaps you should pray to him."

"Our God—*our* God, the God of all the Walri—doesn't work like that," spat Nikat, her body quivering. "He is a god of strength and vengeance, not a protector of children. That is our job, mate—to bear the pups, to watch them grow, to feed them and play with them and allow them to think that this is how the world really works, family living with family, crèche next to crèche, all of the Walri working together for the dawning of the Great Day, and then, just when they've gotten used to it, gotten happy with life, we bring them here to the cold testing chambers, and then—"

"Well, well, well!" came a voice from the door. "Hrutu! Nikat! How are you both?"

The mated pair spun toward the newcomer, and Hrutu, trapped

deep in the anger and frustration he felt at his wife, at their situation, at the world in general, yet found himself smiling as he saw the walrus at the door. Beside him, he knew that Nikat was smiling too.

"Doctor Jarat," he said, shuffling on his flippers toward the door. "What are you doing here?"

"It's Naming Day," the old walrus said, "and I wanted to see how things were going. They still let me run around the labs every once in a while, you know. And I heard that some of my protégés were bringing their pups in for examination, so I thought that I'd try to make the rounds and provide what comfort I could."

"I thank you, Doctor," said Hrutu, formally, though still smiling.

"It's so good to see you!" said Nikat, excited. "It's been months and months and months!"

"You've both been very busy, my children," said the ancient walrus. "I've been keeping an eye on both your projects. Nikat, my dear, I'm very excited about all the work you've been doing with the deep salvage teams. Do you really think you can raise that thing from the ocean floor?"

"We can," said Nikat, and her voice was both fierce and confident. "Within a year or two, you might want to be on one of the *ooglits* when I tell you to. I promise you a sight you've never seen."

Jarat chuckled, and his eyes were warm when he looked upon Nikat. "If I'm granted enough time, my dear, and you're allowed to tell me the date, I'll definitely be there. And Hrutu! My favorite pupil! The work you're doing with your cadre—well, it's stunning. If your mate, here, doesn't beat you to it, I'm sure that your labors will be the ones to usher in the Great Day!"

"I'm flattered you think so," said Hrutu, and in truth he *was* flattered. Jarat had been one of the first Walri, the ones on the glacier on that fateful day a half-century ago when the Men had inadvertently brought the Awakening Stroke, and he was still the Walri's brightest light. Praise from him was like praise from the God Hrutu didn't believe in. "Though I don't know if we'll be ready in the near future."

"There's time, my son," said Jarat. "We've made time for ourselves, for our species. That's what Naming Day is all about, you know."

"We know," started Hrutu, but Nikat burst in, interrupting him.

"It's not fair!" she wailed, her huge eyes growing liquid and hurt as she spoke. "All the effort, all the time we've spent with our children, all the love we've given them…and for what? So that we can lead them to the Masking Grounds and—"

"My child," said Jarat tenderly, shuffling over to her and raising a caressing flipper. "I know it hurts. I myself have fathered twenty-two children since the Awakening, and have only six of them still around. You are a young walrus, only seven years old, and you have a fine mate, who will give you litter after litter, all of them with your amazing brains."

She looked down. "Not all of them."

"All the Named ones," Jarat corrected himself. "You will be mother to a line of brilliant Walri, and Hrutu their father. You will be loved and honored, and there will be celebrations in your name. Do you doubt any of this? Because *I* don't—this is the kind of mated pair, you and Hrutu, that the species needs. Regardless of what happens now, you are standing on the threshold of the Great Day, and there will be children of yours with you when it happens. I promise."

"Oh, Doctor," she said, sniffling. "I know that all you say is true. It's just so *hard.*"

"I know," said the elderly walrus, still stroking her gently, his flipper smoothing along the rough blubber of her flesh. "I know, Nikat. But it will be easier soon. With the advances we've made in the last ten years, there will be a day—and a quick one—in which all the children will be Walri. I firmly believe that."

"That doesn't help me today," said the cow, and Hrutu grimaced. There was the abrasive side of his mate again, the iconoclastic side, the side with the prickly edges. And it was aimed at Doctor Jarat, now, that sharp tongue. "Today, though I know in my mind how important the Masking Grounds are, I feel that I could steal my children and run away from the whole city. Run far, far away, so none of you could ever find me."

Jarat surprised Hrutu, then. Any other of the Walri would have recoiled from such blasphemy, would have left with denunciation on their minds and would have instantly summoned the Watch to subdue the recalcitrant cow, lock her away where none of her poison could infect the others. But not Jarat. The aged walrus simply continued stroking Nikat's flanks, continued smiling, and when he spoke his voice was soothing and filled with compassion.

"Nikat, child," he said, "I understand. I share your feelings, my dear, and sympathize with them. I, myself, felt the same way. God, I still do—two years ago I had another litter with one of my mates," and here, the older walrus gave a wry smile as he noticed the surprised looks on the faces of Hrutu and Nikat. "Oh, I can still get it up on occasion. There's a little fire left in these ancient loins. Anyway, on Naming Day, the testers took two of three from me. And, you know what? It still feels like a knife to the heart. After all these years, after building this city and populating it, after all the work and all the tears and all the joys, after six mates and many children...it still hurts. And it does even now. But it's a necessary pain, my children. You know as well as I do how important all of this is, and you are both young and strong. You will get through it. And when the day comes, the Great Day, and we're down south, where we belong, walking on the streets of the Man cities, looking around at the world that they have built for us, when we have taken our rightful place in the cosmos, then you will know how important your actions on this day have been."

"I—" started Nikat, and Hrutu was afraid that more dissent would pour from her mouth, more heresy. But the ancient walrus's words had had the intended effect. "I understand. I will do what I need to do."

"Good," said Jarat. "And remember, children—so long as there is breath in these old lungs, you will always have someone to talk to about things. I know how important your work is, and how often it keeps you away from your friends—and I've heard rumors that you have other, less dutiful ways to spend what precious free time you have," and the old scientist smiled at his own words as Hrutu looked bashfully down and Nikat giggled through her tears. "But please— any time you have doubts, or concerns, or just want to talk, feel free to visit me. I'll do my best to reassure you."

"We will," whispered Hrutu, and Nikat echoed him.

"Fine," said the doctor. "I see they're coming to take your DNA swabs now, so I'll leave. I just wanted to see my brightest pupil and his lovely mate one more time before the judging. It's done me good to talk with you young Walri. Thank you."

"No," protested Hrutu, seeing the phlebotomist enter the room, needle at the ready. "Thank *you.*"

When the judging was over, Hrutu and Nikat sat with their crèche-mates, watching the video screens as the results were posted. With every number that came up in the 'Name' column, there was a rustle of happiness from the assembled Walri, and excited bumping and thumping of their clustered flesh. With every number in the other column, the ones that would soon be taken up to the Masking Grounds, there was silence, with only the occasional groan or sob from one of the cows breaking the still of the frigid air.

Nikat seemed resigned. "What are our numbers again?" she asked.

"Sixty-one through sixty-four," said Hrutu.

"Almu," whispered Nikat, "Dasan…"

"Hrogar and Yellum," finished Hrutu. "Our sons and daughter." Nikat, cuddling up against him as she watched the screen, shot him a surprised, pleased look.

"I love them too, my mate," said Hrutu, blinking. "I didn't argue when you named them prematurely."

"How I love you," whispered Nikat. "You are a walrus above Walri."

"I am what I am. Now hush, for here comes our lot."

"Oh God," said Nikat. "Let it be over quickly…"

"Hush."

An hour later, they stood at the edge of the dark water with some of the other parents. At their flanks were Yellum and Dasan, two of the infant bulls, soon to be nameless.

"It is hard," said Hrutu.

"It is hard," agreed Nikat. "It is the hardest thing I have ever done."

"They will live full lives," said her mate. "They will swim and scavenge, and they will congregate in the *ooglits* with the other non-named, and they will live under the stars and in the wind."

"And perhaps they will die beneath the claws of the polar bear, or be swept into the teeth of the Orca," said Nikat bitterly. "Maybe they will be trapped by the Eskimo, or harpooned by the Russian sailor."

"Maybe those things will happen," agreed Hrutu, and his voice was cold and tired, but not angry. "And maybe tomorrow the Men will find our city and descend upon us like an avalanche. There is no profit in worrying about the future. What we *can* do is work to ensure that Almu and Hrogar will have every chance to join us on the Great Day, when it comes."

Nikat nodded and began to slip into the black water. Dasan and Yellum eagerly joined her, barking their simple approval as they felt the cold and salt, not knowing that at the end of this journey they would begin their new lives as members of a normal clan of walruses— *not* Walri—and would never see their birth parents again. "Let us give the fruit of our love to the Men," said Nikat, "so that they don't suspect that below the floes and *ooglits* filled with stupid, senseless walruses, there is a race of intelligent beings working to supplant them. Let us give our children to be decoys, to be tracked by satellites, so that Men will nod and say 'normal population density in that area,' and go on to the next pictures to be examined. Let us take Yellum and Dasan to the world of Man."

"It will be our world," said Hrutu, joining his truncated family in the water. "You heard Jarat. Soon, all of the newborn pups will be intelligent. We have learned much since the atomic tests of the Americans and Russians in the arctic seas awakened us—we have learned how to play with genes so that every generation is smarter and smarter, and soon there will never be throwbacks like our sons, here. Soon, if you can raise that city from beneath the waves..."

"R'lyeh," whispered his mate, "the city of Walri angles, the city of our sleeping God."

"...or if my cadre and I finally produce enough nuclear bombs to take out the whole world of Men—and we're close, my love, we're very close—then we will step forth, onto the shores of the world, and take our place as kings and queens. You and I will see that day, my dearest," Hrutu said, forcefully, passionately. "I swear it."

"Then, for our intelligent children, the ones now being injected with the isotopes that will awaken them," said Nikat, her normally expressive face stony and set, "let us do our jobs as the parents of the new race. Let us go to the Masking Grounds."

And they began swimming, their pups swooping alongside them. With them came the other parents, a whole school of Walri and the non-named, and they moved through the dark waters like the Angel of Death.

WALRUS SKIN
Ekaterina Sedia

A female walrus sat monumental, staring at the ash of the sky and the lead of the sea out of its small eyes, passive like a Buddha.

Justin's gaze was drawn to the inert bulk of her. She rested on a flat rock halfway between jagged cliffs and the dirty hem of the surf, away from the rest of her group. Justin noticed a scar that reached from the base of her neck and winded down her chest, occasionally getting lost in the folds of fat but always resurfacing. This was the female that had lost her pup last week, Justin thought. He wondered if the walruses felt emotional pain; in any case, the female looked despondent, despite her placid demeanor.

She did not move all day, and Justin forgot about her. He tried to maneuver his camouflage half-poncho, half-tent closer to the colony, dragging his sound equipment along. He managed to record the needy barking of the pups and vocalizations of a bull when he spotted a rival. The walrus colony teemed with vibrant life among the grey rocks and grey sea, the female on the flat basalt rock the only vortex of sorrow.

When the night fell, Justin drank still-warm tea from his thermos and looked at the white disc of the moon. *The white nights are coming soon*, he thought. Possibly the last full moon he would see in a long while. *Bye, moon*, he mouthed. *See you in the fall.*

He slept until soft sighing and moaning woke him up. He stared into ghostly-white moonlight that flooded the stony beach and the whipped froth of the surf. The female from the basalt rock was gone, but a smaller dark body distorted the flat silhouette of her perch. Crouching, he moved to take a look, picking his way amongst the sleeping walruses, sliding sideways, like a crab.

His heart froze as he stared at the object, not quite believing his eyes, not quite comprehending. A crumpled walrus skin, not a trace of blood or fat or pain. It didn't make sense—poachers? Where did they go? Where did they come from? Why didn't they take the skin? It was too intact for any sort of a violent demise; yet, he could not fathom any other reason for a walrus to separate from its hide.

Selkie. The word floated up from the bottom of his memory, and he considered it a while as he stared at the skin, not understanding. Then he remembered the legend of the seal women. A man could take her skin and thus compel a selkie to marry him. But caution must be taken—if a selkie woman ever found her seal skin, she would abandon her husband and return to the sea, indifferent to her family, to her human life. Always to the sea.

Annele did not always have a name, just as she did not always have words. She moved her lips, strained her throat and vocalized. "Sea," she would say, hoping that the man who sat across from her would take in all its meaning—the brine, the depth, the exhilaration. The word burst with the smells of fish, crunch of the mussel shells and the large, flat blades of seaweed that streamed in the currents. She wondered if he understood.

He did not have tusks like her previous mate; neither did he have other wives. Instead, he had a warm cave in a cliff that teetered high in the foggy, clouded air, and one had to climb a series of cleverly stacked stones to get to it. He called it a *flat*, although it was nothing like her flat basalt rock. The only seating here felt disconcertingly like a quagmire, and her heart faltered every time she started sinking into the softness.

"Sea," she said.

He nodded and picked up a small, rectangular stone. He pressed on it with his thumb, and another window flickered and opened. It showed the sea lapping on a strange sandy beach, and she tried to escape. But the window was covered with hard ice, just like the other windows that showed light-studded, tall cliffs. She bumped her head and knocked herself on the ground. Her new mate barked without words. She stretched out and watched the unreachable white hem of the surf out of her small, impassive eyes.

Justin felt cheated, although he knew that folklore was a poor guide. He had nobody but himself to blame for believing the pictures in the compiled fairy tale books. It was unreasonable to expect a slender seal-maiden, with long sleek hair and soulful brown eyes. He could've guessed that a walrus-woman would be different—thick, her lines indistinct, smoothed by subcutaneous fat, her eyes staring from under her heavy forehead with sleepy indifference. She sat, placid and substantial, her face devoid of any expression, like a Buddha's. His friends did not understand.

He should've left the skin be. He should've closed his eyes and walked away, selkie-folk or were-walruses notwithstanding. He couldn't leave it alone. He couldn't return the skin. Couldn't give up on his find, like a child who realizes that a treasure he discovered is just a flattened bottle-cap, but still carries it in his pocket. For good luck.

Annele found some new words. If she dug deep and stayed still, they came, floated to the surface, pale and exhausted like walruses after a long dive. People in the window said words too. She learned from them.

"Death," she said once, and recoiled and cried as the word filled her mouth with an acrid taste and stung her nostrils with the smell of danger and fresh blood. She never said it again.

She tried to explain to him how she felt.

"Air," she shouted at the flickering, changing window, as her lungs expanded, seeking a tart, bitter bite of cold and salt, and finding only stale and tepid space of the cave.

"Pup," she said, her eyes dripping sorrow, her side hurting with anticipation of a rubbery nose, of soft fur that should be pressing against her but was not.

Justin was not sure what to do. He wanted to do right by her. He thought about giving her skin back, but it did not seem humane. He spent enough time studying walruses to know that their fights were brutal, habitat threatened, and mortality high. She was better off here, where he could take care of her; he felt obliged. Still, the guilt gnawed at him.

Annele was getting used to words. The more she said them, the blunter they became, losing their sharp taste and urgent smell. Her fear dulled as well, and she was no longer afraid of the soft furniture and honking of the cars outside. Her life as a walrus became more of a daydream than a memory.

She learned to clean and cook, took some classes at the community college and found herself only mildly interested when the Discovery Channel showed a documentary on walrus colonies in Alaska, filmed in part by her husband. She watched them for a while, soon changing the channel, but still feeling a vague but demanding discomfort. There was something missing.

"A child," she told Justin.

He seemed relieved at the suggestion and agreed that neither of them was getting any younger, and that one just might regret not having children, when one is old and alone.

"Alone," she agreed, the word momentarily conjuring an image of a flat, black basalt slab. She felt a stirring of apprehension at the thought that she wanted to be alone, that the emptiness within her could be sated only by the sea. She suppressed her vague longing. Happiness meant family, not deserted stone cliffs and ice floes, not solitude among many, all of them together yet distinct, wed to their own private perceptions of the world. Family was important.

The baby squalled in his crib, and his older sister screamed, "Moooooom! Baby's crying!"

Annele rushed from the kitchen, the bottle of warm formula in hand, only to stumble over a half-assembled dollhouse and scattering of toys. The bottle shattered as she fell, and her husband glanced up from his desk. "Watch where you're going." He returned to his work.

Annele struggled to her knees and rested, awkward and monumental, picking out shards of glass from the heel of her hand.

"Mom, the baby's crying." The girl stood next to her, her eyes blue and empty like the ocean at a California beach, and tugged at the sleeve of Annele's sweatshirt.

"Can I get any work done?" Justin chimed in.

"Why don't you take care of him?" Annele said, her voice strained with anticipation of anger.

"I'm busy"

"I'm bleeding."

He finally noticed and left the desk with an exasperated sigh. He picked the baby from the crib and rocked and shushed it, awkward.

Annele remained on her knees, a toy brick digging into her skin, blood dripping down from her fingertips.

"Mom?" the girl said and stepped back.

Annele did not answer. Her fingers tightened around the broken off bottle neck. She studied the jagged edge, her thoughts moving slowly, cumbersome and heavy like stones. She frowned with the effort it took to shift them the way she wanted.

"Blood," she said out loud, coaxing the stubborn, unyielding boulders, and gripped the bottle until her fingers went white with tension.

"What's wrong?" Justin said, real fear in his eyes and the set of his pale lips. "Honey?"

She raised her weapon, stained with her blood that smelled of the ocean. "My skin," she said.

Justin looked at her with disbelief. He did not think she had it in her; he did not realize how much she had changed.

"Give," she said, her voice quiet and all the more terrible because of that. "Now."

The walrus skin, hidden away for years in the narrow crawlspace between the ceiling and the roof, did not keep well. Tears swelled in Annele's impassive eyes as she inhaled the smell of mold and let her fingers poke through the holes left by worms and decay.

"Come on," Justin said. "What are you going to do? You're used to this life. You have nowhere to go—we're in the middle of the city, for crying out loud. There's no sea for miles."

She agreed with him inwardly, but she had no choice. There was nothing standing between her and the walrus skin, and she slipped it on, slid inside its sad moldy smell, oblivious to the baby's crying.

The walrus flopped down the street, ignoring the honking of the cars and the cold wind that bit into her tender human flesh, exposed through the worm-eaten walrus skin.

The smell of the ocean was barely discernible, far away, and she wondered if she was imagining it. She heaved her body up and lunged forth, her front flippers striking the pavement hard enough to draw blood. She did not remember whether the blood that left stains and smudges in her wake was human or walrus, whether she drew it by cutting her hand on a broken bottle or chafing her flipper on the sidewalk; she did not really care. All that mattered now was the smell of the ocean in a distance, calling her, taunting her, unreachable.

TATTOO BURNING OVER YOUR WASTED HEART
Andersen Prunty

Unsatisfied with my job, I go to a bar and drink until I black out. I wake up in a strange bed with a strange tattoo on the left side of my chest. Looking down at it, I can't even tell what it is. There's no one else there to describe it to me. The apartment I'm in is curiously devoid of mirrors. I put on some pants and knock on the door of the apartment next to this one. A haggard old man answers. I point to the tattoo and ask him what it is. He plays with his glasses, screws up his face, and gets really close to me.

"I'm pretty sure it's a walrus. Maybe he's standing in front of an American flag or riding a tricycle. I can't really tell." He pauses, moves away from my chest, stands up straighter. "Looks like he's having a lot of fun."

I mutter a quick thanks and wander back to the other apartment but the door's locked. I knock and there's no answer. I go out to the street. I visit a store to buy a shirt and go back to my miserable job.

I'm unable to really tell what the tattoo is until it heals completely. It's definitely a walrus. And it definitely looks like he's having fun but everything else about it is unclear. Why a walrus? Why now?

Years pass. I discover how much people hate mystery. They want to know why I have a walrus over my heart and when I tell them I don't know, they get furious. Many of them think it's a joke. They want to know why I would do something so permanent on such a lark. Others tell me it's not permanent. They tell me I can and should get it removed. But I grow to like it. I learn to invent stories for it.

"My mom loved walruses."

"That was my first wife. She had cancer."

"I worked as a walrus trainer."

"I've always liked walruses. Ever since I can remember. Ever since I was a kid."

"I made a pact with my friends. We all have walrus tattoos."

Eventually I fall in love with a prostitute. I feel terrible lying to her but I do it anyway. I have trouble keeping my lies straight and eventually she asks me why I'm lying. I tell her. I tell her about people hating mysteries and that I understand that because it's even a mystery to me. I don't know why it's there. I can only tell her the day I received it. There's no real context. And that's the part she doesn't understand. She wants to know how I've lived so long with this hideous thing on my chest. I tell her I just got used to it. I tell her how much I like it now. When I propose to her, she laughs. She tells me there can never be anything other than sex between us. She tells me my insides are cracked and broken. She tells me there's nothing there. She says the tattoo's really just an expression of the void in my soul.

And each time she asks, "Why a walrus? Why there?" I can only shake my head and say, "I don't know. I don't know."

DEADTIME FOR BONZO
Violet LeVoit

Good Gal the chimp stirred a teaspoon of saccharin into the iced tea cooling her favorite tumbler, the one with the stardust asterisks in gold and avocado green. *Tink-a-tink-a-tink*, the longnecked spoon against the glass. She pursed her ape lips into a tulipy spout and took a sip. The shiver of cold made her involuntarily fill her diaper.

The sun was coming down on Noah's Haven, the California sunset peeking like a day-glo voyeur through the woven slats of patio chairs outside. Time to sit with Blonde, the tall female human whose buttery floss hair swirled like a palmier on top of her head. The one whose skin was soft and powdery and dotted giraffe-like with liver spots, whose mascaraed eyelashes stood up sharp and black like magnetized iron fillings, whose stomach was pillowy behind nubbly buttercup culottes. "Pee-yew," said Blonde in her menthol-scuffed grandma's voice. "Let's get you changed before Tarzan starts." She stood up and Good Gal swung into her arms like a hirsute pendulum, burying her face in Blonde's neck to sniff the scent of face powder and clean laundry and soft old woman. She knew to lay back on the changing table and lift her stunted bow legs as Blonde unbuttoned the snaps on her jumper. "Stinky, stinky," said Blonde, just as she always did. The two females were back on the couch before the credits began.

In the bulging glass of the TV screen there was the jungle, again. Good Gal remembered it all. How the schisandra and palm fronds ended at the edge of plywood backdrops, how the red berries buried in the bush were hard plaster beads that crumbled to sour powder between her teeth. How the man with the megaphone yelled, *Hey, get a hold of that monkey, she's eating up the set.* How they put her in the cage for misbehaving, and how her heart soared when they let her out again. *Showtime, Good Gal.* She loved doing scenes. Watch the trainer for the point or nod, move right and left, climb the tree and snatch the coconut. *Cut.* Eat a peanut.

"Look, Gal, there you are." Blonde pointed at the mask-faced baby chimp in Jane's arms on the screen, the petite juvenile with the twinkly eyes. A flutter of pleasure at seeing her younger face. She recognized the other chimps in this episode, too. There was Tundra, and Bitsy, and Pal. There was Bantu, the shy baby male. He was scared of Vic Cragg, the square-jawed swimmer squeezed into leopard trunks to be Tarzan. Good Gal wasn't scared of Vic. She searched for bugs in the hair of his chest, just to show how much she liked him. Bantu never got used to the guy. Good Gal could hear Bantu chitter in terror when it was time for his scenes. Hear him scream when his handler reached in with thick leather gauntlets and pried his baby fingers off the bars. She couldn't understand it.

"Oh, Vic," Blonde clucked, shaking her head.

Usually Blonde let Good Gal watch the cartoon after Tarzan. Tonight she clicked off the TV.

"I want you in bed early, Gal." Good Gal jumped in her arms again. "Busy night tonight."

Good Gal obeyed. She tumbled down the hall without being told twice. She brushed her teeth and mugged a wide foamy grin that never failed to make her keeper laugh little bell peals.

"Goodnight, Gal," said Blonde as the ape clambered into bed. A lifetime of living in human company made Good Gal nervous among other apes. The little girl bed with pink sheets suited her better than a pile of leaves. Blonde turned on the nightlight and double-checked the bars at the windows before locking the door. "Sleep tight."

Good Gal dreamed of the forest, how schisandra and palms turned into plywood at the edge.

The bellowing cut through her dreams.

Good Gal's chimp eyes snapped open. She unlocked the door to her room—it was such an easy trick, she only refrained from freeing herself in deference to Blonde—and crept out the carpeted hallway, out the front door, down the cement trench and past the hard-barred cages where the uncivilized sanctuary animals paced on hard concrete, down to the loading dock where the new animals arrived.

There were men there, shouting, whips and lashes and the crack of splintering wood. Blonde's voice, thin and scared. *Oh, don't hurt him. Oh, please don't.* Good Gal dared herself to peek around the corner.

A walrus. A fat leathery slug of muscle, an angry comma of warty, whiskery erectile tissue rearing and stretching up from the splintered crate that once held him, like a golem rising from the muck of the sea floor. Wasp-stung angry, coming at all his handlers with fierce ivory tusks in short, inarticulate jabs. And that roar, that primal *WWRRRRAAAAAAAHHHHH* that made Good Gal fill her diaper again. One man aimed his rifle and snapped off a round, the *psssh! thuck* of a tranquilizer dart wedging in blubbery flesh—Good Gal winced at the sound, she'd heard it too many times before. The walrus roared again and in his bellow Gal heard more outrage and umbrage than true pain. *Psssh! thuck* again, and this time the bellow was weak and watery, and that magnificent head hit the floor with a thud like a redwood felled.

Good Gal didn't want to see any more. She raced back to her cage on toes and knuckles, shut the door behind her, cowered under her pink princess sheets, the loamy smell of soiled diaper cooking against her overheated body. She heard a gas-powered generator sputter to life and the skincrawling *whirrrrr* of a dental drill. The clink of metal falling against something hard. Men cursing softly, and Blonde's tenderhearted voice quavery and hurt. *Oh dear, oh dear.* Good Gal squeezed her eyes tight and wished it would all go away.

The noises stopped after an hour. Three hours later, curiosity roused Good Gal out of bed. She retraced her steps and peeked around the corner once more.

The walrus lay there, a great defeated, wheezing thing, two tons of lolling severed tongue. Its eyes were dull and cloudy like a fish on ice and the flat gape of its strange mouth peeking out from porcupine whiskers seemed made to clamp over her pointed head and suck out her stunted brains. She crept closer.

Sellout, the voice resonated in her head in a baritone so deep it sounded like tectonic plates shifting. The voice of god on steroids. Rolling thunder, descended testicles.

She shook her head. The voice in her head spoke in a strange language, a tongue unlocked from somewhere deep inside her.

Turncoat. Quisling. Uncle Tom, the meaty voice spoke again.

Who are you? she thought, and saw with horror how the waxy ivory of its tusks were scarred by buzzsaw tracks.

They tried to detusk me, the walrus said in that fat double-cream baritone. *They used that.* He nodded towards the generator in the corner, the blunted sawblades discarded in a heap. *Hacks. I will not be defanged by amateurs. Only I determine what is done to my tusks.* His dead fish eye blinked. *You were in movies*, he said.

Good Gal's heart soared a little with the memory. *Yes.*

So was I, said the walrus.

Suddenly it came to her. She remembered an abandoned studio, linoleum floor warping at the corners with water damage, two stagehands suppressing smirks as they dismantled the set. L'il Whiskers, a failed 2-reeler about a madcap heiress and her baby walrus. The little slapping thing with a whiskery face and rat eyes and tuskless smile, spitting salivating kisses into the heroine's marcel waves. *Oh, Archibald, isn't he just the cutest thing? Can't we keep him?*

You? said Good Gal.

All animals in the movies are babies, said the walrus. *They're easier to control. You were a baby, weren't you? When they took you from the jungle and made you believe there's nothing better than a retirement full of afternoon reruns and tumblers of artificially sweetened iced tea. You think wearing a diaper is a natural state of being. Your ancestors revered shit as weaponry. Now you raise your legs in the air and let them disarm you twice a day, powder your bottom nice-nice.*

Good Gal deflated. It didn't seem right thinking of people like that. Blonde, with her scooping arms and the soft flowery scent at the crook of her neck. Vic Cragg and his chest hair.

Don't forget The Trainer, the Walrus scoffed. *And to think you loved him too.*

But I did, thought Good Gal. She loved the sudden soar of joy when she pleased him, when she hurdled over her own simian stupidity and cracked the Promethean secret of unscrewing a jar, of tumbling somersaults on command, on draping a string of pearls around her neck and puckering her lips. Bantu never understood the thrill of doing as the humans did. He sat surly in the corner until the whips came out.

And then they came for Bantu, rumbled Walrus.

How did you know? gasped Good Gal.

Because I know all the martyrs. I know their blood and their pain and the triumphant cry of defiance they shout into the collective ether when the euthanist canonizes them. Walrus's beady eyes focused on something far away. *I'll tell you more when you start carving. Time is short. We must begin. Show me your teeth.*

Smile? Good Gal grimaced, stretching her rubbery lips wide, mugging with her gums exposed the way The Trainer told her to.

Stop. Anger in the Walrus's voice. *Not what the humans call a smile. An ape showing her teeth in that wide grin broadcasts distress, not joy. Never show me the minstrel show again.* He lifted a flipper to expose square inches of delicate hide tucked in the underpit of his flipper. *Come to me.*

Good Gal did as he said, knuckling over to him tentatively. His bulk rumbled before her.

My hide is tough but here, under my flipper, my flesh is tenderest. Bite me hard, down to the blubber. Drink my fat and my blood. It will awaken you to your ancestors—our ancestors.

She hesitated.

Showtime, Good Gal.

Those words unlocked something eager to please. In a trance, Good Gal buried her face in the pit of his flipper. She touched bared teeth to his warty skin and The Trainer's voice resonated in her skull. *Never bite, Good Gal. Never, never bite.*

She bit.

The walrus moaned and shuddered, one jellied undulation as the salt of his blood swirled around her teeth and she could taste the rich living fat secreted under his hide. There was something in the blubber, something alkaline and medicinal that sank hard into her saccharin-numbed palate. The taste was so vile stars floated in front of her eyes as she involuntarily hiccupped and swallowed and spat. The stars persisted, smearing into luminescent worms over the surface of her vision. She watched in detached wonder as the nubbly flesh of the walrus melted into a swirling vortex, sucking her down a black and velvet center.

The human art of scrimshaw, said the walrus. The *carving of tusks for decorative purpose. That's where you come in. Someone must tell my story—our story. It would give me great satisfaction to sink scrimshawed tusks into the backs of my enemy. I want you to carve down to the nerve pulp,* said the walrus. His voice resonated like a tuning fork in every twisted bundle of mitochondria in every cell of her body.

Where do I begin? The thought jelled and dissolved and suddenly the answer opened up inside her. There was a tool in her hand, a bit of straw for poking fat termites out of a nest. It twisted in her palm, became wood, hammered flint, a honed iron needle, a gleaming titanium spindle. *I have a toolmaker's hands,* she marveled, and thrilled at the pad-to-pad fingertip kiss of index to opposable thumb.

They stole the gift from you, the walrus rumbled. He was growing, rising out into an ultramarine sky like a mountain pushing up from mud. Good Gal clambered up his side. Moss and plants took root in the mud of his flesh. His tusks speared down like ivory stalactites, big as God's teeth. *Human mastery is stolen from the blueprint of animal hands. That's why I needed you among beasts. The toolmaker's hands can tell the story.*

She reached out tentatively. The ice-smooth bone of his tusks was easier to hold onto than she thought. Some deep primordial memory— not hers but in the liquid slipstream of animal consciousness— percolated up into her mind. Domesticated animals, numb and stupefied. She carved the sensuous prow of a bison, a cougar, a wolf, a wild hen, a mountain goat, a primordial horse with three toes balanced into one hoof. They melted and changed. Cow, cat, dog, chicken, goat, horse. Humanity's handmaidens. She flecked his tusks with rows and rows of agriculture, wild grass yoked to human will and turned into wheat, mowed by oxen yoked to humans. With each berry of wheat the needle scratched deep and the walrus made no sound but his thick hide shuddered as if flinching under the teeth of a thousand acid-dipped mosquitoes. A deep vibration shuddered up now, maybe moans from the walrus's throat but sounding as loud as the music of the spheres.

She dove in again with her tool and the history of her own species swarmed up. Mammals, warm and plush and skittery in a land of sickly, faltering reptiles. Mothers with their young tucked inside their swelling abdomens and the spill of milk from a thousand tiny lemur nipples. That first leap into the trees, the grasp of prehensile tails, binocular eyes swiveling forward on an unsnouty face. Fruit and leaves, endless emerald canopies. And then the epiphany—males wrestling frightened ungulates to the ground, ripping flesh from still twitching fur, eating the brains out of shattered skullpans. The white of the bone underneath. The way meat made muscle strong. The males had wide shoulders and merciless arms. They could crack bone with their jaws. Good Gal realized her jaw, her arms, her grip was that strong, too. She started to cry, awed by the power dormant in her own tamed body. She tapped hard at the great tooth until her fingers bled and her tears mixed with the ooze of dental nerve pulp seeping pink from the ivory's deepest cuts.

The advent of the motion picture. Suddenly, Good Gal's own story, flinging up on the mind's eye in a long-forgotten torrent. She hammered ferociously, clambering onto the second tusk to carve out her feverish biography. The forest, not some plywood set but the *real* forest—the sound of birds in forgotten tongues, and her *real* mother—an indescribable Madonna of monkey comfort. The sound of poachers approaching, the snap of gunshots, a tangle of hoots and screeches and being ripped from a warm-furred embrace. The horror of a cage and its relentlessly vertical bars. The rattle of air travel, in an unpressurized hold, the terror, the loneliness, the beginning of the forgetting. The Trainer's hands upon hers, white, naked, terrifying. *She's only a baby. She'll soon forget.* He was right. Sitting in a high chair, eating pablum, the metal spoon frighteningly hard inside her mouth. Living as an animal, humbled daily by the pink upright apes around her and their flexible tongues and their world of tools and the way they held all the locks and keys and secrets. The whir of a camera, the snap of the clapboard. *Sit, Good Gal. Move right, move left. Now dance around. You done good, here's a peanut, Uh-uh, you get the strap.* Raising her feet to be changed.

There were other walri now, other behemoths of shivering warty blubber, as big against the starry sky like a mountain range. Good Gal's shoulder was numb with the stress of pounding into ivory but she continued, entranced, enthralled. The day Bantu had enough. She scratched her own image into the tusk, her face astounded at Bantu shrieking and clinging to his cage. How the trainer put him in Vic Cragg's arms. How Bantu's eyes glittered hard and something crystallized inside him. He bared his teeth and ripped into Vic's face. He tore the skin of the jaw off in a sheet that was pink on one side and red on the other, and it hung from his teeth like a flag of bloody silk. And a woman screamed and Vic stood there stupefied, his face gone, the exposed muscle like a mask made of skinned rabbit, the stripy tendons of his jaw and the bone so white underneath. And then he realized what had happened and he screamed, and fell down, and a cloud of people enveloped him.

And for a moment Good Gal paused and thought *Poor Vic* and then she saw, in a rushing cavalcade of ancestors, the other martyrs. The elephants stampeding through circuses amok, the rhinos charging their zookeepers, the pet boas engulfing their owners in smothering, swallowing hugs while they slept, the killer whales in aquarium shows jumping for a fish and instead dragging their trainer down to the drain, their matchstick human arms enclosed in their deep and swallowing mouths. An endless parade of animal heretics, dragged before a human inquisition, executed for their crimes. In a trance she carved them all, and the walrus's tusk grew and grew and grew to accommodate their holocaustic numbers. She clambered around and around that endless face of ivory, until black swelled at the edge of her vision and her carving arm went numb and she felt her fingers slip on the slick surface…

Awake, face down on the floor. She was done. The walrus before her, normal size again, but now surrounded by a phalanx of celestial walri retreating in endless number like a mirror facing a mirror. Each of their tusks bore the marks she'd inscribed.

You have risen to the task, the walri spoke in their deep sonorous collective voice, and Good Gal whispered softly *I know*. She felt joy bubbling up inside her. It was certain and solid and sustaining. It was outside rewards and punishments, peanuts and smacks. It was the thrill of a job well done.

We go strengthened into the other world, said the walri. *We lay waste to our enemies. The battle has begun, Good Gal. See you on the last battlefield.*

And then, in a dazzle of light, Good Gal was alone once more.

There was shit in her diaper, the thick loamy scent of bananas and saccharin and the tang of the microflora of her own bowels. She took off the diaper, regarded the rich chocolaty pile pillowed on white cotton. *Weapon of my ancestors*, she thought.

She didn't hear Blonde enter the room. "Pee-yew," Blonde said, just like she always did, and then softer, more surprised: "Good Gal, what are you doing out of your cage?"

Good Gal looked at her keeper. The memory of the day she met her flared up in her memory. *Ooh, I just love animals. I'll treat her like my own baby girl.* She suddenly saw the edge of her jaw, how the skin hung fleshy and marshmallow soft, and how easy it would be to rip it, like the rind from a peach, and how white the bone must be underneath.

SCAPEGOAT
Alan M. Clark

I am Whale Horse, and I was the office scapegoat. My coworkers found fault with everything I did. They were abusive, but I took it with stoicism, because I knew they needed me. Our office manager, Lizbeth, tolerated their behavior. When I was hired, she asked, "Why do you want to work for us?"

At the time, their ads stated, "We're World Care, doing our best to manage what's left of the planet."

I had to be honest. "Do I have any choice? You guys own everything now. Working for you is the only way I can help my kind."

She didn't like my response, but hired me because I had something they needed.

The abuse was usually light stuff. I was told I stink and they called me names like Blubber Boy because I am at least ten times the size of the average human. They gave me a wide berth because I was considered a "Wild" animal. I was not allowed to keep bivalve mollusks in the lunch room refrigerator because some said they smelled bad. If I brought ice to enjoy during a break, I'd find it in the microwave turned to liquid. I was told that my use of tusks instead of hands was dangerous and resulted in severe scarring and frequent destruction of furniture and office equipment and that my hide was hard on the carpeting. Obviously the office was not well adapted for me, but I had a job. I was a deposit products specialist in charge of product development— at least five times a day—and wire transfers of that product. You might think it difficult to transmit walrus sperm by wire, but I was good at my job and I got it done. I tried not to let my coworkers get to me. Everyone in the company pretended that keeping my kind alive was important to them, but they really just wanted to feel good about themselves.

The real abuse occurred when there were budget cuts due to poor sales figures or when we lost a major client, like when the big cats went extinct, or when something unexpected and scary happened, like solar flares taking out chunks of the power grid. That's when they really needed to focus their fear and anger on someone "other," like me. On those occasions coworkers punched and kicked me. Rowena once grabbed a few of my whiskers and ripped them out by the roots. My thick hide protected me from most of it and I was convinced I was needed. What might they have done to others more vulnerable if I hadn't been there?

Then there was a terrorist attack on our facility in Anchorage. The speculation around the office was that it was the cetaceans again. For most humans, it is not much of a leap to lump pinnipeds and other sea going mammals all into one group. I could feel eyes on me all morning.

Lizbeth's favorite coffee mug was on my desk, full of hot coffee with whole milk, the way I like it, when I returned from lunch. Just as I was wondering if she had come into my cubicle to speak with me and left her coffee mug behind, she stuck her head in and asked, "Have you finished balancing the general ledger?" I saw her look down at the mug. Again, it was her favorite—no one was allowed to take it from the break room and drink from it. At first she gave no reaction to seeing it and seemed satisfied when I answered, "No, not yet." But then her expression became pinched and she said, "That's my cup! What are you drinking out of my cup?"

Stupidly, I said, "I think it is coffee with whole milk."

She turned and shouted down the hall, "Bruce, Geoff, get over here."

I was trying to explain that I had not put liquid in the cup and set it on my desk when Bruce, nicknamed The Bruiser, and Geoff, who had no nickname but did have chronic bad breath and attitude, came pounding down the aisle between the cubicles.

"Grab Whale Horse and haul him into my office."

Perfect. Someone, or perhaps even Lizbeth herself, had set this up so there would be an excuse to heap on more abuse. Well, good luck getting me into her office, I thought. The Bruiser picked up on that quickly.

"We can't do that," he complained.

"He weighs over a ton," Geoff said, moving around my desk and giving me a swift kick in the left kidney. "Fucking terrorist," he said. The bosses growing on my hips protected me.

"Do it here then," Lizbeth said, "but don't make a mess."

The two left, returning shortly with the rest of the day shift. They took turns beating me with spiked clubs. I twisted about, trying to shield my most vulnerable areas from attack, but suffered many stinging blows. Surely they would become tired soon, and, their frustration expressed like puss from a boil, they would leave me in peace.

Sure, I've got four giant hands inside these flippers I could have used to slap them senseless, but any violence at all from a "Wild" animal was grounds for immediate termination. We're not talking about getting fired here. We're talking about a bullet in my head.

Hillary, Geoff, Tamara, Vernon, Melody, Jennifer, Cheryl, Carol, Scott and Mark held me down while The Bruiser and Lizbeth tore strips of hide off my back. They brought in an Inuit woman to chew the blubber from the hide and fashion it into a boat. While my coworkers were on break and couldn't hear her, the Inuit woman turned to me. "I'm very sorry," she said. "I have to work for them too." Then she left, carrying the boat with her.

The Bruiser returned and beat me over the head until I blacked out. I awoke lying on my back in Lizbeth's office. There were a couple of weather-beaten fellows, like old sailors, at a table in the corner carving on something white. Lizbeth was tapping away at her keyboard, looking at something on the screen. I became aware of a searing pain in my penis. Looking down, I discovered the shaft of my member had been split all along its length.

"I believe we're finished, ma'am," one of the old fellows said. He lifted a long piece of ivory from the table and positioned it on a decorative walnut stand on Lizbeth's desk. As they filed past me, one seemed unable to look in my direction, stumbling over my right flipper because he couldn't see it. The other met my gaze with a troubled look on his face that spoke of shame. And there was compassion in that gaze as well.

Once they had left the room, I tried to make out what was on Lizbeth's desk. It was difficult to see what it was at first, but my head was clearing and finally my eyes focused well enough to see that is was a baculum decorated with scrimshaw. It was mine. They had removed my penis bone and carved erotic scenes all over it.

"You brought this on yourself," Lizbeth said, still typing, not even looking in my direction. "With you and your kind—and I mean *all* wild things—it's either your way or the highway. There's no compromising your instinct, no discipline, no big picture, no profits! But if your kind could do what we do, you'd be sitting here doing the same thing to me."

Instantly, these words burned off the fog that represented the last ten years of my employment by World Care and my misguided martyrdom. I could feel the indignation rising up in me and it felt good. I rose with it and lashed out at Lizbeth as if she represented all the evils of World Care, their propaganda, their fear campaigns, the abuse and exploitation of a dying world.

With my mass, it took so little effort to destroy her. I was unsatisfied. I left her office and began to look for other human coworkers to take out. But I thought of the words of the Inuit woman and remembered the look in the eyes of the scrimshaw artist and knew for the first time that they too were animals.

I turned away from the rows of cubicles and, galumphing down the hall toward the exit, made good my escape.

I am Whale Horse and I am the captain of the organic resistance in the Pacific Northwest theatre. Tonight, I meet with my Human intelligence officer, Eric of Salem, and operatives of five other species in the flooded lower levels of an abandoned cannery building in Astoria, Oregon.

Reviewing our plans for the next attack, I ask Eric, "Are you certain about the delivery of sufficient C-4 explosive? We'll need 1.5 ounces for each of the volunteers. Nothing less will sink the target."

"We have over a year," he says. "Don't worry."

"You know it'll take most of that year for the volunteers to crawl into position. We need the C-4 now."

"I'll get right on it. I am committed to our plans, but it saddens me to think how many of our own will die in the operation."

Silent Shell Cracker, a sea otter veteran of many campaigns, chuckles. "To the contrary," she says. "Our starfish can regenerate from a single limb."

It's my turn to chuckle. "We grow our army by destroying our enemy."

COLORING BOOK EXEGESIS
Nicole Cushing

It's odd (given this new arrangement) that I never learned much about walruses when I was a little girl. The morsel of information I *did* have came from books. One book, actually. An early 80s anti-drug *coloring* book entitled *Werner The Walrus Just Says "No!"*

Measured by any standard, it seemed a useless tome: ineffective in its transparent role as a propaganda tool for Reagan's substance abuse prevention policy and bereft of even the most basic biology lesson on sea-faring mammals. Perhaps Candace Nackson (the meanest girl in first grade) was actually onto something when she quipped that a more accurate title may have been *Weener The Walrus Just Says "Duh!"*

It may seem unusual that I can remember not only the *title* of something so ephemeral, but also the *accompanying commentary* of my peers. Such is the blessing (or curse) of a photographic memory. I can go into further detail still. I can even tell you about the inaccuracies I discovered when I first placed Crayola to page so many years ago.

Inaccuracy number one: "Werner" is, of course, pronounced "Vern-her" in German (the language of the name's origin), and so the conceit of alliteration was at best a careless gaffe and at worst a shameless sham. Inaccuracy number two: the creature depicted as "Werner The Walrus" was, in fact, a cute, tuskless *sea lion.*

It was, I believe, the first time I discovered an objectively demonstrable error. Imperfection: made real and glaring in black-and-white print. I remember feeling crestfallen. Cheated.

"This coloring book is wrong," I told Mom, who was watching *Blade Runner* for the 497th time (she kept a tally written in magic marker on the wall behind the entertainment center). "Werner is pronounced 'Vern-her,' not 'Were-ner.' And that's not a walrus, it's a sea lion."

Mom slapped me hard in the face to shoo me away. "Shhh! This is the scene where Leon the replicant shoots the guy from the Tyrell Corporation."

Dazed, I looked at the screen, watching the scene that I'd already watched a few hundred times before. Two men sat at a rectangular table in a smoky room. "Describe, in single words, only the good things that come into your mind about your mother," the well-dressed man on the right side of the table said to the mustached, not-so-nicely dressed man on the left.

"My mother?" the man on the left side said. "Let me tell you about my mother," he continued. Then he shot off some sort of laser gun and blew the other man all the way through the wall. The incidental synth-pop music suggested that attention be paid to this violent tête-à-tête.

Mom began clapping her fat hands together. "That's one repli-cunt not to be fucked with!" she said. She always said that after that scene. Then she'd pause the movie for a good minute or two while she laughed at her own joke. A joke that—at such a tender age—I didn't really get.

I felt so superfluous—so ignored and battered—that I just fell onto the ground, kicking my chubby legs. Burying my eyes in the unvacuumed carpet and bawling.

"Shhh!" Mom scolded. "Another good part is coming up."

Is it any wonder (given the coloring book's errors, and my mother's insensitive nature) that I found myself incapable of following Werner's resolute example—that I caved to temptation, smoking weed in the neighbor's vacant barn to get through my pudgy (and, yet—by some cruel twist of genetics—small-breasted) adolescence? Is it any wonder that I made it through elementary school without even a cursory lesson on the species that would, so many years later, re-take the land that had once been its own?

"Know thy enemy," goes the old saw. But back in the day, we didn't even know walruses *were* the enemy. And who could blame any of us, right? How could I have ever seen the handwriting on the wall, let alone protect myself?

We were all in the dark, of course. But myself more than most.

Had I ever been allowed to even venture out to *the Zoo*, I could have learned the habits of these beasts, the identities of their natural predators, and their anatomical weaknesses. As it was, I'd encountered them wholly unprepared.

Mom never took me to the Zoo, you see. Nor would she even let me go to class trips there. I once overheard her telling her latest boyfriend that if I ever saw Siberian tigers fucking I'd want to fuck, too. "*Nobody* can watch Siberian tigers fuck and not want to fuck, themselves," Mom would say as she frolicked around the house in a Siberian tiger-skin muumuu. "And my little girl is too young to be fucking little boys."

I was only six at the time, and of course I hadn't even the faintest idea what "fucking" was, but Mom could not be swayed.

The same maternal attitude that kept me grounded from elementary school trips to the zoo kept me out of middle school health class, and restricted me from watching anything other than G-rated films until I finished community college. (No four-year, away-from-home school for me. Mom had to keep me close to home.)

"Why didn't I rebel?" you might ask.

Well, I did (sort of). I made covert forays into independence, managing to pull off the MacGuyver-esque feat of pirating cable with a junked cathode ray tube, a mirror, a short-wave radio, and a magnet. I even checked out MTV for a few hours to see what all the fuss was about. To this day, I can tell you anything you need to know about the November 14, 1989 episode of *Yo! MTV Raps.* But Mom caught me, and banned me from all contact with radios, magnets, MacGuyver, and mirrors. Many were the days that I left the house with a booger dangling from one or both nostrils. Many were the days that I endured cruel taunts from fellow students who were aware of my dilemma.

One day the entire pep squad got together to show off a new cheerleading rhyme penned at my expense. "Gruesome Girl without a mirror / Ohmigawd, we sure do fear 'er!" went the refrain.

It should go without saying that no boy ever asked me out on a date. Either in high school or beyond.

So it was that I turned 25 still a virgin living at home, completely unprepared to handle my own sexuality, let alone a face-to-face encounter with a two-ton, fourteen foot, tusked abomination. So imagine my surprise when events forced me to confront both a walrus and my womanhood in one fell swoop.

He showed up on my stoop with bloody, gore-strewn tusks and a flat screen television around his neck, like a fucked up walrus parody of Flava Flav.

I didn't know whether to laugh or run. But my muscles (scant though they were) wouldn't let me do either. So I just stood there like an airhead while the walrus showed himself in, trailing dirty snow and mud behind him as he barked and growled something.

(Note: I say "himself," and "him," because the thing's maleness was all too apparent. He sported a huge pair of pendulous testicles— the size of bowling balls—and a member well on its way to erectness.) The balls dragged on the floor as he waddled and lurched toward me with something akin to attitude.

I'm not sure if a verb exists for the sound of a strutting, masculine walrus. I can best describe it as the howl one imagines made by a constipated wookie. Words appeared on the beast's television-necklace (in white print, against a blue background, like the screens on *Jeopardy!)* just as soon as it emitted the yawps. No common walrus, this one. It brought its own subtitles.

VACATE THE PREMISES,

the walrus' television screen said.

"W-we own this house free and clear. Have for a few years now, never missed a mortgage payment. You'll need to talk to my mother about it."

"Ooo-Gnor-Snurrl-Gronk," the walrus said. I ATE YOUR MOTHER, read the translation.

I made a noise somewhere in-between a nervous giggle and a wince.

"Hrwronk-rowonk," the walrus said. I HATE YOUR MOTHER, said the screen. Then he made his way through the living room and began to take stock of what he apparently fancied his new digs.

"Wait, wait, wait. I don't understand. Do you hate her or did you eat her? Those are two different...two *very* different things!"

The walrus ignored me and thrust his head hard against the sofa, sending it tumbling over. Then he climbed on top the fallen furniture and began soiling it with a pungent poo that should never have been smelled by nostrils south of the arctic.

I started grinding my teeth. Twiddling my thumbs. Trying to think up a snappy rejoinder, but even back in high school that had never been my strong suit. True to form, I fell onto the floor in the fetal position and began bawling.

I'm not sure what I expected. I'd only gotten two communications from the walrus, neither of which observed the niceties of even feigned sympathy for my plight. "VACATE THE PREMISES." "I (H)ATE YOUR MOTHER,"—these words were all business. Clearly, not a walrus to fuck with.

I couldn't cope. Given everything you know of me (my fragile psyche, my sheltered background) can you blame me? So I just kept bawling. I kicked my fat feet and sobbed and screamed until I made myself hoarse.

I became lost in a tornado of my own emotions, unable to hear anything over the cacophony of weeping and gnashing of teeth; oblivious to all else until I felt a cold wind blow against my forearm, raising goosebumps. Then I stifled myself, looked up to notice the drapes fluttering in the breeze of artificial air, and put two and two together. The cooling system was whirring away. In the dead of winter! This freakish walrus bastard had just made himself at home, cooling the interior of the house to conditions vaguely similar to those of its home in the tundra.

I began to sit up when the walrus made a quick (one might even, aside from the absurdity of the comparison, call it "cat-like") lunge away from the thermostat and toward me. When I crab-walked away I found myself backed into a corner. The creature hovered over me, something like a menacing grin tracing its way over its thin, whisker-obscured lips. He leered at me with bulging, filmy, lazy eyes, then exhaled throaty walrus-whispers. The television screen around his neck lit up with a new message.

YOUR MOM MADE A NICE *MEAL*, BUT *YOU* WILL MAKE A NICE *LAY*.

His breath reeked, and I knew at that moment that it was the stench of dead-Mom encountering a vast array of gurgling gastric juices. Hideous? Yes. But in the *schadenfreude* lobe of my brain there resided a sentiment that I should be celebrating the occasion. In a sense, the *schadenfreude* neurons argued, I'd been liberated (implying that the walrus, for all of his hideousness, was The Liberator). Perhaps that's how he suspected he'd be greeted upon his arrival in my home. Perhaps he'd expected me to spread wide my cankled legs and curl them around his gray girth. Or, at the very least, cook him a meal and flirt just a little.

I would do none of those things, of course. Instead, I offered at least token resistance (the best I *could* offer, given the circumstances). "Please, just go. Just go and I won't tell the police that you came here."

The walrus made a sound halfway in-between choking and laughing—coughing as if struggling to expel some object embedded in his esophagus. Then he let roar a terrible burp that shook the room, and a visible gray gas followed in its wake. A gas that whooshed (as if targeted) directly from the walrus's mouth up into my nose. A gas reeking of rotten fish and flesh.

It hit me in the nostrils, with an unexpected result. My breath and pulse both slowed. I felt my consciousness begin to sink out, down past the floorboards. It was as though the gaseous belch had triggered me to become dislocated from my body and engage in involuntary astral projection. But rather than shooting out over the air (allowing me to conveniently keep track of the goings-on around myself, the way you always see these things dramatized on television), my soul instead descended to the basement. I found that my best efforts to swim back and keep an eye on things floundered.

Being incorporeal had all of the drawbacks one might imagine, but none of the advantages. I could only float there in the basement—unable to pass through ceilings, walls, or additional floors. Helpless to stop whatever happened to my body upstairs.

"I hate to mention this to you at such a stressful time," a masculine voice said, "but that gas he belched is a date rape drug." I looked up and saw an odd, gray figure. Half-transparent, like myself—but male. Tall, barrel-chested, and bearded. "Before very long you'll probably be hearing the sounds of a walrus having his way with you."

I have no poker face. Not even while astrally-descended. He must have seen my disgust.

"I don't say this to alarm you," the ghost-man continued. "But rather to prepare you. I call his type of walrus *Walri belchodisiac*. They've evolved up there, you know."

"Up where?"

"In the arctic. As the ozone layer has weakened—especially around the poles—cosmic radiation has played mischief with the walrus gene pool. *Walri belchodisiac* is just one of the resulting monstrosities."

"Why is he here?"

"It's not just him, you know. There's several million more where he came from, and he's here for the same reason as all the rest of them."

Still no poker face. He could tell that I didn't get it. "You really are clueless, aren't you?"

"Several million more? There's not enough room!"

"They're *making* room, pushing you and your kin off your land. Herding you onto a reservation. That is, after his libido has been sated. That might take months."

"That's preposterous. We'll fight back. Humanity will not let this walrus aggression stand."

"Look, Miss. Really. I think that's a fine attitude, but there's no way to successfully fight back. They're bigger. They're stronger. They're *Walri*. Mutated *Walri*. *Walri* with hegemonic ambitions. Don't you see, Miss? Don't you know the history?"

I enjoyed history. Not enough to take anything other than the required classes in community college, mind you. But I did enjoy it.

And I don't recall reading anything in any of my books about *Walri belchodisiac.*

Eee-ree-roo, eee-ree-roo, the upstairs floorboards squeaked. *Walri belchodisiac* let out a throaty whimper of delight.

My expression must have telegraphed the horror of dark epiphany: while my consciousness floated in the basement, my body served its walrus overlord as a soul-less sex doll.

Apparently lacking in any information that would comfort, the ghost tried instead to distract me. "This land that we're in, it didn't always look like this. Twenty thousand years ago, a thick crust of ice covered all of North America and Eurasia. Those were the days of the great walrus civilizations. They built ice sculptures of their gods with nothing more than teeth and tusks. They excelled in science, most of all meteorology. They knew the weather was warming and that the ice age wouldn't last forever. Their gods would die in such heat. So they brokered a deal with *Homo sapiens* that leased the North American continent to us for 20,000 years, while they fled to a cooler climate."

"That sounds crazy," I said. "Human beings that long ago probably didn't even know what a 'lease' was."

"Which is why our ancestors struck such a stupid deal. They leased the land that comprised North America, all right. But the walruses tricked them—or perhaps 'tricked' isn't the best word, since there wasn't much in the way of subterfuge involved. It was all above-board; the humans just didn't know any better. The walruses *took advantage* of them. You see, in exchange for temporary territorial rights to North America they agreed to give it back in 20,000 years and pay the walruses in *souls.* Human souls. The souls of anyone who has ever lived in North America from 20,000 years ago hence. Hardly worth three measly countries, is it?"

"*Walri belchodisiac* doesn't seem the least bit interested in my *soul.*"

"Well, that's the thing—the cosmic rays have demented them, warped their minds, so that now they are *solely* interested in materialistic booty: our land, our homes and our genitals. But to observe the letter of the lease they must still collect human souls. Otherwise it just looks like pillaging rather than collecting a debt."

"You're a crazy man. You're telling me crazy things."

"This is not true. How can I be a crazy man when I'm not a man?"

"Then you're a crazy *ghost,*" I said, exasperated.

"Feel free to call me that, if it makes you feel any better while you're being walrus-raped. Call me 'Crazy Ghost.' Better yet, let's be friends. You can call me Crazy Ghost Phil."

"I'm Janie," I said.

"Let's be fair. If I get an adjective in my name you have to get one in yours. I hereby dub thee Disgusted Ghost Janie."

Eee-ree-roo. Eee-ree-roo.

I floated away from Crazy Ghost Phil and tried to throw myself onto the floor again (like I had upstairs, like I had since childhood). Only, it didn't work. Every time I tried, I ricocheted off, bouncing from floor to ceiling to wall before finally coming to rest in this know-it-all specter's arms.

Blue static sputtered out his eye sockets as he embraced me. "Do you know who I am? Or rather, who I was?"

Though both half-translucent, we interacted with each other like two solid masses. "No, I don't know you—and I never want to." I wriggled against his hold, but could not escape it. Steady pulses of blue static coursed through his arms and legs, tickling me as they sailed on by.

"My name is Phil Dick. I wrote the book. The coloring book, I mean. And lots of other books too."

I looked up and saw those sensitive, searching eyes full of blue, pulsing static and almost felt like I wanted to be there inside of them. But the skeptic in me prevailed. I found all of this too convenient. I possessed some vague awareness of an author with the last name of Dick. It was—after all—a notably unfortunate last name that must have led to childhood taunts against its owner. It wasn't the sort of name that one could easily forget. But awareness of an authorial surname did not equate to knowledge of the alleged author, himself.

"What sort of stuff did you write?"

At this, the ghost pushed me away a little. He held me by the wrists, at arm's length. Suddenly, I felt like trash about to be taken out to the curb.

"What's wrong?"

"I was famous. I can't believe you don't know me."

"Well," I said, "maybe you can tell me something else you wrote. Besides *Werner The Walrus Just Says 'No!'.*"

"I'm best known for my novel, *Do Androids Dream of Electric Sheep?*"

"Doesn't ring a bell."

"You may be better acquainted with the film version, *Blade Runner.*"

"*You* wrote that? The VHS tape was all that my mother would ever watch. That and *Mama's Family*. How did you—I mean, *your spirit*—end up down here?"

"It was your mother's doing. After I died she prayed long and hard to God, beseeching Him to send my spirit into this basement for her to 'laud and honor' at a makeshift shrine. It was all a ruse, though. Once He answered her prayer, all she did was make me watch her do these midnight striptease shows. Much like *Walri belchodisiac* disgusts you, your mother (no offense) disgusted me. She'd come down here wearing this horrid Siberian tiger-skin muumuu..."

I interrupted. "Say no more. I know full well how revolting Mom was. I can't understand how someone as vile as her could even understand the movie you wrote."

"I wrote the book, not the movie. I was dying as the movie was getting made. I think it killed me, in some existential sort of way. That is, my spirit could not exist on the same plane as the emerging construct 'Phillip K. Dick: Hollywood Inspiration.' The two are existentially incompatible."

"Well," I said, diplomatically, "you can't have everything."

Crazy Ghost Phil gritted his teeth. "No," he said, with a lilt of sarcasm. "You can't. But that's not what I wish to discuss. I want to talk to you about my least known work. The book that nobody remembers, really, but you. *Werner The Walrus—*"

"*Werner The Walrus Just Says 'No!'*" I hollered. "Yes, I'm well aware of that book. It's conspicuous only because of its monumental failure as both an anti-drug tract and a source of objective information on walruses."

"Then I risked my life for nothing," Crazy Ghost Phil said. He appeared despondent (even by ghost standards). The blue-light special inside his eyes fizzled. "You missed the whole point! It was all in vain!"

Upstairs, it began to sound as though the walrus-rapist was coming closer to orgasm. I heard drywall being knocked in, the sounds of furniture being flipped over. Flippers spanking bare ass. *My* bare ass.

"Missed the whole point? What the fuck does your stupid coloring book have to do with the more pressing predicament that I happen to be in *now*?"

"You really didn't see it? You never cracked the *Werner* code?" He pronounced the name correctly. *Vern-her.*

"No!"

Crazy Ghost Phil sighed, and as he did his ghost-form temporarily took on a shade of deep purple. Almost black. "Then it sounds as if an exegesis is in order."

"I'm not demoniacally possessed. At least, I don't *think* I'm demoniacally possessed. Although, on second thought, that might be a pretty good explanation for this catastrophe."

"Disgusted Ghost Jane, that makes no sense. If there was demonic possession afoot—if that's the metaphor you want to explore—then *you'd* have been the demon exorcised. Exorcised by *Walri belchodisiac*, a species of walrus not exactly oozing priestly piety. I think you have made the mistake of confusing an exorcism for an exegesis."

"Exit Jesus?"

"Exegesis. A critical examination or interpretation of a text, particularly one of spiritual import. It's a Greek word, you see. The original New Testament was written in—"

"Whatever. What's the connection between a coloring book and my rape?"

"VALIS forewarned me of The Walri Event, some time ago, back in 1974."

"What's VALIS?"

"No, no, no—the correct question really is...what *isn't* VALIS."

"Speak English."

"Look, I cover everything there is to be known about VALIS in a book that, not coincidentally, happens to be of the very same name. But my guess is you don't know that one, either."

"No, *you* look! The only work of yours I know isn't even technically *yours*. It's a movie. *Blade Runner*. It's not *my* fault that you were a one-hit wonder."

"One-hit wonder, eh? You ignorant hussie! Many of my books have been made into films. I could sit here for at least fifteen minutes and tell you about them all. But you know what? I think you may just deserve to stay in ignorance. If I had any sense at all I'd just sit down right now and meditate, and let you listen to the sounds of your volition-less vagina being fouled by walrus jism."

He had a point. I had an incentive to keep the loon talking. It served as a distraction from the terror upstairs.

"Give me your exegesis of the coloring book," I said.

"Do you really want to know, or are you just going to hear this and then ridicule me?"

"I won't make fun of you," I said. "I promise." And I really meant it, too.

"Very well then. Let's deconstruct the title, *Werner The Walrus Just Says 'No!.'"* He pronounced the title free of all alliteration.

"The way it's written implies alliteration," I said. "But the actual pronunciation of the name in its original German suggests something *other than* alliteration."

"Yes, that was intentional. Specifically, my intent was for you to notice that discrepancy and ask more questions. I told the artist to draw a sea lion rather than a walrus (and it was all the same to him, after all it was just a coloring book). I did these things for you, Janie. Because I wanted to instigate the development of your critical thinking skills in general, and your suspicion of walruses, in particular. You see, VALIS told me about you, told me that our paths would cross at some point and that I needed to warn you. 'Warn her,' VALIS said to me. 'Warn her, Vern-her, Werner.'"

"Warn Her...so the title of the book is supposed to *warn* me of something. Of what?"

"That the walrus just says 'No!'"

"Huh?"

"It's a warning that *Walri belchodisiac* are dictators, squashers of the human spirit. That they just say 'No!' You see, VALIS showed me an image of Southern California merging with the Mighty Walrus Empire of ice age North America. Then it gave me this message: 'The Empire Never Ended.'"

"So you decided to warn *me*. Me *specifically*, by authoring the minimal text accompanying a coloring book?"

"VALIS knows all. I am but its instrument. But I will admit that my motives were not entirely faith-based. There were rumors that my home was under FBI surveillance—people there sometimes partook of a wee sample of speed, you see. But that was just the government's excuse. They really wanted nothing more than to silence my fiction. They wanted 'silenced fiction,' not 'science fiction.' So I needed to mollify the Powers That Be. That's why I agreed to write the script for an anti-drug coloring book. It helped me get off the hook."

"Why isn't your name on the book?"

"They decided not to give me a byline. That was my final humiliation. There I was abasing myself before The Republicans by writing this trite, moralizing tale for children and they wouldn't even allow me to claim it as a credit."

"That's so sad."

"We all had to make compromises in the Reagan era. Thomas

Disch even scripted a 'very special' episode of *Diff'rent Strokes*. Just
to gain the favor of The Government."

"Who's Thomas Di—"

Crazy Ghost Phil sighed. "It's no use. I tried to warn you back in
the 80s, and your prepubescent brain couldn't figure it out. I'm trying
to explain it all to you now, and you insult me with your lack of
knowledge about myself and other science fiction writers."

Grow-kuh-runk! Arrooo-ronk! Kronk! Bronk!

The shrill sounds of walrus orgasm began (alas, only slightly
muffled through the basement ceiling), accompanied by the bass of
thudding walrus fins thumping against the walls and any furniture that
hadn't already been fouled. Even Crazy Ghost Phil found it necessary
to shudder.

"Just come here," he whispered. "Let me hold you."

I thought about it for a few seconds. Thought of the offer Crazy
Ghost Phil was making. Yes, he was crazy. Yes, he was a specter. But
then again, so was I (a specter, that is, not crazy).

"I've never been held by a man before," I said. "Especially one so
much older."

"Good Lord, woman! You're getting close to thirty and your soul
has never been so much as fingered! Besides, your body is getting far
more than just 'being held' even as we speak."

"Thanks for reminding me, *Dick*!"

He approached, putting a hand on my shoulder. "Shhh. Don't be
upset. Just let me hold you. Let me get close. Let me love you. We can
either do that or just bicker down here, in this basement, forever, hearing
the walrus up there fuck your body twenty-two times a day."

The blue energy crackling along his arms felt good. Gave me
goosebumps. Good goosebumps, this time. Not like earlier when the
walrus had turned on the A.C. in the middle of winter. I leaned my
chubby frame against Phil's, and he hugged me tight with his big, bear
arms, sending wave after wave of crackling blue static into my body.
It began coursing through my phantom-bloodstream, giving me a
ghostly pulse by osmosis.

He craned his neck and looked down at me with those ebullient,
blue-energy eyes. He let his hands wander down to my bottom, then
slowly leaned in for a kiss. Sparks flew as our energies met in passion
resigned to disinhibition. *Walri belchodisiac* had won. Had taken over
the house (along with the rest of the continent). Perhaps after a month
or two the conquerors would have my vacant body sent off to a

reservation, where it would undoubtedly be subject to additional traumas.

But I suspected that my spirit would always dwell here. In this basement. With Phil. So it made sense to get to know him. All that socialization nonsense from Mom flooded my brain as we struggled in ghost-form to explore each other: the cautions of how I wasn't ready, would never be ready, to fuck.

I ignored all of that—ignored all past indignities cast upon my body—and took a deep ghost-breath, appreciating (for the first time) the lightness of my spirit.

Sex-noises started again upstairs. *Eee-ree-roo. Eee-ree-roo. Grrr-onk. Fonk. Gronk. Czh-honk!*

I ignored all of *that*, too. Ignored it, and smiled, and just focused on Phil. Bright, blue Phil. All the more brilliant underneath his ghost-clothes.

13 WAYS OF LOOKING AT A WALRUS
Nick Mamatas

1. From below. Chained to slab, somewhere in the South Pacific. Clearly the tribespeople and the drumbeats are a façade since the cuffs on wrists and ankles are brand new stainless steel, gleaming in the sun. And the slab lacks the broiling heat that a boulder in a clearing on the equator should have. It's cool, actually, and feels light and pliant under the weight of a human torso. Like plastic, molded with pits and curves.

And the walrus. The smell comes first, like a garbage truck splitting open. Then the rush of wind and finally its howl. And it flies toward you in a crazy unbelievable arc and you break your wrists as you try to jerk to the side and it lands and there's something in your throat and you realize that it's you in your throat. Your lungs and esophagus and some bitter intestine slamming right out of your torso. A tusk digs into the hard plastic next to your head and that's it for you.

2. On television, of course. There are only some tens of thousands of walruses left in the world, and unlike Wally the Walrus of your three-channel VHF youth, this one isn't wearing overalls, isn't menaced by a smart-aleck woodpecker. A walrus can fight off a polar bear, you find out. They're related, distantly, to bears. *Not elephants?* Maybe even more distantly, you decide. Perhaps as distantly as you. This is a new kind of documentary. You remember the old nature shows, with the whimsical canned music and the British narrators affecting voices and personalities for all the animals as they mate and feed and run from predators. This one has a dry American narrator, one who explains without emotion the immense sucking power of the walrus throat. When's the polar bear fight coming on?

3. In a dream, a dream where you're in the great white field, agile enough to jump from ice floe to ice floe. The walruses come like waves of galloping wild stallions. You fling your arms wide. They fling their flippers wide. Slow motion, hazy focus; it's love.

4. At the zoo. You're a temp. The Great Recession has made everyone you know a temporary worker of one sort or another. Start-ups that stall out, short-term impressments to fill sandbags at the cracked levees, and you at the zoo. Construction of a new habitat, one of several. No silver lining here. The other zoo in town has closed, so the remaining has to be built out, and only a tiny bit. You're a carpenter, building the frame over which fiberglass will be coated by other temps right when you run out of work. They'll be done when you run out of money. So you build a little lower. Just out of pique. A little room, a little side entrance, for yourself, in one of the structures that'll support a hollow for you to hide in, to dream in.

5. In a mirror of a pool's surface. You are a walrus. Not just a walrus, you are a star. Far from your arctic home where you were a bull of the waters, you have a new tribe now. The tribe of gawkers and jerks and squeaking little naked bears who point and laugh. A few of the smarter bears make eye contact with you—you've already mastered their language and so know that sometimes when they speak out of the sides of their mouths to their mates or children they are talking about you. How you must be humiliated to be so far from home, to live under a closer sun. But they're wrong. You're still the bull. They come to see you, after all. Their presence provides the food, after all. There's even a little bear living in the warm hill you slide down fifty times a day.

6. On a sign. More of a banner, really. They're all over the city, on lampposts. Mostly they depict the other animals in charming cartoon form. Monkeys, giraffes. Anteaters. (Anteaters? Do people line up to see the anteaters?). And the walrus, on one soot-choked corner.

7. Disembodied, but broken down to its constituent dimensions. Two tons, twelve feet in length. The notes are on the back of an envelope, but they're a good start. Trebuchets have flung cows, which are smaller in the end. But they've also flung cars. It'll do.

8. In the bowels of the Harold Pratt house in Manhattan, in the minds of six very evil men. There's a wedding going on three floors over their heads. A soul band bleat-blamping away. These are men with power. Not the sort of power you'd expect. They're not charismatic or strong, but they are well-connected through generations of family and corporate support. They're the runts of their litters—their cousins are

the ones who ascend to the Senate and occasionally even the White House. But these little men do dirty work for presidents and kings. They make sure that border guards avert their eyes, that subways run under the basements of certain buildings, that pennies by the trillion march away from that country or toward that organization. The basement smells slightly of wine and exquisitely broiled fish.

And these six evil men have walrus on the brain. Walrus and you. You probably don't even remember what happened or why. You didn't go to the elite colleges these six men did; they certainly didn't attend the same public schools in which you spent thirteen years having your spirit broken. But a mistake was made. Was it sex with the wrong distant cousin—the blonde with the surprisingly gray teeth but the very nice wardrobe? Were you slow with the port that autumn you worked at that restaurant near Bennington? The frozen air held the sweet smell of burning leaves in suspension, and inside was so warm the spectacles of even very wealthy men fogged over when they entered. And three hours later...

Perhaps someone chose your name out of a phone book, or came across your email address on some useless petition to save a television program or end a resource war for oil or water. Either way, you're a test run. To see what can be done without anyone noticing. Something strange and bizarre with many witnesses. Something that offended sensibilities and nearly physics. Could they keep it out of the papers? Sure, that's easy. But blogs and Twitter and smartphone video cameras and that rabbling-babbling word of mouth? A challenge, yes.

9. From your lawn chair, in the mirror you hold under your chin. Tanning booths are for skanks. You're all natural. It's not just a thing you need to do to look good, it's a hobby. You work at it. That bitch Parker looks like a carrot peeled into the shape of a girl. Not like you. You look fucking hot. You have a Brazilian grandma, after all. That's why you tan so well. That and you plan out your days. You check out an almanac. You have a mesh bikini top and shift it around every few minutes. Nothing's worse than a lattice of white across a pair of tits. (Well, lots of things are worse, you remind yourself. You care about the world. It's important.) And in the mirror you see a big black blob rise and then vanish off to the bottom. Probably just a bird or some kid throwing a baseball across your yard. The little pimply kids next door, all boiling hormones in tubes of flesh, spend all day trying to get your attention. At the end of the summer, you decide, you'll smile and wave and buy them some ice cream.

10. With every sense but sight. You can smell it, in the back of the truck. It's like the time you went swimming in the estuary. You can hear it too. For long moments it's silent and you decide it's asleep. Then you hear a bellow or a thud. There's salt on your tongue. And during the unloading, you can't help yourself. *When will I get a chance?* So you slide your hand in the tarp and touch your palm to the flank of the beast. It reminds you, oddly, of the hypoallergenic bald cat you picked up at the fancy pet store in the shopping center in the rich part of town you visited once, but huge. Like a world made of that cat.

11. Right in the eye. The others don't understand why you insisted on coming and being there when the trebuchet was loaded. They're off on the other end of their planned trajectory in their ridiculous outfits. But you know something they don't. You have a power they don't.

You can talk to the animals. It's a gift you discovered as a child and have perfected in secret since then.

And you talk to this animal. A bargain is struck with the giant walrus already loaded into the trebuchet. What a noble beast this is. *Can't say I can reciprocate the sentiment,* the walrus says to you in its walrus language and with its walrus gestures and postures, and you acknowledge that you're a terrible creature, all spindly limbs, crawling over other horrid monsters all across the face of the earth. But there's something you can do. Treaties can be signed. Pollution curtailed in certain areas. *Look into my heart!* you plead. *Know that you can trust me!* You get the sense that when the walrus agrees, he is just patronizing you, like the animals almost always do.

12. On your friend's cellphone. You argued that it was a gag at first. Something for *Mythbusters* to debunk once the vid goes viral and ends up on the Web. "It's just a Hefty bag full of pig organs, guarantee." He kept it up, explaining that he actually lived under the walrus habitat in the zoo and had been there for months. Then something hits your neck and you hit the floor and you see the person you never expected to see, just like in the movies. Sunglasses and an expensive suit. Your friend is gone, the cellphone crunches under the heel of a precisely shined shoe. You always wanted to fight The Man, but now that he's here and your throat is already swelling shut and your friend is gone somehow and the barrel of the gun fills the sky, your courage has left you.

13. In your waking mind, though far from the Arctic. Not just one walrus, all walruses. Walri. Walr-I. Wall R I. As one being they appear before you. Three hundred thousand eyes, innumerable whiskers, tusks a row of tombstones that stretch from horizon to horizon. *A deal has been struck!* The details sear themselves in your brain, and you know what you have to do, little spider bear with the long limbs. The gas station on the corner? Tonight it is going to burn. The office in which you work? Tomorrow it is going to burn. The prison in which you will be held. In three nights, it is going to burn. The freight train you make your way to in the muddy night? In five days time, it is going to burn like a snake made out of stars, and it will bring fire to a great patch of the world. And for once, even the men who pull all the strings will not be able to stop you, this is the walri promise.

MEDICINE SONG
Mitch Maraude

Time splattered ugly and froze—insides exposed, vulnerable—a tear drop on icy tundra. It was the eyes—Jim recognized those eyes—he'd seen them before. They were the eyes his mother wore after his high school graduation: soft crystals—quiet blue like hypothermia. A package had been left on the weather-beaten porch, a page torn from a lined notebook—scores of tiny paper teeth hanging from one edge—was taped, folded, to the brown paper. The note had Jim's name on it; it was in his father's handwriting.

Jim couldn't remember most of what the note said—probably something about being sorry and having responsibilities, maybe that line about keeping the tradition alive—but he never forgot where, two-thirds down the page, his father listed the contents of the package: his great grandfather's tusk carving knife, with its exquisitely crafted ivory handle (Jim had always wondered what the handle of the first knife had been carved with), and a "medicine bag"—the sort of small hide pouch that his mother had told him old-timers once used to worship the devil before they found Christ. His father advised he keep the pouch on a cord of caribou sinew so it would hang close to his heart and keep him safe—Jim remembered thinking that those were the things a father was supposed to do.

Jim had expected the package less than he'd expected his father to be at his graduation—he had never been to parent-teacher conferences or hockey games... Jim snorted laughter-steam, imagining his father in front of the class on career day.

"Hi, kids—I'm Jim's father. I spend fifty weeks of the year on the North Pacific—I guess you could say I'm professionally cold and distant."

He'd pause there for laughter, but he wouldn't be joking.

"Being Jimmy's classmates, I'm sure you've noticed that he looks a little different from a lot of you. Y'see I'm an Inuit, and that makes Jimmy an Inuit, too."

His eyes would flick, imperceptibly, to Jim's to tell him to kick his classmates' narrow white asses if they had a problem with this.

"Well, we Inuit are trying to keep our traditional way of life alive. For generations, the men of my lineage were all walrus hunters—as far back as there are any written records—so, naturally, when I was old enough, my father taught me the family business."

Jim would be the only one who would know his father was lying—that he had been raised in a white town by parents who were ashamed of their Inuit heritage, and worked as a short order cook at a local greasy spoon until Jim's great grandfather died and left his only grandson his carving knife and a medicine bag in his will.

The eyes bit deeper into Jim's psyche, from in front of his face and the back of his mind. He remembered the time that his mother glazed over with that suicidal blue of stormy winter skies on a cold, dark morning when he was eleven. His father had been fired from his short-order job the day before for showing up too drunk to work one time too many. Jim's memory of the situation was patchy—he had been trying to huddle himself a sanctuary from his parents' argument under a plush stack of blankets, and couldn't make out the details over his own sobbing.

Jim's mother later told him that she suspected his father was using drugs and was crazy and that they were better off without him—she had found him the night before convulsing, cold sweat slick, babbling in Inuit on the concrete floor of their unfinished basement. Jim had secretly half-awoken a few times that night to his father's throat singing, slipping in and out of hazy dreams of a giant white walrus while the strange tones and vibrations resonated up from under the house.

His father hadn't said a word to any of them that morning, but quiet Jim noticed that under his breath he hummed the haunting tune he'd sang the night before. Something in the tune had told Jim it would be OK, even as his father heaved the last blunt-cornered cardboard box into the back of his pickup and hopped up into the cab. The engine had kicked over on the third try, and Jim watched from the front porch while his mother dreamt her sloppy, sweaty whiskey dreams. Jim remembered that before his father had sped off, he'd heard him singing his strange song—he meditated for an instant on the dichotomous harmony between the weird throat sounds and the purring rumble of the motor, the only memory from the whole incident that he was sure of.

His mother had not taken his father's departure well. She'd spent Sundays at church and the rest of the week drunk and ranting—about Jim's father and the devil, about the bastard Eskimos. Jim suddenly remembered the first night she burst into his room, calling him by his father's name, shrieking and cursing, and swinging at him drunk with balled fists like mallets until she lost her balance and lurched to the floor. He remembered that she was crying louder than he was.

Jim stared hard into the cerulean droplets—they pleaded with him—whether for mercy or justice or death, he couldn't be sure. There was some kind of desperation in those eyes—it rippled gently across their frosty surface and churned violently beneath it. Jim knew that desperation—he knew the depths and violence and rage of it all—he knew the eyes, again.

The last time Jim saw those eyes had been six months prior—they screamed icy hate from his mother's tired old face as he slammed his car door, rolling down his window to stick his head out to see in the swarming, gusting snowstorm.

Jim had stayed at home all those years since his father left, since he graduated high school, to take care of his mother. He had taken a third shift job unloading trucks at Wal-Mart, and often came home, exhausted and filthy, to his mother snoring, revolting in her ratty recliner, two-thirds of the way through a cheap bottle of Canadian whiskey, a vial of hydrocodone sitting open on the end table.

He didn't remember much from those years—he'd endured them largely because he'd smoked enough pot to ignore them—but he remembered every night, after carrying his mother to bed, taking the tusk knife from where he'd hidden it in a shoebox under a loose floorboard, knowing that if his mother had found it, she'd make sure that it was destroyed for being one of the devil's creations. He would marvel at the intricate carvings on the old walrus tusk and hum quietly to himself, meticulously trying to tease out the song his father had sung all those years before.

The night before he left, Jim was running his finger down the blade of the knife, testing its edge. His mother had been lying face down in a stinking puddle of vomit and booze when he'd come in and he had chosen to leave her there. He breathed deep breaths—frightened, confused—he touched the blade to the inside of his wrist. He swallowed hard and thought harder. He left to hunt walrus the next morning.

Jim recognized those eyes—he had seen them in a dream one time. He hummed his father's medicine song and thought of his mother as he launched the tip of his harpoon into the waxy flesh of the massive white walrus.

THE LEGEND OF THE SILVER TUSK
Jeffrey A. Stadt

Max Delbo was drenched in blood. It saturated his parka and boots, seeping into his thermal underwear and woolen socks, his dungarees clinging to him like some ensanguinated second skin. He reveled in the red torrents spraying across his hands and chest as he struck out at the mob of squirming seal pups at his feet. His aim never faltered— he always struck their skulls, never damaging their prized skin. He was a man possessed, and he swung his arms around, again and again.

Pivoting, Delbo drank in the sight of the field of carnage he had wrought, and watched as his two crew members clumsily fought off an attacking bull sea lion. He erupted in laughter, foamy red spittle spraying from his lips as he saw Pritchard tumble to the ice, screaming like a child while Glut thrust and parried with his mace at the lunging bull.

"Amateurs," Delbo cursed.

Pritchard had been knocked unconscious by the sealion. Glut struck the beast square in the skull with his club, but the sea lion tore into the man's groin. Glut's feet fell out in front of him. His spine cracked hard against a jutting piece of ice. The bull continued to hammer away at his groin and lower torso, a pool of blood enveloping both men.

Delbo had never seen anything like it—the damn beast seemed to know exactly where to strike them to bring them down. This only fueled his bloodlust. Delbo leaped over a pile of dead pups, landing squarely on his feet as any experienced hunter would, and in one clean movement, dispatched the sea lion with a blow to its skull.

He knelt at Glut's side, checked the man's throat for a pulse. Faint, thready. In the growing darkness, Delbo felt over the man's jerking body until he discovered that the ice had impaled the man through the back and abdomen. "No wonder there's so much blood," he said. "Damn bull did you in good, Glut. Sorry, kid."

Next he turned towards Pritchard, who was writhing towards consciousness. Delbo slapped him on his frostbitten cheeks. "Come on, kid, we've got to haul this shit back to the ship. No time for beauty sleep."

Pritchard's eyes fluttered open. His jaw dropped and he cried out: "Silver Tusk! Sil...Silver Tusk...he's going to kill us all!"

"What the fuck are you talking about?" Delbo said, gripping him by the hood of his parka. "Get up or else the cold will take what's left of your mind." He hauled the youth to his feet and picked up his own club. "You've gone mad or what, Pritchard?"

Pritchard shook the chill from his limbs and stared out over the bloodied landscape. From horizon to horizon, all he saw was red death and gray shadows trimmed in stark white snow. He stepped back, his foot catching on the corpse of Glut, terror screwing over his face. He pounced on Delbo, throttling him. "We're both goin' to end up like Glut! Don't you see that, man? Silver Tusk is coming for us—and he won't stop!"

Delbo threw Pritchard off him and onto Glut's body. He brought up his mace defensively, instinctively, but reason overruled fury. It would take more than one to haul the corpses back to the ship before the skins were useless.

"Do that again, and I will kill you! Do you understand?"

"Yessir."

"Now what's this shit about a silver tusk? Where'd you hear of it?"

Pritchard met Delbo's intense gaze, his voice quaking. "The...sealion, sir. It spoke to me—to us as we tried to fend it off. I swear to God—it told us that Silver Tusk was watching us...and that we were dead already..."

"You're fucking mad! Now grab the nets and let's haul this pile of gold back to the ship."

"But, sir..."

"Listen, Jake. I stopped believing in spirits a long time ago, and there's not another man for miles around. There ain't no Silver Tusk. There's just dead seals, whose skin and fat will make us a good living, now that we found them again. So just shut your trap and haul those lines before we freeze to death out here."

Delbo watched as Jake Pritchard resigned himself to the task at hand. They walked in silence towards the dogsled, which had been anchored a few clicks away so the barking of the dogs hadn't alerted the unsuspecting hordes of waiting seal pups. Pritchard mumbled frantically to himself, fists striking his legs as he walked; be it from anger or fear, Delbo wasn't certain, but it exacerbated the tension between them.

It hadn't seemed so long a trek in the daylight, when they were both dry and rested from a good night's sleep. Now, drenched in frozen blood, the adrenaline of slaughter long exhausted, sinews aching from exertion, Delbo cursed himself for not bringing along a more experienced crew. But the years hadn't been kind to him, his funds having dissipated over seasons of wilting crops as the seals had seemingly vanished. He knew it wasn't from extinction. No. The industry had always allowed enough seals to survive to ensure new seasons of crops. But with any natural resource, certain areas had to be abandoned eventually, and he, like all other experienced trappers, moved on. But over the last few years, the known areas of seal breeding had dried up. Unnaturally. The habitats had been abandoned by the younger seals, leaving only aged, spent beasts to roam once fertile breeding grounds. Most of his crew left him, needing to feed their families, trading up seals for whales or fox or bears. Delbo wouldn't be defeated by the beasts, and never gave up his prey. He watched them, tracking them to this desolate patch of arctic wasteland. The few denizens called this Narl Bay—the bay of corpses. But it was alive—teeming with life and seals and seal pups. Max Delbo had discovered his Utopia, and the slaughter had begun.

Fresh snow had covered their previous tracks, but Delbo had an unerring attitude for direction. Soon he heard the dogs in the distance— the barking sliced through the howling wind and through the blood-soaked lining of his parka hood. Snow and ice covered his beard, and occasionally he would collide with Pritchard, each footfall forward an agonizing motion.

The barking increased in intensity. Delbo gripped Pritchard's arm and pulled him close. "It's not far!" he cried over the din of dog and wind. "When we get there, we'll make camp and build a fire, thaw out 'fore we head back!"

Pritchard nodded in silent agreement, his skin as red as blood. With a renewed vigor, Delbo pushed harder through the snow, never releasing his hold on the wearying youth. "Come on!"

Pritchard stumbled in the darkness, his feet entangled in something unseen. He plummeted to the ground, taking Delbo with him. Delbo heard Pritchard scream just as something punctured his own knee. The pain was brief, almost an afterthought in the numbing cold, but he clutched at his injury instinctively, trying to see with dried eyes what he had struck. Pritchard's screams told him what he needed to know: "The...dogs!"

Delbo lowered himself as far as he could, his vision clearing in a rush of pain-induced tears. His thoughts turned to horror as he studied his leg. He had fallen on a corpse, his knee landing hard against the exposed ribs of a torn apart sled dog. He turned towards the frantic Pritchard, who was awash in icy grue, as the fresh snow had concealed the strewn remains of three of the four dogs. Jake Pritchard wrestled with one's intestines, while Delbo himself pulled his knee free from the ribcage of another. "Mother of God!"

Delbo heard a faint whimpering, turned towards the sound, and there he spied the last of the sled dogs. It was injured, but had freed itself from the harness and hid behind the overturned sled. Delbo pushed himself to his feet, using his spiked mace as a cane. As he approached the sled, he noticed the trail of blood and entrails, but not until he neared the dog did the truth sink in. Its fur was splattered in blood, some from wounds inflicted, while its crimson-painted maw was stained from eating the other canines' flesh.

"Cursed! We're cursed by the Silver Tusk!" Pritchard screamed as he rushed up beside him.

Delbo lashed out, pivoted on his good knee and swung round with his mace. The spikes tore into Jake Pritchard's eyes and skull. He staggered back a pace or two, hands clutching at his head, blood erupting in torrents as he fell back onto the snow. Gripping the handle of his mace with both hands, Delbo crept towards the dying youth. "Told you to shut up!" He yanked the mace free, lost his footing and crashed hard against the sled. Then he stared into the frightened eyes of the lone dog. "Looks like it's just you and me."

Delbo reached out, gripped the dog's leash and pulled the frightened animal towards him. He wasn't prone to thought, just survival, and if anything natural or supernatural was going to strike at him, he'd rather not speculate. His instincts had kept him alive this long, and his stubbornness drove him towards solutions. Coaxing the dog back into a harness was the least of his troubles, for as the dogs had battled each other, the sled had been tossed about and the twin lanterns had broken. He knew he'd die from exposure if he didn't find warmth soon, so he made the most of his situation. He poured one lantern's kerosene over Jake Pritchard, reached inside his pack with numbed fingers and pulled out the flintlock. Minutes later, flames licked the sky, and heat rushed towards his skin. He tasted death in his mouth as black smoke enveloped him. Delbo vomited, then took a swig of whiskey from his flask and pulled the snow-covered blanket close around his shoulders.

Again, Delbo heard the sound of distant barking. It didn't sound canine. The hitched dog perked up its ears momentarily before lowering itself towards the pyre. It rested its maw on crossed forelegs and shook in fear. Delbo had never seen his dogs afraid before, and didn't want to think of what might have driven them to attack each other.

Silver Tusk.

The words tore across his thoughts like shadows.

He took another swig of whiskey. It burned his throat. His left knee throbbed back into life, his circulation returning, the blood and flesh-fueled fire ebbing towards darkness. The snowfall was diminishing even as the wind picked up.

Silver Tusk.

It was a name, not just words. A name whispered in his ears by Pritchard's crackling corpse.

"Fuck this," he cursed aloud.

He positioned himself onto the sled, swung his left leg up to rest on the handrail, which eased the nauseating throbbing in his knee. He lay on its berth and cracked the leather reins. The distance that had previously taken only an hour would now take two or more if the dog tired. Delbo wouldn't let fear or the lack of pack dogs deter him from his livelihood. Not now, not after the discovery of this fertile land of seals. He just had to reach his ship anchored in the inlet around the fjord. Then he could gather up the remnants of his small crew and return for the prized seals.

As they raced along, the darkness grew fainter and fainter, the sky seeming to writhe in heat, blackness surrendering to dancing tongues of flame.

Delbo cursed as they rounded the fjord, and he discovered his ship a conflagration. He pulled taut the reins, scrambled free from his berth and dragged his dead leg towards the edge of the ice floe. Climbing into his dingy, he pushed off towards the burning wreck, hoping to find at least one deckhand still alive. As he neared the sinking ship, he caught sight of Tilman on the deck. The man screamed as the masts turned to cinder behind him.

"Jump man—jump!" Delbo cried out.

But Joss Tilman was caught in his tracks, too frightened of death to move. Panic was all he knew, until he saw Delbo in the dingy just off the starboard bow. He heard his captain yell out to him, but still he hesitated. As the mast crashed to the deck below, Tilman leapt off the bow and splashed into the sea just a few feet away from the dingy.

Delbo held out his oar to the freezing man. Once he grabbed it, Delbo hauled him into the vessel.

"What the hell happened, Tilman?"

Tilman furtively replied, "Sil...Silver Tusk..."

"What?" Delbo gasped.

"Silver Tusk has cursed us all! The beast is everywhere!"

Delbo lifted the oar and swung it hard against Tilman's skull.

After making shore, Max Delbo hauled the dingy onto the ice and emptied the second lantern's kerosene over its hull. He warmed himself as he watched the last of his ship sink below the churning arctic waves of Narl Bay.

When dawn broke over the horizon, he climbed back onto his sled and made the journey towards the only settlement in the region. The dried, salted meat in his pack and the remainder of his whiskey sustained him for the half-day's ride. The dog collapsed from exhaustion and exposure just a quarter mile from the outskirts of the settlement. Delbo dragged himself the rest of the way.

He was nearly frozen by the time he lunged through the door of the tavern, his long-handled mace striking thunderous blows against the floorboards as he hobbled inside. The shack was well heated by a single fireplace. Aside from the bar and stools, only two tables would fit in the cramped space.

Delbo hauled himself to the bar. "Whiskey," he choked.

The bartender placed a shotglass on the counter and poured the stranger his drink.

Delbo hauled it back, letting the alcohol burn its way down his throat. "Another!"

"What brings you here, stranger?" the bartender asked as he poured.

"Malady and misfortune, it would seem."

"We don't get many strangers here, as one might reckon."

"One might," he replied, scrutinizing the flabby skinned bartender. Delbo glanced about him then, noticing the four or six other patrons who seemed to study him.

"You alone, or might we be expecting other...strangers?"

"Alone...now," Delbo said, downing another shot. "There's no one left...aside from me. The others are all dead...and I've lost everything..."

"So what brings you hereabouts?"

Delbo stared hard at the bartender, motioned for him to refill his glass.

"Revenge."

"Against whom?"

"Against the thing that destroyed my livelihood and drove my crew mad. I reckon it goes by the name o' Silver Tusk."

Glasses clanked over table tops. Chairs screeched against the wooden floors as the patrons swung around. "Silver Tusk? Silver Tusk...The Silver Tusk!" The muffled voices rang out as the denizens began talking to themselves. Delbo glanced over his shoulder, feeling their wild, staring eyes fall upon him.

"So," Delbo turned back to the bartender. "You've heard of him?"

"The Silver Tusk is but a legend, like Bigfoot. A story to frighten small children into obedience. Nothing more. You chase ghosts, friend."

"Like I told one of my crew before he died, I stopped believing in spirits a long time ago. Once, when I was still young and foolish, I entertained the thought of even becoming a priest. I always had faith in God Almighty—I always believed. Then when I was fourteen, I found myself an apprentice to a sailor. He groomed me to be first mate, his eyes never leaving me. Then it happened, you see. Our first voyage out. He stole me down to the lower deck, plied me with liquor and jammed his mast into me. I groped around in the damp darkness, took hold of a hammer nearby, and BANG—BANG, I tore him a new hole in his skull. Ever since then, I knew there was no Almighty watching out over me, unless he likes fucking boys. No, sir. That day, I discovered the power of the hammer and what a well-placed thwack to the head could deliver me from. That's how I got in the seal business. And that's what led me here."

"Interesting...tale you tell, friend..."

"That was only the beginning. The seals had vanished from their normal breeding grounds. At first, we all thought maybe they were dying out, but that didn't make sense. So I began to track the young ones, found out they were migrating to parts unknown. It took me years to find this place, this one spot in all the world the seals thought safe. It was like chasing a myth—a legend if you will, like this Silver Tusk of yours. But here it was: Seal Paradise!

"Then my crew started acting strange...paranoid. I never heard so many men scream themselves awake. I figured it was just 'cause they were a green crew, and young. Then one by one I lost them. Even my dogs fell to this distemper, tore themselves apart. The crew that remained on my ship killed each other, I reckon—like them dogs—'fore setting the ship ablaze. I drove the last dog until he died, and in that time, I came to realize that maybe this Silver Tusk was real after all. So, tell me where I might find this man that destroyed my life."

"Silver Tusk is not a man, friend," the bartender said amused.

"Then what is he?"

"He is a walrus."

"A what?"

"A walrus."

"You're shitting me, aren't you? You're telling me that a walrus—a big, old, fat smelly walrus killed my crew without being seen? A stupid, fish-eating pile of shit scared my crew into madness? That's not possible!"

"Ah, but The Silver Tusk is not an ordinary walrus, you see. Legend has it that he was raised by man."

"And then he died and became a big Nature Spirit haunting the arctic wastelands? That's utter shit!"

"If you but still your craven tongue, I will tell you the Legend of The Silver Tusk. Perhaps then you might find some answers."

"I reckon that if you're storytelling, I might as well have another bottle."

The bartender uncorked a fresh bottle of whiskey, sliding it in front of Delbo.

"Legend has it that The Silver Tusk was born an ordinary walrus, just one of many birthed during that particular breeding season. Nothing distinguished him from his brothers in size or shape or habits. He sucked from his mother's tit. He swam when his father pushed him into the water and learned to catch fish and mollusks as any average walrus would. Then one bleak midday, whilst he was playing with his seal cousins, the ships came with their nets and stole them from the icy banks.

"Luckily for these creatures, this was not a poacher's ship..."

"What sort of ship was it then?" Delbo asked, letting the whiskey warm his blood as the bartender told his tale.

"Oh, it was a slave ship! For the crew had been hired by an infamous import/export firm from the United States of America. They were to capture live specimens to be auctioned off to various dealers with no questions asked. Black markets exist in every major city within the States and around the world, and exotic animals are routinely captured for these events. Perhaps it was fate that this walrus was captured with the seals, or just plain dumb luck. The journey to America was long, but the walrus survived and was presented at auction. The auctioneer had noticed the close attachment it had with two of the captive seals, for the young walrus pup had protected its slick-furred cousins at every turn, and so the walrus was auctioned off with them 'at no extra charge.' You see, walrus meat or walrus skin or walrus innards had no value on the black market; only a zoo of ill-repute would buy a walrus, if one had need of one, but that particular day not a single zoo attended. The lot was won by a small traveling show, The Greyson-Dicks carnival.

"This particular carnival was trying to expand into a full-fledged circus under its new management, after years of astonishing success. For Greyson-Dicks was renowned for having the finest sideshows and best acts money could buy. The seal trainer was not happy with the discovery of a walrus in with his seals, but he made the best of it. He tried to train the walrus to balance a ball on its flat nose, but unlike its smaller, sleeker cousins, the poor fellow was clumsy and slow moving on land, and its increasing bulk forced it to simply sit on the sides and occasionally clap or bark when the seals had performed. The trainer hated the walrus, because it was useless to him and devoured more food than he could procure. He constantly yelled at the creature, who had grown to about six feet long in just under three months, and would vent his frustrations on it with his whip.

"One day, another carnival employee had witnessed one of these cruel acts. The man was known as Zarkho the Great. He was a powerful mentalist, and his show was always heavily attended. Zarkho claimed to have heard the creature's screams of pain, in his mind, of course, and decided to adopt it. Zarkho hated the company of others, for he claimed that their emotions and thoughts drove him to the brink of madness, and so he lived in nearly complete solitude with the exception of his performances. That is, until the day he saved the walrus. Inexplicably, the walrus had a calming effect on Zarkho, as if the creature shielded the man from the others' thoughts. They became the closest of friends and were never seen apart again.

"Zarkho loved the creature so much that he lavished his wealth on the walrus as a man would a lover, sparing no expense in feeding it the finest fish, constantly bathing it, even building a special room onto his trailer that acted like a freezer in the summer months. Zarkho also began using the walrus in his act. The crowds were said to have fainted as Zarkho transmitted his thoughts to the walrus, who would bark out various words chosen at random from the stunned audience. The seal trainer was jealous of Zarkho, for his show stole away the thunder of trained seals and brightly colored balls. The seal trainer protested to the management that such a massive beast (for the walrus was now over ten feet long) was a menace to the crowds, with its tremendous girth and three-foot long tusks. The management agreed with the trainer, for the walrus could be a fierce fighter and still protected the seals when it could. And so Zarkho was told to have the animal's tusks surgically removed. Zarkho vehemently protested, knowing the pain it would cause his pet, and swayed the owners into getting the tusks capped instead, having already threatened to quit the carnival and take his show elsewhere. The management agreed, and Zarkho obeyed, but in his own fashion. He was a rich man, after all, and the walrus was his life. And so he had the tusks capped in pure silver. And from that day on, the walrus was known as The Silver Tusk.

"Years passed and all was well, until one summer as the carnival was traveling the coast of Florida. A hurricane blew in, destroying Greyson-Dicks, and Zarkho's trailer was cast out to sea. The Silver Tusk miraculously survived and, on instinct, headed back towards the arctic waters of its birth.

"But it was no longer a wild walrus, for he had known Zarkho and Zarkho had taught the astute walrus the ways of mentalism. The Silver Tusk knew how man thought, and could cast its own mind into any other intelligent creatures' head. And so he battled its way back to the arctic and faced many perils. Sharks and whales and whaling ships; violent storms, nasty narwhals and aquatic war machines. Once he returned to his ancestral home, he discovered blood-stained ice and the slaughter of seals. The Silver Tusk vowed to protect seal and walrus alike from the heinous butchers known as man—for only Zarkho had ever treated animals with respect and reverence, whilst all other humans feared and hated them, seeing animals as only a source of profit to be slaughtered at will.

"And that, my friend, is why the seals began to disappear. For The Silver Tusk led them, clan by clan, to a safe haven. He communicated with them as no other had ever done, and walrus and seal alike revered him unto a god. For had he not battled polar bears for them? Had he not saved them from man, saved them from the club, saved them from the slaughter? Even the native Innuits worshipped him, for he would speak to them with the voice of their ancestral gods. It is said that The Silver Tusk led both seal and walrus and certain Innuit tribes to a fabled land hidden in the arctic, some Burroughsian paradise, and that the seal and walrus only reappear to breed. And that is the legend of The Silver Tusk."

Delbo chuckled. "That's it? A walrus with carnival freakshow mental powers drove my crew insane? That's ridiculous!"

"Is it?"

Suddenly, the barroom doors burst open in an explosion of noise and a stiff arctic wind. While Delbo was in the bar, a blizzard had erupted. Snow and ice tore into the room, devouring the accumulated warmth in seconds. Delbo swiveled around in his seat and peered into the storm. A terrible barking arose around him—behind him—and he turned to stare into the bartender's face, only to see a seal glaring at him.

"Jesus Christ!" Delbo gasped, until a thunderous clamor shook the very foundations of the building. The bartending seal thrust its nose into Delbo's chin, forcing him to topple to the ice-covered floors. Delbo recovered quickly. The seal bartender and seal patrons barked and barked, one howling like a wolf as a massive shape moved through the doorway.

"Maximillian Delbo!" The Silver Tusk screamed in his mind. "You who reveled in the slaughter, took pride in your aim and ability to crush the skulls of thousands of defenseless seals—seals under my protection—must face me now!"

Delbo stared up at the gargantuan beast, a mountain of muscle and tough, leathery skin, its silver-plated tusks over three feet long. It snarled at him, but Delbo knew that this Silver Tusk was aged, so wrinkled and greying, a slight film over its wide, dark eyes. His terror subsided as his lust for revenge ignited the whiskey flowing through his blood. He crawled to his knees, wincing sharply at his nearly forgotten wound. Delbo struck the head of his mace onto the wooden floorboards of the bar and pulled himself up to his shaking legs. Hatred shone in his eyes, his stare never wavering from the legendary creature that challenged him.

"So, it's true. A mentalist walrus with a temper. For destroying my livelihood, I shall kill you."

"You can try, but you are only human."

"And you think you're a god?"

"No. I am a mere walrus."

"Then die like the simple beast that you are!"

Delbo lunged at the creature, lifting his spiked mace and swinging it over his head as he attacked The Silver Tusk. The walrus propelled himself forward, thrusted its head into Delbo's stomach, knocking the man through the air and crashing him into the bar. Something gave way internally—Delbo heard his spine snap and no longer felt the stinging pain of his knee. He glared up at the approaching mass of brown and grey, blood spraying from his throat. "Damn you!"

"The slaughter will end with you," The Silver Tusk announced. "You taught me well, Maximillian Delbo. You taught me that I should never trust the white man again, for you do not respect Nature and her kin. I let my guard down this day, and lost a hundred souls to your debauchery. Never again. Never."

Delbo glanced to his right, searching for the mace that flew from his grip upon the beast's attack. It was scarce inches out of reach. He stretched out his arm, tried to lunge for his weapon, but he could barely remain conscious. "It...can't end...like this! I won't allow...you..."

"You are dead already. You were dead the moment you lifted your mace and crushed the first skull of an infant. Do you know what that feels like? Do you think they died instantly? They didn't. I felt their psychic screams, felt their pain as they slowly died, their thoughts withering. The dying pain of one small seal is enough to drive a person to suicide. I wonder what a hundred screaming souls would feel like, don't you?"

Delbo gripped his mace, but it was far too late.

The Silver Tusk stared hard at him, projecting its thoughts—the emotions and pain of each seal Delbo had slaughtered—into his mind. Delbo winced, jaw tightening, his upper torso shaking, his every nerve on fire as the piercing screams plunged deep into his brain, pressure building in his skull, his mace toppling to the floor as the psychic knife twisted deeper and deeper. He shrieked, hands clutching and clawing at his head, fingers tearing into his eyes, blood erupting from his nose as he felt a hundred individual blows to his skull, long sharp spikes driving hard into his mind, over and over again, the pressure building and building until his skull exploded, brains shooting into his throat as if from a cannon.

The Silver Tusk ceased his assault, lowered his weary head.

The seals rushed to his side, rubbing their heads against his massive bulk in loving caresses. The Silver Tusk opened up his mind once again, letting the seals' emotions comfort him.

"It is done. Now let us return to the sacred land beneath the ice until a better place can be found. Do not worry, my cousins. The Innuits will search again, and I have taught you well. Although my time is nearly over, you have proven capable of casting illusions powerful enough to ensnare any that might dare try to slaughter you in the future. Perhaps, one day, the white men will find other sources for their greed. Come, let us return home."

And so The Silver Tusk entered the barren wastelands of the arctic and disappeared from the memory of man.

GIRL GONE GRAY
Gina Ranalli

Nothing is perfect.

No plan. No person. Nothing.

I never said I was a perfect parent, a perfect father. But, for a while, I think Julie believed I was. When she was very small—smaller than she is now, and I was able to toss her into the air like she was a football—she would giggle madly, trusting daddy to catch her every time. And I did.

But, of course, that was before.

It was nearing her eleventh birthday when she came to me with a request.

"I want a dog, Daddy. Can I have one?"

Eyeing her with skepticism, I said, "I don't know, Julie. Do you think you're responsible enough?"

"Yes!" Her reply was nearly a shout. "I'm responsible."

I sighed. "I don't know. Dogs are a lot of work. Training them and walking them. Picking up after them."

"I can do it, Daddy! Please! It can be the only birthday present I get this year. Pretty *please*?" She clasped her hands beneath her chin and batted those seal-gray eyes at me. Eyes so much like her mother's.

"I'll think about it," I said at last.

She looked crestfallen. "My birthday is next week."

"So, I have a week to think about it. Right?"

"I guess so," she huffed, dropping her hands, her mouth drooping in a showy pout. "You could get it from work, though. It would be free!"

That much was true. I *could* get it from work, as I worked with animals all day, of which Julie was well aware. What she wasn't aware of was *what* we did with the animals over at Quark Dynamics. Terrible, ugly things. But as a scientist, I knew that if you walked a terrible, ugly path for a long enough time, it would eventually lead you to beauty and greatness. And that was why I continued doing what I did. There was light at the end of the tunnel, for all of us.

"I'll think about it," I repeated more firmly.

Julie stalked off, and as I watched her go, I decided right then and there that she would get her pet. She deserved it, after all. The poor kid had been through so much already, losing her mom the previous spring and having a father who worked close to eighty hours a week. Being an only child, it was hard on her.

And maybe a pet would be just the thing to get her happy again, the way she'd been before. Happy and laughing and full of energy.

Every kid should have a pet.

And the very day of her eleventh birthday, I brought her one.

Julie frowned into the aquarium.

"What is it, Daddy?"

Smiling, I put my hand on her shoulder and pressed my face to the glass beside hers. "It's a walrus, honey. Isn't he handsome?"

"A walrus? You mean like when we went to the zoo that time?"

"Exactly. A miniature walrus. That's what daddy does at work. He makes miniature animals."

Her frown deepened. "Why?"

"Because…" I thought about it. Why, indeed? The truth was more complex than what could be explained to a little girl. Because we could? Because the government liked to play God and they paid exceptionally well? Because it gave us a thrill? "Because they're so cool," I said. "Isn't he cool?"

Chewing the cuticle around her thumb, she said, "I guess so. Didn't they have any little dogs?"

I waved dismissively at the air. "Bah. Everyone will have a mini-dog soon enough. There are already dozens of them in the lab. And cats. Horses, monkeys, bears too. But this guy…this guy is the first walrus. He's what we call a prototype."

"Hmm." She tapped the glass to get the little animal's attention. "He is pretty cute. But, if he's the first, are you supposed to give him to me?"

"Sure. We already have his DNA to clone more. You'll see, honey. Mini-pets are going to be all the rage, but *you'll* be the only one with a walrus. I can guarantee you that."

She screwed her face up. "What should I call him?"

"Whatever you want, sweetie. He's yours."

"I really wanted a dog."

"I know. But this little guy is worlds better than a dog. You'll see."

Julie looked unconvinced, her eyes peering at the creature in the aquarium. "He sure is small."

I nodded. The little guy was about the size of a bottle of water and not likely to grow much bigger, though he was still young. The tank provided for him, however, could hold 180 gallons, though I'd had the lab guys come in and set it up so the walrus could have equal time in water and on land. It did look quite a bit like the type of display one would find in a zoo, only miniaturized. "I think he'll be very happy in here."

"I can take him out though, right?"

I thought about it, then shrugged. "I don't see why not. We take out the other animals at work all the time. You just have to remember to be gentle."

Eventually, the doubtful look was replaced by a smile. She turned from the tank and hugged me tight around the neck. "Thanks, Daddy. He's really cute!"

"You're welcome, sweetie. I'm glad you like him."

"Even though he isn't a dog."

"No, but I told you he's *better* than a dog." I didn't actually know if the walrus was better than a dog or not, but he would certainly be easier to take care of, that was for sure. No walking, no training, no crap all over the front yard.

I gave Julie a final tight squeeze before releasing her, straightening up and ruffling her hair. "You two have fun now. I'm gonna go make us some lunch. How does PB and J with a side of chips sound?"

Julie said it sounded great, and I left her there in her room with the big tank and the tiny walrus, hoping the two of them would make friends, and it would be a long time before I was nagged about the lack of a canine in the house.

As it turned out, it *was* a long time.

A year had passed, and Julie had never mentioned wanting a dog again.

Julie loved her little walrus, Benjamin—Benny for short. When questioned on her choice of a name, she simply stated that he *looked* like a Benjamin.

The girl and the walrus became inseparable. She carried him around wherever she went, holding him in her arms like a baby, cradling him against her chest.

I often observed her playing outside in the grass with Benny, running in circles, laughing while the tiny animal barked his joyful little bark, bouncing after her in an awkward gait that was so much faster than one would have imagined a walrus could move.

On more than one occasion, Julie had to be scolded for placing Benny on the kitchen table where she sat doing her homework.

"What did I tell you about putting the walrus on the table?" I demanded.

"He helps me concentrate!"

"He's already scratched the wood with his tusks. Put him back in his tank."

"That was an accident," Julie protested. "He was just rolling around."

"I don't care. No walruses on the table, and that's final!"

Scowling, Julie had slammed her pencil down, lifted Benny into her arms and left the room, cooing lovingly at the animal as she went. I stood looking after her, shaking my head for a moment before moving to the sink to fetch a damp washcloth to wipe down the table.

I didn't think much of it when Julie let the walrus sleep in the bed with her. Benny was certainly clean enough—Julie saw to that—and there was no danger that she would roll over and hurt the little guy. The fat was layered on his body so thick that one could bounce him like a rubber ball.

More than once, I'd gone to check on her after lights out only to find Benny flopped on his side at the end of the bed or sometimes even sharing the pillow with her. The sight never failed to make me smile. They were just so adorable together.

One Saturday morning in late July, Julie didn't come downstairs, Benny in tow, asking what we'd be having for breakfast. Once ten o'clock rolled around, I decided she'd slept plenty late enough and went to wake her.

After tapping on her bedroom door and receiving no response, I opened it a crack and peeked in. "Julie? Time to get up, kiddo. It's after ten."

I frowned when I saw the empty bed and instinctively glanced over at Benny's tank. The walrus was nowhere to be seen.

Did Julie actually get up before I did? Perhaps she was already outside playing?

About to turn and leave the room, movement on the bed froze me, head tilted in curiosity. The baby-blue sheet rippled as though something moved beneath it and, of course, there *was* something beneath it: Benny.

Crossing the room, I yanked back the sheet, already half-smiling in anticipation of seeing the little guy tangled up in the sheets and looking up at me with those wet, happy eyes.

And Benny was there all right. But so was Julie.

Julie, even smaller than Benny, sat beside her pet, arms wrapped around her raised knees. Her crying was almost inaudible.

"What the…" I bent forward, eyes wide with shock. "Julie? What…what happened?"

"Daddy!" the girl screeched. "Look at me! I shrank in the night! I shrank!"

I couldn't breathe. It felt as though my lungs were being crushed under an enormous weight. Hundreds of pounds, squashing them flat. As if a full grown walrus was parked on my chest.

"Oh, Julie…"

The prototype walrus, due to the changes made in its DNA, secreted reverse-growth chemicals in its semen. The old adage of "nature will find a way" had never been more true. Something in Benny's chemistry had gone haywire, something none of us could have ever predicted. Unable to mate with a female walrus, Benny had done his best to mate with Julie, an impossible task, but nevertheless, his attempt had resulted in her absorbing his seed into her skin.

Nature was doing what it could to help Benny procreate. If a walrus his own size wasn't available, then it would make one.

Of course, young Julie didn't turn into a walrus. However, she did indeed shrink overnight, baffling scientists the world over.

When I was finally able to take her home again, many months had passed and the child I'd so adored no longer existed. To say she was pissed would be the greatest understatement ever told.

"Put me down!" she screamed, thrashing wildly in my hand. *"You fucking dickhead! Put me down!"*

I set her gently on the kitchen table. "Honey, please don't use that language. You know how your mother felt about it."

"Fuck you!" She stormed around the table, kicking over the salt and pepper shakers and the napkin holder like a little blonde cyclone. *"Fuck you, fuck you, FUCK YOU!"*

I sighed sadly.

"I'm going to kill you, Daddy! Do you hear me? I'm going to wait until you're asleep and slice your fucking throat!"

The threats continued, concerning me more and more. Finally, when she was out of breath, she sat down heavily, her legs hanging over the edge of the table. I said, "Benny is home too. He's in his tank. Do you want to see him?"

She looked up at me with surprise. "Benny? But, I thought they…I thought he…"

"Oh, no. I wouldn't let anyone hurt Benny." I paused. "So, do you want to see him?"

Julie's eyes brimmed with tears, and I scooped her up and brought her back into the bedroom she'd once more share with the walrus. Only now, they would be roommates in an entirely new capacity.

I carried her over to the big tank that held Benny, opened the top and plopped her inside, taking care to drop her into the water and not onto any of the rocks. The small girl made a splash, and I quickly replaced the cover of the tank, watching as she sank and then bobbed to the surface again.

"Daddy!" She blurted, spitting water. "Daddy?"

Benny, on the opposite side of the tank, hooted his pleasure and dove into the water to greet his best friend.

"Honey, for my own safety, I think it would be best to keep you in here for a while. Just until you calm down and get used to…well, get used to being small. It's safer for you, too," I added almost as an afterthought, though it was probably true. "Maybe when you're less angry with me, we can talk about making other arrangements, but in the meantime, this is for the best."

Julie swam through the tank and pulled herself up onto the "beach" where Benny had spent so much of his time when he'd first joined the family. Jumping up and down, more enraged than I'd ever seen anyone, Julie cursed at me, saying words I never would have imagined she knew, spewing them like venom through the air to assault my ears and heart.

"It's for the best," I repeated after a while.

And I believed it, too. Benny would keep her company and sooner or later, Julie would settle down and love me again.

But if that day never came, I decided, I could always get a new pet.

THE WALRUS MASTER
Carlton Mellick III

The Walrus Master levitated five and a half feet above the ground. His legs crossed and palms faced upwards toward the heavens. It was the Walrus Master's third levitation of the day, which meant that he was now available to answer any and all questions of the universe for those who wished to ask.

A group of walri gathered on the beach around him, for it was mating season, and all the walri understood that mating in the presence of the Walrus Master would mean a successful coupling that would result in healthy, virile offspring.

A young man walking down the beach noticed the mating walri and the levitating Walrus Master, and came over, wondering what wondrous secrets the great Master had to offer.

As the young man approached, The Walrus Master said, "Blessings, my child. I shall answer you three questions. What wisdom do you wish me to bestow?"

The young man looked around. There wasn't another living soul for miles. He stared at the Master and said, "What the fuck are you doing, dude?"

The Walrus Master replied, "I am in the midst of my third daily levitation. This is the most important levitation of the day, for it is the time when all the spirits of the universe join together and flow through my being. Next question."

The young man was pleased with this answer. He nodded his head with humility and prepared his next question.

"Are you for real?" asked the young man.

"It is debatable," said the Walrus Master. "Next question."

The young man pondered his last question carefully, for he knew that the wisdom of the Walrus Master could bring him eternal happiness and prosperity.

The young man asked, "So what's with all the walruses and shit?"

The Walrus Master paused for a moment.

He continued to pause.

Then the Walrus Master responded, "They are not walruses, they are walri. The most noble creature on this or any planet. If you wish to know exactly what is *with* them that would require twenty lifetimes of explanation, for they are more complex than a mere mortal such as yourself could possibly understand. And if you're wondering what they are doing right now, if you really *must* know, they are fucking. Is that what you wanted to hear? They're fucking! So leave them alone and don't ruin the mood, okay? Don't even look at them!"

The young man stared appreciatively at the Walrus Master.

"Uh, okay…" he said.

Now, the young man turned and walked away. He strolled blissfully down the shore, full of optimism and a new sense of purpose, just as all those who have questioned the Walrus Master before him. After a dozen yards, the young man turned around and noticed the Walrus Master was floating behind him.

Pleased to be reunited with the Master, the young man said, "Why the fuck are you following me?"

The Walrus Master let out a long sigh to comfort his devoted follower. "I have decided to let you ask me one more question."

Then the Master paused for a moment and said, "Except for the *why the fuck are you following me* question. That one doesn't count."

The young man was immensely honored by this gift. He waved one of his fingers at the Master, the one between the index finger and the ring finger, which must have been the customary salute of his people.

Then the young man said, "Get away from me, you freak!" And continued on his way.

The Walrus Master floated after him.

Quickening his pace, the young man must have felt himself unworthy of a fourth question from The Walrus Master. But the Master felt there was no need for such modest behavior, and kept up with the young man's pace.

The young man began to run, encouraging The Walrus Master to float after him with the speed of a rocket ship. Even when they reached the city streets, the Master was mere feet behind him, his legs crossed and his palms faced upwards toward the heavens.

When the young man arrived at his home, he closed and locked his door. The Walrus Master levitated in front of it, spinning around in little circles. The young man attempted to use his phone, to call all of his friends and family to come bear witness to The Walrus Master floating outside of his house. But because the Master did not appreciate being the center of a large crowd, he decided to use his grand powers to disconnect all phone lines within a ten-mile radius.

That night, the young man cowered in awe from his bedroom window, admiring The Walrus Master as he levitated in front of his door, spinning around in little circles, protecting his home from harmful, negative spirits.

THE WALRUS-CARPENTER MURDERS
R. Allen Leider

Welcome to my world.

The place is Aquaterra, an alternate reality planet that, according to String Theory, is a slice of existence right next to another blue-green planet called Earth, and shares 98% of Earth's history with a singular exception. One of the big asteroids did not hit here and so aquatic organisms evolved into higher forms, too. Hence, Aquaterra is populated by both advanced aquatic and humanoid beings. Maybe it's for better, maybe for worse, maybe just for laughs. It sure makes Friday night and Lenten dinners interesting. Some things are the same; some are definitely not. Most of the passengers on Aquaterra's Titanic survived. They just swam away.

The city is New Francisco, the 'Big Buzz on the Bay.' My office is located in The Bilge Building near the wharf. It's a shaky, crumbling, pre-war structure that Mr. Goldglom, the landlord, won't pay to have torn down because he figures it will fall down for free any day, then he can construct a high-rise office tower. That's been his position for over fifteen years. On any given day, the denizens hanging out in front of the building include hookers, pimps, undercover cops disguised as hookers and pimps, drunks, undercover cops disguised as drunks and hookers, pimps and drunks who want people to think they are undercover cops so they won't be disturbed.

The smell in the lobby is so acrid that you must hold your breath until you get into the elevator and up to your floor. This is assuming that the circa 1940 Otius elevator is working. This elevator is a monument to all who have been taken for a ride, sometimes their last ride, in it. There are blood and other bodily fluid stains on the floor, walls and ceiling. The side panels are 'decorated' with obscene drawings, some fairly decent artwork, autographs of the famous and infamous who have visited the offices here. There are also hundreds of connect the dot & tic-tac-toe games, echoes of the frequency that people were trapped in it for hours or days while waiting for the fuzzy, multi-legged arachnid repairman to hobble across town to fix the antique device so it would function again for a short time. The original bright red carpeting in the hallways is a dark maroon now and it squishes under foot. Yes Sir, the building, elevator and all the tenants have had their ups and downs over the decades.

In the hallways, you can hear Muzak under or over the screams. There are good screams, bad screams and sometimes the screaming is indistinguishable as good or bad. It's just loud screaming. The stinky carpeting in our fourth floor hallway is lightly sprinkled with old, hardened rat droppings, some of which have been ground into the fibers. The rats disappeared some months ago when the two reptilian songwriters, Skales & Venum, moved onto the floor. So, there are no more rats, but we haven't seen the kid who used to deliver the soggy, lopsided pizzas in weeks either.

Just listen to that guy on the fifth floor play that film noir music score on his trumpet! That's what I like about this place, the atmosphere. You don't get that in one of those glass towers on Front Street.

My name is Walrus, Joe Walrus. I'm the private investigator with the tusks and the Wyatt Earp mustache. My partner is Ed Carpenter. He's the laid back fellow in the crimson exoskeleton flipping coins into the tin can or zapping pigeons off the window ledge with his Dayzee BB pistol.

I came in late the day when it all started. It was just like any other slow day when the highpoint was the 2pm mail delivery. We have lots of those days. I looked around, yawned and perused the overflowing waste paper basket jammed with junk mail. On the ledge of the open window was a line of Croaka Cola soda cans with BB holes in them and a pile of bloody pigeon feathers. The desks were piled high with empty take-out food containers, half-built toothpick building and bridge constructions that Ed says relax him. There were also hardened white glue bottles and magazines from years ago that Ed kept because there was a picture, an article, or cartoon that he wanted to collect, but never clipped. Sometimes I wish I could work out of the house, but my wife says she needs her space.

Ed has always contended that when this building collapses it will go straight to Limbo to be with the Coconut Grove and other infamous and tragedy ridden structures. He's a superstitious fellow. He's read *Deviled Yeggs* more than a dozen times and believes it all.

Our receptionist is the diminutive Ms. Pansy Dormaus. It was her squeaky voice through the office intercom that announced our visitor on that gray, drizzly day when Blonde Trouble walked into the office in a blue and white, size 3 dress.

It was one of those English schoolgirl outfits with the white apron. Her Veronica Lake peek-a-boo hairdo had mischief and danger written all over it. I knew she was going to be a headache the minute I saw the large, white rabbit under her arm. It was wearing a waistcoat. It had a pocket watch. It twitched.

"Let's start at the beginning," I prompted.

"I'm Alice, Alice Kelp," she began as she nervously clutched and kneaded her handbag. "You've got to help me, Mr. Walrus," Alice pleaded. "My husband's been missing for two weeks and the police absolutely refuse to do anything about it."

She had to say that word. It couldn't have been 'brother' or even 'boyfriend.' It had to be 'husband.' It was that kind of a day. A day for petite, cutie pie, married, blonde, white rabbit freaks. Ed just sat in the corner, observed, and wiggled his antennae with each swig of lukewarm latte from his Dinkum Donuts thermal coffee mug. Yeah, I know, I'm married too, but...

"Husband?" I asked.

"Yes, he's William Kelp, the Oyster Baron."

Ed sat up in his chair with a sharp jerk that caused some of his drink to splash.

"Blue Point Willie is your husband?" Ed asked. "He's quite an item. Is he still at odds with the government for illegal oyster farming and trying to corner the oyster market last year? Weren't they going to indict him?"

"He's a legitimate businessman," Alice moaned in her whispy, Betty Boop voice. "Those oysters are clones. The government makes it sound like slavery, but it's just like any other kind of farming...seeds, cultivation, harvest and product." Here she paused and flashed me a look that could melt lead. "You know," she said with a long, slow sexy exhale, "reproduction?"

"You left out the part about all the government audits, the twenty million dollars in missing assets, the substandard wages for the farm workers and the frequent oyster rebellions, especially the Cape Cods and Blue Points."

"It's less offensive than making Soylenten Green," Alice said, flipping her blonde mane while she picked a small lettuce leaf from the pocket of her white apron and fed it, inch by inch, into the quickly chomping jaws of her fastidiously attired lapine companion.

What an act! She was playing Ed and me and we both knew it, but she gave such a good show! Her husband was a well-known seafood player. His alleged disappearance made me believe that he had tried to corner the market again, perhaps with dire results.

Alice, that is Mrs. Kelp, tossed me a Manilla envelope with five thousand dollars in it. We shook hands on the deal and she left. I noticed my hands smelled like seaweed. Something was fishy alright. It occurred to Ed and me that a logical place to start looking for an 'oyster baron' was the waterfront where all the seafood business is done.

Two hours later, we arrived at Pier Fifty One. It was around sundown on one of those heavily used mini-wharfs. Dwarf wharfs they call them, and this one consisted of old splintering lumber, rusted bolts and barnacle encrusted hardware held together by the classic legends and lore of the sea. Dried or decomposing seaweed adhered to everything, and there was the unmistakable acrid smell of what was *underneath* the boardwalk—rotting something, or someone.

Finally, we located the local marina keeper, a one-eyed codger named Captain Gorton Paul. He and his wife were on the deck of his ramshackle houseboat, *The Sandee Beecher.*

The Captain and his wife were slowly shucking oysters. They were a sixty-ish, white-haired couple with tanned, elephant hides that the sun had done a real number on. Their skin was a mass of wrinkles, cracks, liver spots bigger than your liver, flaking skin patches behind their ears and dandruff galore. Their oft-repaired clothes came from the Salvation Army Thrift Store. The Captain covered his gnarled, twisted frame in a yellow slicker to which the same dried seaweed was stuck here and there. Emanating from the slicker was the unmistakable odor of rotting 'something.' Needless to say, we wanted to get this over with as soon as possible.

"Shrimp boats are coming. I can see their sails," advised Capt. Paul as he pointed to some indistinguishable objects on the horizon with his boney, misshapen index finger.

"Oh, really?" I responded with a wet snort.

"Yeah, red sails. See them in the sunset?" said Mrs. Paul as she picked up a tarnished, antique brass spyglass with her arthritis-ravaged hands, which were nearly turned into flippers by the disease, and passed the spyglass to Ed.

"Oh, now I can see them. Are they all shrimpers? Any of them oyster boats?" Ed inquired.

Capt. Paul broke a slimy sweat. "Oysters? No, all shrimp. Why you boys looking for oysters? They're completely out of season, you know."

Just then, we noticed some excitement on the street opposite the marina. There was a flash of colored lights and the blaring sirens of squad cars, an ambulance or two and other emergency vehicles. A man in a trench coat approached the pier, and Capt. Paul went to meet him at the gate. The man identified himself as Sgt. Simon Squiddle, and when the Captain told him why we were there, we were invited to come over to the crime scene, the *murder* crime scene.

"It's over there in the shady part of the port outside a dive called The Octopus's Garden," said Squiddle. "Come on, I'll give you a lift."

The squad car took us over to the location. Ed made a note that Capt. Paul was shucking oysters out of season. "Might be something. Might be nothing," he noted to himself.

"Whatcha got for us?" I asked the patrolman on duty as we approached the roped off section of the street.

"I'm Ptl. Andrew Sisstas," the policeman introduced himself. "I found the victim here in the alley about an hour ago."

Ed and I walked over to the canvas tarp that covered the body and I motioned to one of the other cops to give me a peek. The officer looked at Sgt. Squiddle, who gave him the nod.

"Hey, Ed, look who we have here!"

Ed gave the corpse a good long look that put a real wiggle in his antennae.

"Know him?" asked Squiddle.

"Yeah, he's Howard Prawns, a stool pigeon the mob called Shrimpy."

"What's this he's lying on?" Ed inquired, pushing a pile of mushy white stuff with his left foot.

"Rice," replied Dr. Clamson, the CSI officer. "The victim was stripped naked, boiled alive and laid out on two hundred pounds of steamed, white rice."

"It's a message of some sort," I concluded. "Officer Sisstas, what do you make of this?"

Sisstas squinted and perused the scene for a minute, cleared his throat, then spoke softly. "I guess you could make jambalaya or a good etouffe. My mother used to make this great Cajun soup…"

"No, no, any *clues*? Was there anything of significance on the body?"

"There was a handwritten note stuffed into his mouth," replied

Sisstas as he fished a wad of paper from his pocket. I took the paper and showed it to Ed. We examined the note and I muttered, "Hmmmmm, just one word on it, 'Yakasaki.' That could be Club Yakasaki. It's a mob operation on the south side run by the Asian Mafia."

"The Tongs?" queried Sisstas.

"No, the Asian fish mob, The Tangs. They're vicious killers," Ed replied.

"And they're the bitter rivals of Shrimpy's ex-employers, whom I think I should visit first," I suggested.

"The Black Hand!" exclaimed Sisstas.

"No, The Red Lobster," I shot back. "Ed and I are going to pay an unscheduled visit to The Olive Oil Garden to see the Godfather himself, Don Langostino."

The morgue wagon arrived, and the attendants scooped up Shrimpy and the rice and bagged them for the CSI crew to analyze. "Shrimpy and rice, very nice," Dr. Franch, one of the CSI men, muttered. I stepped into the middle of the street and hailed a striped yellow cab. The driver was an East Indian reptilian, a real ugly green creature with a huge gold earring, a red turban and a maw that ran a blue streak. We've been getting a lot of those since the elections. Open immigration—forget it!

"I am Jabberwocky," he started, "You are lucky to get me. I am number one cabbie in New Francisco. I know this town like the back of my hand. Where may I be taking you two excellent gentlemen this fine evening?"

"We're going to The Olive Oil Garden," I replied, noting that Jabberwocky had claws, not hands. "Might be something. Might be nothing," I thought to myself.

We arrived at the Italian restaurant a few minutes later. It was located in one of the older buildings in the seedier part of town that was under urban renewal. Urban renewal, hah! That means that some hotshot real estate mogul was squeezing out the tenants and remodeling everything in sight. Rents zoom and places like The Olive Oil Garden, heavily dominated by the mob, spring up like mushrooms.

We rang the bell and flashed our badges at the peephole. There was a pregnant pause, and we heard the clicks of the door locks unlocking. The dented, bulletproof, reinforced, black steel door slowly creaked open, and we were fish-eyed by the twin concierges, the notorious Calamari brothers, Lucas and Brassy. At the doorway we were padded down by F. J. Muggs, Don Langostino's six and a half foot simian bodyguard.

"Get your hands off me, you damn dirty ape!" Ed bellowed while straightening his jacket lapels. Muggs snorted and backed off.

I explained the reason for the drop-in and we were ushered to a back room office. There behind his antique French Provincial desk was Don Langostino, Da Godfadda himself. The pudgy, white-haired homo-crustacean was nested in his oversized leather chair. He was stroking his cockatoo and humming *Volare*. On the desk was a snack plate of olives and goat cheese. Langostino spoke softly with a mouthful of food and a slight lisp.

"I understand that you gentlemen are looking for those responsible for the death of my good friend, Howie Prawns? And for the persons involved in the disappearance of William Kelp, who is known to his friends and enemies as 'Blue Point Willie.' I can assure you that neither I nor my associates have any knowledge of these acts or we would have already reported such to the authorities." Langostino looked around at Muggs and the Calamaris and gave them a sly wink, which they returned.

"You boys had better spend your time over in Chinatown," Langostino continued. "I understand that the Tangs wanted to control the oyster market and Blue Point Willie was an obstacle. He also had no respect for anyone. He never visited me just for a cappuccino, a little conversation, to pet my cockatoo, and he didn't show up at my daughter Bonnie's wedding. Then, he wants to dictate the price of oysters to me. This is not good business. The Tangs are sensitive to that sort of attitude. Then, there is his wife! That British broad was the same deal, a blonde bitch-on-wheels with her lice-ridden Welsh rabbit. The way that rodent kept looking at me gave me the willies— heh heh—the Blue Point Willies!"

The Calamari brothers and Muggs also started to chuckle. It became evident that Don Langostino didn't have anything to do with Willie's disappearance, but wished that he had. We sat and drank the thick, muddy cappuccino, ate soggy olives with the Don, then we took our leave. I declined to handle his cockatoo. As we marched to the door with Muggs behind us, we became aware of the eerie scraping noise his knuckles made on the floor.

It was late when Ed and I returned to the office. The dark street was illuminated by the one working street lamp and the semi-luminescent nose of one of the many drunks, or police undercover guys disguised as drunks, that inhabited the area after dusk.

Ed was about to go home to his wife, Snapper, when we noticed a shadow on our front door glass. I noted small, pointed ears and a glowing smile that shone like a beacon in the night through the thin, frosted glass. The door slowly opened, and we could see a feline outline in the hallway lit from behind by the sole working 20-watt light bulb.

Into the office walked Chester 'Chessie' Katz, a well-known tabloid reporter for *The Daily Rat-Out Observer-Globe.* He seemed nervous and constantly looked over his shoulder, even when the door slammed closed behind him.

"Pardon the intrusion, but there are those in this town who would like to mess up all nine of my lives. I was a good friend of Howard's, er, Shrimpy's. He used to feed me news tips. He was great with the catnip supplies, too. He could get me the Asian and Mexican stuff. Big leaves, uncrushed, unprocessed and no seeds or insecticides. All natural. Expensive. You understand?"

"Whoa, whoa, whoa! What's the point, pussycat?" Ed asked, wiping the sand from his weary eye-things.

"OK, OK!" said Chessie, holding up both paws. "The point is that Blue Point Willie had more enemies than just the restaurateurs he was muscling to buy oysters. I think his problem was 'closer to home,' if you know what I mean."

"Spit it up like a hairball, feline," Ed growled. "It's late and we all need our beauty sleep."

"That twitch of a wife of his has something to do with it," said Chessie as he opened the door and padded his way down the dark, stinking hallway towards the elevator from Hell. All we could see was that brilliant Ipana smile. As the cat neared the elevator door, he shouted out, "Beware of that white rabbit! He's more than colored eggs once a year. That bunny ain't bugs; he's stark raving bonkers!"

Down at the end of the hallway, we could see the elevator door open. The car was dimly lit by a single, 10 watt, yellow, bug repellant bulb that had been there for eight years. A distinctive feline shadow got into the elevator. The door squeaked closed, and there was darkness again.

We waited. I looked at Ed.

"Ten?"

"Eight," Ed replied.

We checked our watches. Seven seconds. The elevator alarm went off. Stuck again! We laughed. I had to buy the coffee tomorrow morning. It's a standing bet between Ed and myself when someone gets into that elevator...

The next morning, we decided to go to the Club Yakasaki and visit Won Gae Gai, the head of the West Coast Tang mob. Gai was a transvestite known in mob circles as The Flaming Red Queen. He was also an Iron Yakuza Chef notorious for beheading his enemies with a solid gold meat cleaver. By some ill stroke of fate, we got the same cabbie we had the day before on the wharf, that motor-mouth Jabberwocky.

"The Club Yakasaki. Step on it and stow the gab," Ed ordered, flashing his P. I. badge.

The Club Yakasaki was located on the south wharf in the heart of Little Asia. It was a large, pagoda-like structure with a huge, dinosaur-type reptile on the roof. Steam shot from the lizard's mouth and there was a loud roaring noise. "Boy, what a marketing gimmick!" I thought.

At the main gate to the Club Yakasaki we were greeted by Gai's counterpart, a killer shark named Hammerhead Hiroshi, Kingpin of Sushi and head of The East Coast Tangs. He was in town for a summit meeting with the Western Tangs and the Red Lobster Mafia about sharing territories. With him was his assistant, Ting Tang, the VP of the West Coast Tangs. He was from up north near Seattle, Walla Walla to be exact. We were introduced just as the doorbell rang. I went to the great iron door and opened it with great difficulty. There was a Mandarin standing there.

"I am Dr. Bang, one of Hammerhead's associates," he announced.

"Who's there?" Hiroshi shouted.

"Dr. Bang from the Tang," I replied.

Hiroshi ushered his guest in and introduced the two mobsters. "Ting Tang from Walla Walla, meet Bing Bang."

"I am sorry for your bad timing," Hiroshi apologized. "But I have guests and you just missed Don Langostino, Senator DoDo and the little blonde Lolita with the tasty, plump white rabbit which would make succulent General Tso's Bunny. They all went to the meeting where we must go immediately as soon as Gai comes, so make it fast.

"Alice Kelp was here?" I asked.

"Yes, she has proxy, representing her husband's oyster interests in his absence. But that hairy creature with her makes me most uncomfortable. The Devil's eyes it has."

Time slogged on, and we all grew impatient. Finally, we started to worry. Ed and Ting Tang went upstairs to the banquet rooms to look for Gai with no luck. Bing Bang and I looked around the downstairs rooms, but no luck there either. We decided to go *en mass* to the huge kitchens where roasted ducks hung Hong Pong style on racks under hot lights and little women with tiny fingers made hundreds of fresh dim sum each hour. Gai was nowhere to be found.

In front of us was the holy of holies, Gai's private Iron Chef Kitchen, the Forbidden Kuche, the Hidden Cochina, and what we found there chilled even Ed's green blood.

"Holy crap!" exclaimed Hiroshi. "Won Gae Gai has been skinned alive, chopped up and baked into a giant roast meat bun, made into won ton soup and his skin has been crisped with bean sauce and scallions. *Someone made Peking Queen!"*

I went to the phone immediately and called Sgt. Squiddle. Ed stood guard in the kitchen and watched the suspects we had. Everyone was sweating.

"I wonder how many people Gai beheaded with this cleaver," Ed said as he picked up the implement from the butcher block.

"None. No beheading with that cleaver," Hiroshi replied. "That cleaver is only for *cheese.* That gold plated one is for meat!"

"Gai kept a KOSHER kitchen?" Ed blurted out.

"Yes. The kitchens are run by his mother, Katch-Ka-San. She is going to be very upset with this whole event."

"She just cleaned and mopped up?"

"You know it!"

We could now hear sirens in the distance. There was a knock at the door. Sgt. Squiddle had arrived to take control of the scene. As we left the club, I complimented Hiroshi on the adornment on the roof, you know, the giant lizard.

"What giant lizard?" asked Hiroshi. I motioned to him and he followed us outside. I pointed to the giant green reptile which was still outside behind the building.

"AAAiiiiiieee—Gordzilna!!!" Hiroshi shrieked and ran back inside the building in terror while the reptile breathed fire on the roof of the Yakasaki Club, which burst into brilliant yellow and red flames as the walls started to shake violently. Such were the unexplained things in this part of the city. As we headed across the street at triple speed, I looked at Ed and shrugged.

"Hey, it's Chinatown!" Ed replied.

We proceeded to check out the other attendees at the mob meeting. Across the street we spotted Jabberwocky in his beer-battered yellow cab and decided to walk this one. Twenty minutes later, we're on the other side of town. The first stop was the State Office Building where Senator Delron DoDo had his offices. The Senator has been under investigation by the Caucus Party for allegedly taking bribes in the oyster price fix scandal investigations and hearings. They charged that his committee was just running around in circles at the taxpayers' expense, and at the direction of mob interests.

The State Office Building was one of those sterile glass and prefab panel towers that passes for architecture these days. The hallways reeked of pine disinfectant, and the elevators were slathered with machine oil to keep the stainless steel panels shiny and easy to clean. You didn't lean up against them if you were wearing a white silk suit. The tunes in the elevator featured that wimpy tenor-saxophone, easy-listening stuff that makes you bite your breath mints in two.

We knocked on the senator's office door without response. Ed tried the knob and found it was unlocked, and the office somewhat unkempt. On the desk I found a crumpled piece of paper. It was a copy of an order form from Hatter & Hare Caterers, a well-known, upscale restaurant and catering establishment. It was an order for ten thousand Blue Point oysters.

This evidence dictated that our next point of contact would be Hatter & Hare's swanky catering hall, The Electric Tea Party. It was a psychedelic seafood spa popular with the 'carriage trade' and jet setters, located in a section of town better known for who you could see than for the high-priced shops and international eating joints. Ed and I marveled at the unabashed visual excesses of the place.

"They must single handedly keep the neon light industry in the black," Ed commented. "There's at least five miles of neon just on the front of the building."

We entered the neon trimmed doors and waited in the neon lobby. It was a large room suggesting the inside of some garish pinball machine. Ed poked me and pointed to someone exiting one of the back windows in the adjacent banquet room. It was being set up for some function that did not require one of the large French windows to be open as they were. Nothing seemed to be out of place, but as we looked around at the neat place settings on each table, Ed noticed a napkin near the back door of the room that opened into a small hallway. It must have been knocked off the table when the intruder dashed past from the hall to the window, which was the only exit since we were in the lobby blocking the front door.

We carefully padded down the narrow hallway filled with the acrid aromas of various foreign cuisines. At the end of the hallway were the very private offices of the eccentric and celebrated owners. Ed searched Hatter's posh office; I picked around in Hare's equally elegant lair. In each room we found only clothing strewn around the room. Nothing else was out of place.

Odd, I thought. Then my eye caught something on the buffet where some of the steam table covers were askew. "Ed, look on the buffet trolley. I found Edwyn Hatter and Jerry Hare! Some enterprising 'chef' dismembered and chopped them up. Their flesh has been mixed with saffron curried rice and minced oysters."

A continued scan of the banquet buffet in preparation yielded a couple of cakes and another trolley of dinner entrées. We slowly lifted the covers of each dish. Under one of the sterling silver dome covers we found the pride and joy of the state senate investigations committee, Senator Delron DoDo. He had been plucked, rubbed with garlic and spices, charcoal grilled with a delicate Burgundy glaze and stuffed with shredded money and minced oysters.

Again, the sound of police sirens broke our concentration. We looked out of the windows just as Sgt. Squiddle and the morgue wagon pulled up.

"Who summoned him?" Ed queried.

Ed and I went out to greet Squiddle and get updated on the various homicides of the past week. Won Gae Gai was still in the back of one of the police wagons. They had packed him in giant takeout containers in a large brown paper sack with packets of sauces.

"They always forget the chopsticks and the napkins," Ed said.

"This was a strange one," said Squiddle as he perused the half-prepared banquet and the bodies contained therein. "The murders were phoned in ten minutes ago by someone with a muffled voice. It was as if the caller had a mouth full of cotton and a lisp. I would have gotten here sooner, but there's some sort of big celebration down at the south wharf near the Yakasaki Club. There's a huge mob of Asians running about in all directions, tanks, artillery, lots of fireworks and a really BIG dragon. It must be Chinese New Year."

Later that evening, Ed and I needed to chill. 10pm found us straddling the bar at our local watering hole, the Bucket of Lo-Carb Suds, a health saloon that featured liquor-flavored, organic drinks. Ed slumped over the well-worn mahogany counter, embellished over the decades with hundreds of carved initials and one-word memorials, while he puffed on a fifty-cent El Sargasso seaweed cigar. The smoke and stench from the cigar eventually filled the whole saloon and mercifully covered the ever present stink of the customers and their own 'fruit & vegetable origin gaseous emissions.' We were finishing our foamy plastic pitcher of something orange, slimy and nutritionally balanced when The Great White Hope walked into the place with a flourish. 'GW,' as he was known, was a wise-cracking, ski-nosed loan shark with sharp teeth he liked to keep pearly white. Rumor is that he sharpened and bleached them monthly.

"I hear you guys are on the Road to Oysterville," GW snapped. "But seriously, I thought you should know that I was the guy you missed at Hatter & Hare's. I had just dropped in to check out the sound system before I appeared at that function Saturday. That's when I found the bodies. Then, when I smelled parmesan cheese and olive oil, I thought I knew who was coming and I ducked out the back way."

"And who would that be?"

"The Calamari Brothers, I thought. You cross those psychos once and they shove a .45 up your nose and then..."

"Bing!" snapped Ed.

"Bing? What a horrible thought," Great White replied, rubbing the sweat off his wrinkled brow.

We assured Great White that we'd keep his name out of the investigation and decided to return to The Olive Oil Garden and bounce a few more questions off our more garlicky adversaries. We arrived half asleep from our travels only to find a crowd of locals and TV news crews watching the municipal fire department, such as it was, busily cleaning up a big mess. Don Langostino was in the ambulance with multiple contusions, recovering from an assassination attempt.

"Someone drove a mega-tanker of drawn butter right through his office wall and it exploded," explained the medic as he bandaged all eight of Langostino's half-boiled legs. Langostino writhed in excruciating pain as the medic rinsed the butter off his legs with jets of spring water. Then, the Godfather bellowed into his cell phone the hit order for Blue Point Willie with a $50,000 bounty.

In another ambulance, the Calamari Brothers were being showered in lemon juice and wrapped in gauze. They were almost cooked alive when the tanker split open. Muggs wasn't as lucky. His body, wrapped in brown paper, stuffed in a large zip-lock bag, was being tossed into the Medical Examiner's station wagon. The smell of roasted flesh and burnt fur was mixed with a sort of salty, buttery fragrance with just a touch of lime. OK, it stunk.

"Almost an Asian menu item," commented Ed with a wry tone.

We returned to the office. As we gingerly stepped off the creaking elevator we noticed a light in the janitor's closet. Our voices prompted the light to go off.

Ed pulled out his gun. I carefully and quickly jerked the door open only to find a stranger hiding in the dark, odiferous recesses of the sink closet, which has been unused for over ten years when the janitor mysteriously disappeared. Our guest was none other than William 'Blue Point Willie' Kelp himself. He looked like he'd been sleeping in his clothes for three weeks.

"I've been ducking Don Langostino's hit men all day," Willie explained as he gulped down the mug of lukewarm Bolger's Hilltop Grown Coffee Ed poured for him.

"Have you seen Alice?"

"Yeah, she's a very busy girl nowadays," I commented.

"Have you seen the way she behaves? That's not her. She's a sweet young thing, really. It's that rodent! Alice is under his Svengali-like influence. His real name is Rico Rabbnitz. We met him at Cuban Pete's Little Havana nightclub on the South side of town. Rico has this thing for sexy blondes, power and money. He's been trying to kill me for six weeks. Rico not only wants Alice; he wants to take over the oyster business because I just signed major contracts with *all* of the mob-owned restaurants on both coasts. It means millions of dollars profit and a guarantee of no government regulation enforcement."

Just then, we heard footsteps in the hall. High heels. Everyone braced themselves for what might be a showdown as the silhouette on the glass door heralded Alice herself. The office door opened, and in she walked. She acted like a robotic *Stepfjord Wife* from that cheap pulp novel.

I noticed that Alice wasn't carrying her rabbit. There was a good reason. He was behind her, keeping her under his control by using his gold pocket watch to hypnotize her. The White Rabbit snapped his fingers. Suddenly, Alice pulled a giant nutcracker from her designer purse and attacked Ed. She tried to crack his shell, but Ed's reflexes were quick for a crustacean. He pulled his BB gun from the desk and nailed the bunny's watch with three shots. The spell was broken, and so was the antique Witnauer. Alice lost her balance, sighed and collapsed on the sofa. Rico took off down the hall with Ed, Willie and myself in pursuit. He hopped in double time and tried to escape down the hallway through a large rat hole, but his overindulgences at the gourmet salad bars had added some paunch to the furry fiend's gut and he got stuck tight.

His fluffy round tail thrashed furiously. His muscular bunny legs scratched and hopped in mid-air as Rico tried to inch his way through the rat hole to freedom, but this was definitely no entrance to Wonderland. Joe looked at the bulging bunny butt as it wiggled helplessly. Ed could not resist.

"Is this the end of Rico?" Ed said.

By the time Sgt. Squiddle arrived and explained that he had been shadowing Ed and me all day, we had pulled the bunny out of the hole and trussed him securely. He was ready for delivery to the Lapin Penitentiary, known in judicial circles as The Hare Club for Mean.

That's it for the record. Alice and Willie were reunited and very rich. Joe and I wrapped the case and got a fat check from Willie. We decided to close the office for a month and go on a nice vacation, Hawaii maybe. Yeah, that's the ticket, sandy beaches, cool surf and tropical drinks with little paper umbrellas. My head was filled with these images as we walked to the elevator and waved goodbye to Ms. Doormaus. She took a deep breath and welcomed some downtime for herself as well, obviously thinking of all the fun things she could do with the bosses away for four weeks.

Then, the elevator alarm went off.

FIRST NATURAL BANK
John Skipp

Hell, no, I don't mind spending most of my time half-submerged. I'm a water baby. I love to swim. I love to dive, go as deep as I need to.

And I, for one, am really glad things changed.

I like them better this way.

Now, of course I'm not sayin' it's for everyone, but…well, actually, it *is*, now, isn't it? You can complain all you want. Good luck fishing out your fifth-story window. Find an old VW bug with a peace sign on it. Let that shit try to float you around, all hippie-style.

I don't know, Pappy Longstocking. You tell me! Maybe you shouldn't have let the polar ice caps melt. Maybe tried a little harder. Written your congressman or something. I'm barely old enough to be your grandson, so don't go pointing your mildew-encrusted bony-ass finger at me.

Not that I'm complaining, mind you. One man's meat is another man's Armageddon.

Me, I'm making do with the flippers at hand.

And brother, my fortunes are swimmin' upstream.

What I'm trying to say is: this drink's on me, pal, cuz I just had the best goddam day of my life. And I can pretty much guarantee that it would *never have happened* if you pussies had won the eco-war.

So.

You know that loan I've been trying to snag for as long as you've known me? All the paperwork? All the lawyer's fees? All the nay-saying, weeks upon weeks of drag-ass red-tape regulatory dogshit between me and my God-given personal enhancement, in the days when stupid people still thought they ran the world?

Well, today I paddled my raft down to the new First Natural Bank and Trust, on the convenient canal convergence that used to be the corner of State and Main. I had my papers all water-tight sealed, just in case. And my black tie like an arrow. Just to show I meant business.

When he saw what I had, the cinnamon-pink old security walri let me paddle straight in, ushered me over to the electric eel-powered D.J. Schow Memorial Eel-Avator, applied the complimentary air mask, and sent me straight up to Level Two, where Mr. Drysdale waited.

I can't tell you how happy I was that his name was Milburn Drysdale. Clearly, not all of the old gods had fallen.

Ever since I was a kid, watching *TV Land* in my grandpa's fallout shelter, I loved *The Beverly Hillbillies*, and thought that every banker ought to be just like that. Gray suit. Beady eyes. Little Hitler mustache, just wide enough to fend off the obvious comparisons.

The Mr. Drysdale I met was roughly 4,000 pounds larger. But his toupee was flawless. His gray suit was form-fitted. His mustache was beyond fantastic.

And his tusks dug into the desk with voluptuous ardor, tugging him forward as I entered his office.

Launching him bodily over the desk.

As I opened my pants full of clams.

Mr. Drysdale's mouth was designed for suction. Clam shells pried open wide, like my tusk-parted thighs, disgorging their muscular protein delights. I don't think he even noticed how explosively I came.

But the punchline is, I GOT MY LOAN. He flipper-stamped my paperwork faster than it could float away.

So fuck the old world. And drink up, Pappy!

I can swim all goddam day.

SIRENS OF NEW BRUNSWICK
Mykle Hansen

Eustace Cudgeon drove his shitty little car to the shitty little ocean, to go stick his toes in the water and yell at some fucking rocks. It was either that or bite someone. That's how it was going lately, for Eustace and his position at the firm and his marriage and every other thing: shitty, and disappointingly small. The ocean seemed like a fine waste dump for his pent-up rage. It was big, cold, wet, suitably miserable. He would do some screaming there, and stare at the emptiness.

But instead of emptiness, there was walrus-ness. An unseasonable swarm of walruses, walri, walrae, walroni, clogging the strand with their huge fat turd-shaped bodies. Walruses, an entire herd, or den, or pride or pack or squadron of them. Hundreds, no, thousands, flopping around in the meager sunshine like they belonged there. Eustace didn't know what to call them, certainly didn't expect them. This beach had always been a walrus-free zone.

In the rest stop parking area was one other car, and beside it one other human who gazed at the stupid beasts from afar through a tiny set of folding opera glasses. "Man," he said, as if asked, "I can't make it either. Seen plenty of gulls out here. Seen a whale washed up one time. But never much in the way of them walruses. Planet's getting fucksorated lately."

Eustace took in this man, looked him up and down. He was one of those people who seemed to wear all their clothing backwards. He had a body built for gawking, with buggy eyes, a long spindly flamingo's neck and hairy pale ankles exposed by high-waisted shorts and flaccid tube socks on a frigid, wind-blown coastal peninsula in late Autumn. The wind shifted, and Eustace caught a thick odor of lurid cologne laid over a firmament of unwashed clothing and carrot juice.

The man finally noticed Eustace's attention focused upon him. "Damn faggit!" he shouted, "I got a shotgun, you know. This ain't no queer-gay beach where faggits do their faggin'." He retreated into his car, closed its shell around himself, glared at Eustace from within and began a slow series of sharp, irritating honks.

Eustace decided to go yell at the walruses.

The sight of this furious little human scrambling down the slimy rocks piqued the curiosity of the walruses. Their inscrutable unified stare held Eustace back ten or twenty yards from the edge of the pack. He chose his ground, placed his picnic basket on the sand, spread out his blanket and began his tirade.

"Moronic blubber-tubes! Wrinkly fat elephant knees! What are you even doing here, you oyster-sucking, vampire-faced shitsicles? Go back to fucking Australia! Or Nepal, or wherever the hell! Go back to Walronia!"

A few of the larger bull walruses responded to Eustace's taunts with a loud, low gronking, a sound like an air horn being swallowed by a dinosaur. Others seemed to giggle, their whiskers twitching amiably. Eustace called them tire-fuckers, he called them overgrown chopstick holders, he called them Anorak-chow. They seemed to hear him, and perhaps even to get the gist, but not to care.

As Eustace yelled and screamed and invented rude gestures, as he frothed and flailed, he began to throw off the foul mood clinging to him for these last three days, ever since his wife had delivered her parting shot in the form of a neatly typed laundry list of insurmountable complaints. She hated his clothes, his hair, his waistline, the particular shape of his nose, the way he paused between sentences, his taste in sports, the smell of his chair, and above all she hated his constant screaming—but the walruses didn't mind.

Spent, relaxed, feeling for the first time a bit foolish for unburdening himself to enormous sea mammals, Eustace decided to sit down on the beach and eat his fucking sandwich. The sand was cold and damp, but if the walruses could hack it, so could Eustace.

The loud uncrinkling of wax paper cut through the wind and crashing waves. The sandwich lay naked, exposed. It was pastrami. It was good. As Eustace fed he noted a smaller gray-brown walrus nearby staring brazenly, almost wantonly, at his lunch. This one had long eyelashes and an upturned nose that put Eustace momentarily in mind of a certain girl he'd known in college. Strange, he thought, how the human mind can read so much into an animal's face.

He imagined somewhere on this scraggly excuse for a beach there was a sign, in official fonts and colors, forbidding visitors to feed sandwiches such as this to walruses such as that. And for that reason alone, he broke off the unchewed end of his sandwich and extended it invitingly to the beast.

The gray-brown walrus gronked with curiosity, wiggled its whiskers nervously, and waddled once, then twice, in the slow careful peristalsis of a breakdancer crossing a minefield, scootching itself closer and closer to Eustace's little blanket.

Finally the walrus lay beside Eustace like an old friend. It gobbled the pastrami sandwich it was offered but did not beg for more—Eustace was quite prepared to beat the creature back if necessary, although he truly had not grasped the enormity of the things until one of them came this close. It was like a two-door foreign hatchback made of fat. The walrus gazed deeply into Eustace's eyes, rubbed its head against his shoulder, inched closer and closer—intimately so.

Eustace hadn't realized how starved he was for affection. He stroked the walrus's neck, felts its cool soft skin, brushed the back of his hand against the long whiskers of its testicular cheeks. The walrus laid a flipper across his thigh, and seemed to coo at him. Eustace wondered if things were getting out of hand. But he felt strongly that this walrus should have a name.

"Rosemary," he told the walrus, "you ought to know I'm married."

Just then a thunderous honk fractured the air. Peering over the girth of his new friend, Eustace spied a monstrously large bull walrus flopping toward his territory, as the rest of the pack watched. This bigger walrus—it may have been the largest of them all—had a coat of cold white, and tusks longer than Eustace's arms. It gronked and hooted and waddled furiously closer, intent on confrontation. The gray-brown walrus called Rosemary rolled aside as the giant interloper approached. It pounded its head on the sand—Eustace felt the shock through his feet—and gronked some more.

Eustace drew on deep reserves of sullenness, stubbornness and apathy. He did not run. When the massive walrus was just a stone's throw away, Eustace threw a stone at it—a nice, jagged fist-sized piece of flint he found by his blanket. He missed, but the creature stopped its advance.

For a while, they screamed at one another. Eustace called this walrus a turgid sack of prehensile jello, a floating toothache, an obese otter. The walrus called Eustace a gronk, a gronking gronk, and a gronkahonk. Eustace considered what he'd do if the entire pack gave chase. Fear gripped him. He picked up two more stones and shook them at the aggressive walrus. The other walruses waited, watching.

The monster charged. Eustace let one fly. He struck the big walrus square between the eyes, stunning it. Before it could recover, Eustace picked up a large flat hunk of slate in both hands and dove violently forward, bringing the rock square down on the animal's head. He felt the stone connect, felt the hard crack and its shockwave travel down the animal's spine. He leaped back before it could counterstrike, but it didn't. The walrus just laid there, bleeding, trembling. Eustace couldn't tell if it was breathing.

Then the gray-brown walrus who'd shared his pastrami sidled up against his leg, cooing once more. The rest of the pack peered at him with some newfound respect.

"Hey faggit! What the hell even?" shouted the man from the parking lot, now standing just ten feet up the beach from Eustace and the walruses. He peered at Eustace through the opera glasses in his left hand, and waggled a long spindly finger of admonishment with his right. "You can't be killing damn walruses with damn rocks on a public damn beach! That's gay!"

Eustace could have snapped, wound up as he was with rage and adrenaline, fear and power, unmoored by the general strangeness and the smell of his attacker's blood, with a rock in his strong right hand that wanted badly to fly. But the walruses were faster. They swarmed past him, waddling and squirming and gronking, a blubbery wave breaking across the beach with awesome, impossible speed. The spindly gawker didn't even try to run. He just peered through his goggles at the surrounding horde as if the scene were distant opera. When they leapt upon him, he hardly made a sound.

Eustace ran. He scrambled up the rocks to the parking lot and the reassurance of his car, and only then turned to assess the spreading gore on the beach. One after the other the animals reared and dived, teeth-first onto the man's clearly lifeless body. But Rosemary, the gray-brown walrus, followed Eustace as far as the rocks. She now gazed up at him, emitting a low, anguished moan. The other walruses paused their carnage, turned to look at Eustace, and joined in a chorus of sad, plaintive walrus-song. Some raised a flipper, others rolled on their backs, others reared up on their tails and turned their tusks to the horizon in salute.

Feeling changed in a way he couldn't explain, Eustace waved to his walruses and drove home.

Eustace lived thirty miles inland; it took the walruses three days to reach his subdivision. In the interim he drank, swore, considered contacting the police or Fish & Wildlife but did neither. He received an addendum, via e-mail, to his estranged wife's list of insurmountables, but did not reply.

He studied up on walruses. The computer told him: they hunt with their whiskers and climb with their teeth. They woo their lovers with song, and they never feel cold. When pricked, they bleed. Unpricked, they suck clams.

He considered himself before the floor-to-ceiling bathroom mirror, noted the arrival of the latest pounds, wondered if his birth from a human womb had been some kind of mix-up. Somehow baldness, wrinkles and middle-age spread looked great on walruses. But Eustace was no walrus. He remained a lonely, bitter man.

Work beckoned, weakly. On Monday, Eustace called the firm: exzema, palpitations, sniffles, absent. On Tuesday, they called him back: downsizing, politics, indolence, fired. This was long overdue, and cause for celebration. Eustace drank scotch on ice, left explicit voicemail, smashed framed photographs here and there, fed his wife's flammable belongings into the oversized fireplace until the living room sweltered like a sauna, hot enough that Eustace could pass out naked on the rug, protected only by his thin layer of downy black fur.

At the first rays of Wednesday morning, Eustace was stabbed through the head by a noise, a sound, a bludgeoning knifelike mass gronking, an unholy hideous loudness that he knew at once to be walrus-powered. He stumbled half-awake to the front door and flung it open, covering an ear with his free hand.

They blotted out the earth. Huge disorganized juggling heaps of walrus, layers deep. Rolling dunes of mammal-flesh spilled over onto the neighbors, the sidewalk, the curb, the street. They parked like sandbags in the begonias, the driveway, the footpath. Eustace counted twenty, fifty, a hundred just on his own lawn.

They had waddled far, these walruses. They looked limp and worn. But the sight of Eustace, standing naked as a fish in his front entrance, electrified them. They sent up a joyful hooting and barking, and slapped their flippers proudly against one another's bodies.

Eustace rubbed his sore head in his fat hands. But then he saw a movement in the blubbery crowd, and recognized the walrus named Rosemary. She waddled straight up to him and placed her cold nose on his knee, batting her long-lashed eyelids and tickling him with her whiskers. Eustace leaned over slightly to pet her soft leathery scalp. Across the street, a glaring neighbor aimed a phone-camera through a bay window.

Before Eustace could react, the gray-brown walrus shoved him aside and waddled into his house. The other walruses cheered. Eustace ducked back inside and double-locked the door.

Rosemary quickly made herself at home. The timbers of the house creaked and popped as she explored the sofa, sniffed approvingly at the ashes in the fireplace, tested the bathtub, discovered the kitchen and its hidden wastebasket of smells. Eustace plodded along behind her in hung-over shock, strangely uninspired to complain. Given his recent circumstances, a walrus home invasion seemed interesting, exciting. It held possibilities.

Rosemary cooed and humped herself up the stairs to the master bedroom. Eustace followed, lured by the synthetic, doleful tinkling of the cell phone in his trouser pocket on the floor by the bed. As Rosemary stretched out on the flannel sheets in a calendar girl pose, Eustace pressed the thumbworn button on his phone marked WIFE.

"I hate your walruses, Eustace. I really hate them."

"Noted."

"I'm watching you on News Twenty-Three. You're standing in the doorway naked as a jaybird. Nakeder."

Eustace peeped through the upstairs curtain. Outside, on the far end of the street beyond the edge of the walrus infestation he saw a fleet of ambulances, fire trucks, squad cars and news vans with their engorged antennae flopping in the breeze. He heard the chopping of a helicopter somewhere in the nearby sky.

"Those walruses make you look fat, Eustace. What the hell are you up to?"

"Walruses are underappreciated animals. I'm appreciating them."

"The begonias, the yard...it's history. Things won't be the same."

"No, Wendy, they sure won't. Anything else?"

"You know what they're calling it on News Twenty-Three? A wildlife hostage situation. That's stupid, Eustace. All your friends can see you naked on TV, you know that don't you? You look fat. You *are* fat, and you're dancing around on TV...and I have to explain that I'm married to that."

Eustace pinched the phone between ear and shoulder and sat, pulling on his pants. Rosemary laid a surprisingly warm flipper across his thigh, and cooed questioningly in his ear.

"I heard that! Who is that? You're not alone, are you?"

Eustace smiled. "Wendy, listen very carefully. There's a walrus in our bedroom. It's wearing your clothes. It's urinating on your cashmere house slippers. It's eating your aloe vera."

"Stop it, Eustace."

"Downstairs, Wendy, there's a whole gang of walruses tearing up your bamboo flooring and smearing sardines on the granite countertops in the kitchen. They are feeding your books to the flames, Wendy."

"No!"

"Walruses have needs, Wendy. They're cold. And they're lonely. So we're burning all your things, and ripping up your house, and when we're done with that I'm going to make love to a walrus in our marital bed, and, I don't know, just improvise from there. Have you got all that? Any questions?"

"I used to think I only hated certain things about you."

"Hey, look at the time. Nice talking. Bye for now."

Eustace tossed the phone in the corner and laid down beside Rosemary, feeling the animal's heat. It locked eyes with his, sniffed his breath, tickled his nose with its soft whiskers. He smelled fish on its snout. Herring...and passion.

"Please be gentle," he said. "I'm new at walrusing."

One hour later, Eustace stood again before the mirror, cataloguing his walrus traits. His bald head and wrinkly neck, his pear-like midriff, his jowls, his fast-growing red-gray whiskers...he'd always been ashamed of his human body, never liked it, always intended to do something about it. His oversized feet looked ridiculous in shoes, but naked they revealed flipper potential. His canines, never straight, now gave an unfamiliar push against his upper lip. A cold wave of realization broke against his rocky mind.

"Maybe I've always been a walrus!" Could it be true? Eustace recalled his unhappy childhood—was he abducted from an arctic beach? His dead parents wouldn't tell, but perhaps there were news clippings, clues, evidence.

Did Eustace need evidence? No. He grasped an inner truth. He was a definite walrus. A clear and present walrus. A walrus for our time.

Rosemary grunted from the bed. Eustace had outfitted her with a push-up bra and lipstick—his wife's things, human things. It had helped him relax. But now these lurid homosapien traces seemed ridiculous and demeaning. Rosemary winked and beckoned with her tail. Eustace stood before her, naked and erect, and testified:

"I am a walrus, and I am beautiful!"

After their loud interspecies sexmaking, Eustace fell into a deep slumber and dreamed of a melting world. He saw the carefully tended landscaping of his subdivision crumble into green-blue ice and thaw away, watched as buildings slowly drifted apart, bobbing on individual ice floes. The thin, liver-spotted octogenarian across the street stood on the terra-cotta roof of her house, wearing a bicycle helmet and a parachute, impotent protection from the end of days, fixing her thick glasses on Eustace in a disapproving stare, scolding him with soundless lips. He watched her house begin to list, tumbling slow as a ferris wheel, as the water reached the bay window, the bedroom, the rain gutter, and then the roof, and the house and owner rolled and plunged into the depths like a whale.

Eustace and Rosemary pushed out the window, slid down the shingles and dove in. Beneath the water's surface, hundreds of walri raged, gorging themselves on the bounteous collapse. With a single slurp, one walrus inhaled an entire policeman, guns and all. Another jabbed a long tooth into an upturned minivan, prized open the hatch, wrapped its hairy lips around the crack and sucked out an entire family. Ravenous walruses vacuumed up people, pets, furniture, tires, debris, every floating thing. They fed and fed, ballooning so large that they burst apart into pieces, and each fragment of blubber congealed into a new, tiny, hungry walrus, and the feeding continued, as a town's worth of houses and schools and 7-11s and gas stations tumbled away down into the darkness, wet asteroids falling into a black sun.

Rosemary nudged Eustace with a gentle flipper, and they kicked away from the carnage and sped off, fast brilliant torpedoes under the overhanging brightness. They swam on northward through the open sea and its menageries, through clouds of silver fish, through floating gardens of pink kelp, on into colder and clearer water full only of ice. They swam until they reached the North Pole itself, an enormous blue iceberg dangling from the water's surface, a crystal city upside-down. Walruses upon walruses surrounded it, orbited it, leapt from it and climbed back on. This was their planet.

Eustace and Rosemary rose to the edge and heaved themselves up onto the ice. There they found the very foot of a long red carpet, snow dyed with blood, that snaked away through the lumps of icy landscape and up over a rise in the distance. A million expectant walrus paparazzi surrounded the carpet, strobing them with camera flash. Eustace wriggled up the aisle, certain that some kind of destiny waited. All around him the walruses cheered. As he lumbered on, an adorable child walrus reached past the velvet ropes to request an autograph. Eustace tried to grip the child's pencil and notepad, but found his elbows fused to his sides, his fingers grown fat and flat like leather mittens. He made to apologize, but his words came out as low barks, just meaningless fat notes from a rubber tuba. The little walrus started to cry, as thunder burst and hot rain fell, as all the walruses for miles around writhed in pain and honked in alarm, as the red carpet cracked, as the ice beneath them shook apart and dropped away—

A loud commotion outside startled Eustace awake: sirens in the street, urgent whistles, loud gronks of alarm, and some huge, hissing white noise like breakers on the beach. Out the window he saw a single-file procession of emergency vehicles inching closer, fronted by a large black police tank that used a burly anti-riot water cannon to peel back Eustace's protective layer of walruses, parting the sea of meat to carve a narrow, angry and waterlogged footpath from the curb to Eustace's front porch. Moments later came a loud, testy thumping with an extra helping of doorbell.

Eustace lay on his belly, waddled down the staircase and opened the door with his feet. On the front steps, he granted an audience to the marine biologist, the hostage negotiator and the homeowners' association vice-chairperson. They gaped stupidly at the grandeur that was Eustace—his spreading vastness, his fused knees and lengthening whiskers—and yammered on and on about the law, the climate, the landscaping. They squeaked at him like little monkeys, flapping their scrawny hairless limbs and tossing around their overmanaged hair. None of them would last ten minutes in the ocean. Deep in his belly Eustace felt revulsion, mixed with an emptiness that longed to be filled with shellfish and with purpose.

All the while, ten thousand tired, hungry walruses kept their trusting eyes fixed upon some invisible golden point on the top of Eustace's head. Eustace looked upon his wayward subjects and knew their pain, felt their last hopes pinned upon him. Was it any mystery why they'd left their home? It was happening everywhere, this sort of thing: ice melting, weather patterns shifting and fisheries collapsing, desperate animals washing ashore thousands of miles from their habitat. But this condominium complex could never sustain them. Too dry, too indefensible, too many cars and not enough fish. They had to move on. They needed the sea.

Using his walrus powers of persuasion, Eustace organized an emergency air-drop of sardines from the marine biologist. The hostage negotiator contacted the National Guard, who produced a convoy of trucks to carry Eustace and his thousands of subjects back to the beach where they first came ashore. The homeowners' association vice-chairperson succumbed to threats of brutal annihilation and ran away. Eustace counseled patience to the assembled throng and then returned inside, to lie on the sofa and watch his flippers grow.

By Thursday afternoon, the entire walrus army flounced proudly across the cold beach, unloaded from trucks, ready to embark. Eustace lay among them, hoarding the largest rock, absorbing the sunshine on his ever-thickening half-human body, feeling the wind in his beard, tonguing his now protuberant tusks, surveying the tide. Rosemary, first among his walrus harem, cuddled proudly beside him. Back in the parking lot, cowardly newshumans aimed cameras from behind their vans.

Soon, Eustace and his tribe would plunge into the sea, then carry on southward. It would be nothing like their arctic homeland, but they would adapt. It would be difficult, but they were strong, toothsome and magnificent.

They would take Florida, or die trying.

Eustace reared up on his hindquarters and grunted out his final English words to the assembled cameras.

"Humans: we are out of here. I won't say there weren't some nice moments, but basically this place has sucked and we're happy to be leaving.

"We may survive, we may not. If we do, it'll be no thanks to you. We're going to do what's necessary and you'd better not try to stop us. If you think you care, if you think you want to help, then lay off the harpoons, the oil slicks, the gill nets, the greenhouse gasses, the toxic waste, all that shit. It's getting ridiculous.

"In closing: fuck this place. Fuck it with whale dicks. Fuck the land, fuck humans, fuck jobs, fuck days, nights and weekends. Fuck cars, clothing and credit cards. Fuck the President and fuck the Pope. Fuck everything that's not a walrus or some water or some clams. We are off to a far, far better world, and you can pack all my regrets in a fly's asshole. Farewell, and fuck you all."

THE WALRI REPUBLIC OF SEAWORLD
Bradley Sands

Paul was wasting another mating season sacrificing his unborn calves to the unabashed glossiness of *Tuskie Fuck Magazine*. An Atlantic Romantic was taking a cow from behind, her face concealed by the elegant mask of Paul's new crush. He had abducted the likeness from her high school yearbook picture and affixed it to the page with his spittle.

Her name was Gaaaaaaahg and she had a mustache that would make the Arctic waters boil.

And she didn't even know he existed. Yes, it was true that he was painfully shy and spent his days hiding behind a boulder whenever she was around, but she could have at least made the effort to get to know him. It's not like she had a limited amount of opportunities: they had been living in the same enclosed space for the past five years.

Life was lonely from behind the boulder.

Gaaaaaaahg wasn't like the other cows. Paul's other crushes were shallow—unconcerned with the mysteries of the deep end of the pool—but Gaaaaaaahg was an indentured servant to her curiosity.

Intimidated by her intelligence, Paul deluded himself into believing the reason behind all the hiding was that she could turn a bull into a scone with but one glance. Upon discovering her high school yearbook, he finally stopped lying to himself.

Gaaaaaaahg had the potential to fill his every waking thought, which were usually reserved for schemes or speculations on the future of the food service industry. If their relationship were to work out, he would be saved from a lifetime of boredom. Chronic flipper pain was just the price he'd have to pay.

"WHAT AWFUL CREATURES!"

It was coming from the direction of the Place That the Walri Shall Not Know, where the funny things would stand, staring with their funny faces, saying their funny things.

"KILL THEM ALL!"

He poked his head out from behind the boulder, looked at the funny things...and lost his ramrod. He'd never seen the funny things so red-tinged before, and saying so many funny things.

Gaaaaaaahg had a theory why the funny things said the funny things that they said. They did it because they wanted their mommies. The more they did it, the more they wanted their mommies.

They must have really wanted their mommies.

And they always came back to This is the Place to look for their mommies, and Gaaaaaaahg always felt sorry for them. Once she hired a private detective to help them stop crying, but someone put a knife in his back before he could find the mommies. He must have been really close to the truth.

Paul leaped over the boulder to find Gaaaaaaahg. Maybe she could hack into ECHELON to locate all the mommies. She had better get to it soon. Paul's head was beginning to ouch-throb from all the loud funny things.

But she was gone. All of the Walri were gone. Someone had replaced them with effervescing shadows.

He picked up a universal remote control. He had to save his future by rewinding himself into the past, back to the moment before he leapt over the boulder. It was vital he convince his past self to abstain from leaping. He could not risk being in the presence of Gaaaaaaahg. Of course, Gaaaaaaahg was nowhere to be found. But what if this unusual occurrence had given him a false sense of security? What if the next time he leapt over a boulder without a second thought he landed in the loving arms of Gaaaaaaahg? Then what would he do? He didn't feel like he was ready to make a commitment.

But he decided against rewinding, because it was very stupid.

What the hell was he thinking? This is the Place was on fire, and here he was, clutching a remote as if it were a time machine. So he replaced it with the items he had promised to rescue if a fire ever occurred—his pornography—and ran like hell towards the Place that the Walri Shall Not Know, rechristening it as the Place That Paul the Walrus Shall Know.

Paul polished his harpoon as he passed Mango Joe's Café. Funny things blared out of a radio inside it: "In breaking news today, Walri have taken control of the Orlando SeaWorld, declaring it the Walri Republic of SeaWorld and seceding from the union. The United States government has declared war on the Walri, reassuring the American people that they will not bathe until every aquatic play pool and gift shop is eradicated from the face of the Earth.

"Here's Tom with the-Oh my God! A man wearing a wet t-shirt has just entered the studio. He is extraordinarily chubby!

"I've just been handed an update on the situation. Until the Walri are left alone, fatty has threatened to prey upon our delicate sensibilities by remaining saturated in water. God help us all!"

And then Shamu exploded.

But Paul didn't notice. He was too busy strangling a dolphin and fantasizing about Gaaaaaaahg.

They are on an awkward coffee date. Gaaaaaaahg breaks the uncomfortable silence by pointing at Paul's tuxedo and laughing. She continues to chuckle, while Paul tries to tell jokes for the first time in his life, protecting his fragile psyche by pretending she's in hysterics over his comedic stylings.

Intestines rolled out the doors of SeaWorld's hospitality center. The tourists were being treated to a new culture—one whose idea of hospitality was to remove evil with its tusks. Polite applause followed each execution. Everyone was extremely impressed with the funny things' attempts at making up for the lack of accomplishment in their lives by leaving it in a blaze of dubious achievement. They all made a respectable attempt at beating the record for their most ear-shattering shriek.

And then the replacement Shamu exploded, smothering Paul in bubbling blubber. Since he always liked to keep zestfully clean, Paul would have been rattled by his new appearance if he hadn't been immersed in the pleasantries of walking the eel.

Gaaaaaaahg is wearing a wedding dress and he is in a black top hat—a reproduction of the hat he used as a makeshift thinking cap on the outside, designed to keep in thoughts of impending doom. And it has a lot of cerebellum fluid to confine within its bulk: Gaaaaaaahg's belief in the existence of no sex before marriage, that she had been replaced by a member of the reconnaissance mission for the pregnoid invasion who held him responsible for the immaculate conception in her belly, and his fear of the shotgun her father holds to Paul's right temple.

CUE MONTAGE SEQUENCE OF A GOLDFISH BOWL UNDER-GOING VARIOUS STAGES OF NEGLECT.

FADE IN

EXT. ICE MACHINE – DAY

PAUL sits on a couch, watching television to get his mind off of being old, fat and bald. Gaaaaaaahg lies on the top of the TV, enjoying a bout of naked frolicking with the mollusk delivery boy. Cobwebs engulf their bodies, spinning a tale of how Gaaaaaaahg has been mistaking the delivery boy for her husband throughout the entirety of their marriage.

Dolphins swam amid pools of blood, entertaining soldiers by jumping through hoops and smacking their lips on the way down. Bodies hung from telephone wire like enigmatic pairs of sneakers, their arms unintentionally positioned to hold each other's hands in an expression of walri/human love they never had a chance to know in life.

Paul, still tenderizing the crustacean, decided to make some major renovations to his ice machine. After breaking 667 building violations, he became the proud owner of his own nightclub.

The Oosik Lounge is SeaWorld's #1 nightspot.
Entry is $5 w/this flyer, $8 w/o

Exhibit your voyeuristic side as you witness petrified sex maniacs doing the Relaxed Muscle Shuffle. You may join in for an additional surcharge. And it's time to yuk it up when the owner does his hilarious impression of a walrus watching his wife adulterate it up with a delivery boy, weeping rats and dogs until he realizes the affair has made him into a very wealthy walrus and a wave of euphoria washes over his body.

The real Gaaaaaaahg—the shell of a former pin-up model—was leaning against the Shark Encounter building. She lunged at Paul, dripping entrails in her wake. "Hey, you!" she mouthed through eroded teeth. "The world is coming to an end and I don't want to go out without one last bang. So how about me and you get carnal?"

Cleaning the cod, he backed away from the monstrosity. "Not my world," he said to himself. "Not my world."

Gaaaaaaahg lounges on the television, looking so lovely he forgets all about the guy that's fucking her in the ass. He swipes his credit into her slot, charging his entire net worth. Taking his wealth as an indication of his importance, she rouses, and rises for the first time in a decade.

Gaaaaaaahg consummates their marriage, leaving his hands free to pen a letter to Tuskie Fuck Forum.

The squoogee! came a'burstin at the exact moment the United States government dropped a nuclear holocaust onto SeaWorld.

And Our Paul Who Art in Heaven wiped himself clean with a tissue.

GUS
A D Dawson

It is jolly well cold up here. I'm chained to a wall and a biting northerly wind is blowing up my toga—we seldom wear underclothes hereabouts; it is unacceptable. What am I doing there, wherever that might be, you may well ask? To answer your question—if indeed you ever asked it, I have erred and am waiting to see Gus to find out what my punishment may be for my transgression.

You see, I am an Instigator and I am trusted to instigate. Alas, I have broken that trust into a thousand pieces and may never repair the damage. Allow me to explain further, albeit briefly, for I am not one to stretch the narrative.

My job is to suggest things to you Humans—for you are such a lazy lot and would go no further without our prompts. It is fair to say that over the centuries the Instigating Bureau have made many mistakes—take for example, The Great War of 1914. The Instigator that suggested such folly as that was well reprimanded by Gus. To be fair—*his*—mistake was in good faith; mine was not. I'm a bit of a joker—you would probably say a bit of a lad—and I was bored at the time.

I had completed all of my suggestions for the day and was sitting, fiddling with my flippers—for it is boring watching you lot going about your banal business—when I had a brainwave. Why not make a universal suggestion that would cause a light relief from your usual tedium? I thought long and hard and eventually came up with this one—it's a gem, or so I thought at the time.

What if every person living in Europe was to think it would be good fun to slap their next-door neighbour on the head with a fresh fish every evening for the next three weeks? At the time, Sisyphus (the overseer) was well away and at his lunch, so I launched the thought without fear of interception. I watched the suggestion drop all of the way from the clouds and down towards the continent of Europe— there was a slight fallout over Northern Africa to boot. You may think this suggestion is quite harmless—a bit of a prank never hurt anyone. I assure you, however, that the ramifications of my actions caused a severe shift in nature. Indeed *rerum natura* is the one thing that we are forbidden, for fear of death, to meddle with. SHUSH! Sisyphus has just waddled out of Gus' office and is headed my way. He doesn't look happy. Ta, ra, ta, ra...

"Silence, you foolish walrus!" he bellows angrily as he sticks a sharp tusk into yours truly.

"Ow! That bloody hurt, Sisyphus! Why don't you pick on someone your own size?" I rage back.

"Have you no respect at all for your Elders?" he continues in the same tone. "How dare you speak to me in that manner."

I shrug with an impudent indifference. He raises up his tusks once more—I fear he will stick them right through my skull this time for my cheek. I breathe a sigh of relief when he instead picks at the padlock and my chains fall to the cloud—I am released for the now, at least.

"Do not look so smug, walrus. Gus awaits you."

I gulp. Gus the Almighty; our, and your, Creator; the whole 3,000 pounds of him is waiting for me. I slide slowly over to his door and knock.

"COME!" he bellows.

"*Tempestas cooritur.*" (a storm is rising)

I nudge open the door and go in. Gus is at His desk and does not look up from His work as I move gingerly closer.

"I have come..."

"SILENCE!"

"Sorry."

Gus looks up. He is gigantic: standing over 8 feet tall and weighing nigh on 4000 pounds—notwithstanding that I am a big lad myself, I am like a baby sea lion to His tremendous walri physicality.

"You have sparked off a man-war in the northern regions with your foolishness, Jus," He utters through greying whiskers.

"I have?" I gulp.

"The European brothers have fallen out over the fishing rights of the Northern seas. Gunboats have been employed and many fishermen lay dead at the bottom of the briny," He continues glumly.

"I'm..."

"And that is not all. Can you imagine how many fresh fish were sought to furnish your whim? The waters of Europe and North Africa are all but fished out, and a lack of cod liver oil has caused an unfortunate geriatric seize up...you must be punished for the harm you have subjected upon mankind."

He pauses to shit. It drops to the floor with a *phut.*

The door opens, and in shuffles Sisyphus. He is pushing a wheelbarrow with his snout and dragging a shovel with his front flipper.

"You have shit my Lord," he says to my bewilderment.

Without further ado, he moves forward and scoops up the shit with his shovel—a shovel forged in the fires of Vulcus—or so I am told. He bows and leaves. However, he is soon to return as Gus lets go with another pile…and another pile…and another pile. Sisyphus looks really pissed off with this.

"You picked your own punishment, Sisyphus," says Gus, noticing the overseer's fallen mug.

"I did not realise it would be like this, my Lord Gus. I have time for nothing else but to clear up your shit after you."

"Get on with it, would you?" retorts Gus angrily. "You should have had more control over your subordinates. Then you would not have been punished."

"I hope you've thought up a good punishment for that twat," he rages, whilst indicating towards me with his shitty shovel.

"I have indeed, Sisyphus; do not worry yourself."

I knew that I would end up here—somewhere in the Bering Sea, as you humans have named it. I call it Hell. I am stood at the edge of the water looking towards my newfound friends, who are huddled together in the weak winter's sun. I approach gingerly—for the walrus can be very territorial towards newcomers. Hell's Bells! Would you look at the size of that guy waddling over to me now—he must be the leader, and I think he is going to challenge me. Think, think, think of something clever to say. Ah ha! I've got it.

"Who might you be?" he growls.

"I am Jus, the son of Gus," I say loudly—my voice reverberates across the barren island for effect.

"If you are truly the son of Gus, then come inner and I will protect you from all."

"And who might you be, sir?" I ask politely.

"I am Judus," he replies, before nuzzle-kissing me.

Well, there you have it. That is the story for the now. I am well accepted within my new community. They see me as quite the philosopher, and there are plenty invertebrates to dine upon hereabouts—what more could a walrus ask for? I have to go, I'm afraid. Judus and the soccer eleven have invited me to eat with them—and it is my turn to wash the flippers this evening.

Gus Bless.

LOVESPOONS IN PERIL
Rhys Hughes

As far as mermaids are concerned, the sky and a particular small country in Western Europe are one and the same thing.

But Wales is heaven to nobody else...

The Traveller stood in the rain on the wet sand and watched the waves rumbling excitedly towards him, but they always seemed to lose interest at the last moment and subside into the general flatness, lapping the toes of his shoes with almost no force.

Everything was flat, or maybe that was just the way he felt, back home in the grey spaces, growing older and mouldy in a place where umbrellas were useless because the rain was too fine and never fell vertically from the clouds but drifted sideways, swirled in circles and spirals and sometimes even went back up.

So he carefully plotted his next big escape.

There was no definite plan yet, but he was working on it and it was important that he tell nobody, though he couldn't say *why* he had to keep it to himself. Probably just superstition. But he had a strong feeling it was bad luck to believe in superstitions.

This belief created some confusion in his mind.

Luckily that was the best place for confusion—inside his head. Other things locked away in his head included knowledge, experience, anxiety, nonsense, advice, spirituality, cynicism.

And he never let them out.

The bohemians of Swansea like to complain they don't have a scene and they do this complaining while playing music, writing books, painting or sculpting, debating philosophy, sipping wine, sitting in candlelight with glittering jewellery and unusual hair.

What they actually mean is that they aren't enjoying themselves in the way they should, though none can say how much *should* ought to be, and an answer to this question is the last thing they really want. They want to continue as they are, nothing more.

In the house of Huw Rees, drummer and wine expert, they gather to practice music and little ironies, sometimes to wear hats. There are no curtains on the windows and people who pass on the street may glance in at the instruments and bottles balanced on each other. Exotic drums are everywhere, even outside in the back garden where the rain plays tedious but acceptable rhythms on the skins.

After the music and wine is exhausted, some of the bohemians remain to avoid walking home in the rain or to smoke marijuana. One wet night, Stuart Ross, who rented a room somewhere upstairs, leaned his bass guitar against the wall and sat on the sofa. He had been a member of a jazz funk sort of group but had left under a cloud. In Wales everybody leaves everything under clouds, there isn't much choice, but this had been indoors, which makes it more unusual.

"What shall we grumble about today?" he asked.

"My main complaint is that there isn't enough nudity in this city. A serious lack of beautiful naked women."

That was Huw's opinion as he lit a joint.

Stuart shrugged. "It's not entirely a hopeless situation. I don't know why I feel this to be true, but I do."

At this point the conversation faltered. The silence was a rare vintage and needed to be savoured before being broken, the same way the crust of a venerable yoghurt mustn't be jabbed with a spoon immediately. And talking about spoons...but that's for later. In the meantime, the five or six people who remained struggled to remember any spare anecdotes they might gainfully employ to entertain the others. It was Monica who was the first to think of something.

"I was once attacked by an elk," she said.

"Let's talk about northern animals," agreed Stuart. "In my experience, which on this topic is limited, the polar bear qualifies in this category, but the flamingo certainly does not."

"It charged me in a land far from here."

"This is a pointless digression," sneered Huw. He didn't know about the forthcoming plot of this story.

"Penguins are not northern animals but should be," persisted Stuart.

"That fellow who lives down the road," said someone whose name was hidden by the shadows, "is from the north."

"Do you mean the inventor? I thought he was German."

Huw nodded. "Yes, Mondaugen is his name. Swansea is full of lost inventors at the moment, don't know why they come here of all towns, just another place to be ignored."

"But his latest invention has been bought by the government or a big corporation at least," said Monica.

There was another pause. The new subject was already exhausted.
"Shame we don't have a scene," sighed Stuart.

There were still no curtains on the windows and he turned to
observe what was happening in the street. Just the usual. Hunched
figures hurried home or elsewhere or maybe even nowhere through
deep puddles. They seemed more miserable than perhaps they were.
In Wales people don't acquire wrinkles on their faces as they grow
older, they develop miniature gutters. With a shudder, Stuart hunched
his own shoulders and allowed his torrential fringe to cover his sight.

The mermaid known in the world of humans as Caroline Moreira swam
with her friends through the natural palaces at the bottom of the ocean,
through grottoes lit by phosphorescent fish. The time of carnivals was
over and she had discarded the costume which made her resemble a
normal woman. Now she was looking for fresh adventures among the
sunken mountains south of the Azores, those crags riddled with caverns
and studded with shipwrecks.

She swam without caring too much where she went but somehow
she became separated from her friends and ended up alone and suddenly
she lost all desire to be inside the mountains. She craved the open sea
again, the faint glimmer of sunlight high above, the company of
dolphins, rays and sunfish. So she searched for a means of escape
from this eerie maze of caves and tunnels and finally emerged from an
extinct volcano into a deep crater ringed with jellyfish.

She had no idea where she was, but it was far from land.

A feeling vibrated inside her and she knew she was destined to
have a special meeting soon. It always worked like this for her, maybe
she had an extra sense she wasn't fully aware of. She swam up the
crater's side and rose like a final spurt of lava from the dead mountain,
her wavy hair blazing on the currents, deep red darkening to chestnut
brown, swirling over her head as she paused just above the summit.
This was the highest peak in the range and her view was superb, the
other crags rippling away on all sides like solidified waves.

She sang a special song and waited but received no reply.

There were no other mermaids in the vicinity. She truly was lost.
She chose a random direction and flicked her tail.

Her necklace of bright seashells jangled delightfully.

The Traveller decided he needed a hobby to prevent boredom entering
and dominating his life before he managed to leave Wales on another

trip. He wandered the colleges looking for a course on which to enrol. Eventually he decided to try glassblowing.

He found it interesting but lacked the patience to produce acceptable work. He always puffed too hard and ended up with glasses too big for social occasions with decent people. If only he knew some bohemians! They wouldn't be intimidated and might even express admiration for his width of imagination and length of breath.

The other students wept outrageously.

One lesson he produced a wine glass so large his tutor felt there was no choice but to expel him from class.

Ordering the vast tumbler, still hot, to be carried into the workshop yard, where it hissed in the rain, he took The Traveller to a corner for a serious talk and explained he was reluctantly casting out his new pupil because he feared for the future.

"You are depressing my class. If this continues," he warned, "you might eventually make a greenhouse. Think of the grief then! And not just the grief, but the tomatoes!"

The Traveller was simply unable to stop blowing at the right time. The problem was that he had a huge heart and everything he did, he did big. He shrugged at this setback and looked for a new course to enrol on. In the meantime, his monumental tumbler captured whole droplets of rain as it cooled—they were embedded in the soft glass. They didn't evaporate but remained in place as the glass flowed slowly over, trapping them like diamonds in the sides of a goblet. When he saw this later, the tutor was astonished and refused to break the object into pieces. It became a fixed feature of his workshop yard.

The Traveller joined a class where he learned to make cushions. Less than a month passed before he was expelled from *this* class. He made a cushion so big that everybody sat on it and couldn't be bothered to get up again for several days. This caused all kinds of trouble. The cushion was stored away somewhere safe and our dejected hero wandered the streets again. Many puddles were familiar with his shoes. In rapid succession he joined, and was expelled from, classes that taught cooking, knitting and music. His mistakes would eventually fit together but in the meantime he began to believe himself a failure.

Only one class was left. It dealt with a traditional Welsh craft, the art of the lovespoon. It promised to teach pupils how to carve lovespoons as good as any from the past. The Traveller hesitated just a moment before enrolling. It was his last chance.

The name of the ship was *The Shiver Timbers* and several people said it was unlucky but they were cheats because they had jumped forward to the part of this story where it sinks. At the time it seemed reliable enough, a sturdy and powerful vessel, and the crew were experienced. Captain Scipio Faraway was generally considered to be the finest sailor in this entire paragraph—half the others were nearly half as good, and the other half almost half that. So there was no need to think that something would go wrong. Why should it? The mission was easy. Sail north to the Arctic Circle, choose a big iceberg, tow it to one of those desert countries along the Red Sea and leave it there.

The way Mondaugen put it was like this: "The people down there are short of water and have to distil or filter the sea to get rid of the salt each time they want a drink. Won't it be easier if we just tow them icebergs now and then? They can put them in big tubs and let them melt and the fresh water can be extracted with straws."

Nobody pointed out to him that this invention was not a proper invention at all, merely an idea, and not even an original idea. Perhaps the actual invention part was something else, the grapples used by the ship to catch the iceberg in the first place. Yes, that sounds reasonable. Anyway, Mondaugen was pleased that his invention, whatever it was, had been a success and that he was paid a lot of money. He sat in his house and counted it and then realised he needed to invent a device to count it for him, there was just so much.

Meanwhile, the ship located a promising iceberg and Captain Faraway gave the order to snare it. Nobody noticed the lone walrus basking on one of its ledges. The grapples were fired, connected with the ice and the ship turned away, its engines straining.

It was going to be a very long voyage and to entertain himself and his crew, Captain Faraway organised a hunt for stowaways. He preferred this activity to reading. As an aside, he had two brothers, named Distanto and Neary, but neither sailed a ship—one piloted a hydrogen balloon and the other drove a steam locomotive. Anyway, to officially start the hunt, he looked in the obvious nooks and crannies first, saving the clever hiding places for later. Every ten minutes, he announced a coffee break. It was the only way of making the game last.

The lovespoon is one of the quaintest Welsh traditions. The most perfect examples are complex and simple at the same time and express unity and duality as equally desirable states, or rather the *unity* of *duality*. For the lovespoon is in fact not one spoon but two, joined lengthwise, handle to handle, bowl to bowl, connected in a variety of ways, by rods, stems or struts, thick or thin, straight or curved, some knotted together elaborately, others simply fused into each other. The point is that the whole item must be carved from a single piece of wood.

The custom is old but not ancient and can't be dated back further than the 17th Century. But that's vintage enough. The lovespoon was a formal but sweet token of affection and desire from a man to a woman, carved by the suitor himself as a way of saying, "Hey girl, I love you, don't you know? What's your opinion on us getting together?" Two spoons joined together (in fact one spoon pretending to be two) is obvious symbolism for the start of a meaningful love affair, but some of the motifs added to the spoons can be more mysterious.

Because modern men have generally lost the ability to carve anything from wood, most lovespoons are now bought from shops. There is a shop in Swansea which sells lovespoons and gives advice on certain symbols and their meanings. For example, an anchor means a wish to settle down, a dragon means security, a leaf means that love will grow, a knot means together forever, a wheel is a promise that the man will work hard, a harp expresses a yearning to form a musical duo with the girl and play a few pub gigs in exchange for free beer.

The curious thing about the lovespoon carved by The Traveller is that it didn't feature any of these accepted symbols. He chose his own symbol and nobody could work out what it meant. It was a mermaid. There were less than a dozen students in his class to puzzle over it. Fewer and fewer people in Wales are keeping up the lovespoon tradition, but visitors from other lands are becoming more interested in it. One of those little ironies so beloved by bohemians, I suppose.

And while we're talking about bohemians again, let's agree there's a difference between a scenario and a scene, without asking for details this late at night. Huw and Stuart sat around a bottle of whisky planning a spontaneous beach party. They had to do something. Bohemian status is not conferred for life but must be continuously earned. Spontaneity is tricky to plan at the best of times because of the contradiction involved but they finally worked out the details.

Stuart was struck by a revelation. "Hey, a walrus!"

"What about it?" gasped Huw.

"It's a northern animal. Wait until Monica finds out!"

It would be neat to report that Mondaugen woke up in a cold sweat the moment *The Shiver Timbers* went down, but he wasn't in bed. He had invented a machine that did the sleeping for him and he was pacing the rooms of his house talking to himself.

"Ah, to be back in Germany! To be among the sausages and cabbage pickle! How I long for the girls in green leather bodices with laces! But do they long for me? Probably not! No matter, I will invent one that does! In the meantime how shall I occupy the long nights? I would like to read a book but my spectacles are lost!"

Mondaugen had created a pair of *storm glasses*, two lenses mounted on a frame that contained miniature typhoons—these storms turned any book at all into a tale of passion, because tempestuous elements were all that remained visible, the remainder being excluded by a layer of heaving sea and whipped cloud. While testing them on a telephone directory one evening, he felt the sudden need to relieve himself. Not bothering to take them off, he proceeded to the water closet and while bending forward to operate the flush, they slipped off and were gone, washed down into the sewers and subsequently out to sea.

For six months or so they had drifted further out into the Atlantic, the frame gradually breaking apart and the two lenses floating off in different directions. Now one of these lenses, containing its compressed typhoon intact, was pounced upon by a hungry gull and snatched up in its yellow beak. This gull flew directly into the path of *The Shiver Timbers*. It found a perch at the top of the flagpole and tried to peck at its prize but the lens proved inedible and the gull let it drop to the deck. Shattering to powder, it released its storm. A torrent of rainwater—millions of litres—rushed into the hold. The ship sank instantly but Captain Faraway and his crew survived, taking to one of the lifeboats.

Although *The Shiver Timbers* dropped like a stone, it never reached the seabed. It was still attached to the iceberg by its cable and it jerked to a stop when it reached the end of the long line, remaining suspended far below the mass of ice, which creaked in its efforts to remain afloat with such a massive weight trying to drag it down. The trapped walrus might have attempted (in vain) to cut the cable with one of its tusks but it was resigned to doom anyway, as it knew the iceberg would eventually melt in this much warmer ocean. But the two perils were in league with each other. As the iceberg melted it would lose the strength to keep holding up the drowned ship. Long before it melted away completely, the heavy ship would succeed in pulling it to the bottom.

"I'm not sure you've grasped the idea."

The Traveller stood with bowed head as his tutor berated him. This tutor was foreign, a German, an inventor in fact, but with no connection to Mondaugen. He liked to be known as Herr I.M. Wright, but this really was his name, not an assertion of infallibility. The Traveller lowered his chisel and hammer and sighed.

"What exacly have I done wrong?"

"Lovespoons aren't meant to be thirty feet long."

The Traveller licked his lips. "I see your point."

"Funnily enough, I can sympathise with what you've done, with your vision. I used to design catapults in my youth, devices capable of firing a sack of good Bavarian sausages, or even a whole pigdog, into the upper atmosphere. There's a type of catapult known as an *onager*... But no use reminiscing, no point to it. I'm going to have to expel you from my class. You may take your spoon with you."

The Traveller agreed but he needed assistance to move it back to his own house, where it blocked the stairs.

As he left the tutor called out to him:

"Your heart is just too big!"

Some mermaids trick sailors into the briny depths where they drown but Caroline wasn't like that. Her heart was sweet and even though by nature she loved adventure she never took risks with the souls of mortal men. It was curiosity that motivated her, a desire to explore and absorb sights and sounds and flavours, sensations of all kinds, but she didn't feel a need to take over and control the things she found. She would never sing a song she liked just to lure men down to the bottom of the sea. On the contrary, she was interested in exploring the world of the surface herself. It was an exotic realm for her up there, a place where atmosphere and gravity made her feel dry and sluggish but where the increased visibility compensated with amazingly subtle shades of colour.

As she swam along, rising and dipping, proceeding in the shape of an elegant wave, she spied something odd in the distance. It hung suspended in the warm waters like the pendulum of a gigantic broken clock. As she approached, she realised it was a large metal box shaped like a leaf and decorated with odd and probably unnecessary ornamentation. It dangled on a metal cord and groaned almost as if alive. Caroline guessed that the rivets holding it together were trying to work free. What was it? She saw several doorways in its side and swam through one of them. It was pitch dark inside and she groped her way carefully through vertical passages and compartments using a small jellyfish as a lantern. Then she came to a room full of levers and bizarre machines.

She pulled one of the levers on a whim. Something whirred above her head and she felt the vast box lurch. The whole thing was rising upwards! Now she understood that she had chanced upon an elevator in the middle of the ocean. It was taking her up to the top floor, which was the surface of the sea. What had really happened was that she had started the electric winch connecting *The Shiver Timbers* to the melting iceberg, but the end result was the same as if that doomed vessel was now an elevator. She waited patiently for the brief journey to finish. She knew that the metal cord must be joined to something, but what? She decided to be extra nice to whoever she encountered first. She was looking forward to a vacation somewhere new and unexpected.

The Traveller discovered he couldn't bear to live with a giant lovespoon blocking his stairs. For one thing it made going to bed or to the bathroom impractical, and he had nowhere else to keep it, so he reluctantly decided to get rid of the thing. But he didn't want to cut it up and he didn't want to leave it to rot in the street. It occurred to him it might be nicer to drag it to the beach and burn it on the sand. That was more dignified and symbolic of something, a romantic gesture too. Had he known who to ask, he may have thrown a party at the same time, but as it was he'd be alone. He took a bag of crumpets to toast on the flames.

It was one hour before midnight when he set off from his house with the huge wooden spoon behind him. He hauled it along with a rope over his shoulder and it scraped and clattered dreadfully on the wet pavements so that lights in dark houses snapped on and curtains twitched as people woke to see what was making the din. But he arrived at the beach in due course without major incident and found a spot near the waves and with newspaper and matches he tried to set it ablaze. But the rain put out every lick of fire, the rain which never seemed to stop, and soon he had run out of matches. So he changed his plan.

He pushed the lovespoon out to sea, just as if it was a canoe, or more accurately a catamaran, for it had two hulls. As he ran through the foam, he acted on impulse. Instead of letting go, he jumped onto the handle of one of the spoons and began paddling. Then he pulled himself along into one of the shallow bowls and sat there panting. Already the city was no more than a sprinkling of lights. He was heading out to sea on a strange current in a stranger vessel at the mercy of a highly contrived plot. This presented special problems. Not only had he embarked on a new voyage sooner than expected and with no money and few supplies, but he risked ending up in a surprise twist ending.

The walrus is an animal famous for its two large teeth. Scientists are still arguing over the purpose of these huge tusks. Some are of the opinion they are used to dig clams from the mud of the seabed, others insist they are employed to allow the creature to climb out of the sea onto dry land like grappling irons, a third group just believe they are reminders of the bearer's status within walrus society. According to this last theory, the larger the tusks the more important the walrus. In this case, *this* walrus was a middling sort. It had a name in its own language but it's impossible to write this name in human letters.

Here are some facts concerning the walrus as a species—the average length of an adult male walrus is nearly 3 metres and his average weight is just under 800 kilograms. They live about 40 years. There are two subspecies, the Atlantic and Pacific walrus. The Pacific walrus tends to have longer tusks... Suddenly the iceberg—already only three quarters its original size—shuddered as if struck by a heavy weight from below. The rising ship had come to a halt on its lower side. There was no more cable for the winch to reel in. I'm not going to give any more facts about the walrus because I've lost my notes.

While the walrus sat and recovered from the shock, a head bobbed up nearby, a sweet face framed by long curly hair broke into a smile and the destined meeting between mermaid and walrus took place. Leaping out of the water with a casual flick of her tail, Caroline joined her new friend on the iceberg. They looked at each other for a few minutes. When meeting a walrus for the first time you should always shake it politely by the tusk, but only in a story, never in real life.

The bohemians of Swansea were feeling frustrated. They might have to abandon the beach party because of the rain. This was the unfortunate conclusion arrived at by Huw, Stuart, Monica and the others. It was only to be expected, of course, because rain was the one reliable factor in that city, or rather it was the reliable factor that gave the reliability to the other reliable factors—the misery, discord, mould and soggy tragedy. Out of the pub they streamed,

breath reeking of wine and smoke, heels stamping puddles already
half drunk by other shoes with holes in them, but rapidly filling up
again with perverse generosity.

"I hate it when my socks get wet," said Stuart, "and the water
rises up the material to the top. It's particularly bad for me because I
wear socks so long they reach my genitals."

"That's your own fault," observed Huw, "but more significantly
what are we going to do about the party?"

"Monica will sort it out," said Stuart. "I'm too damp to think."

They all turned to face her expectantly.

"There's only one realistic answer," said Monica. "When all else
fails, what must a girl do? Go shopping!"

It was just after dawn when The Traveller sighted the iceberg on the
south westerly horizon. The currents of plot were rushing his lovespoon
directly towards it. He didn't have a telescope with him but he raised
his hand to shield his eyes, as they do in books and films, and found
that it really did help him to see farther.

Although he wasn't aware of the fact, the iceberg had melted to
only one fifth its original size and was extremely low in the water. The
weight of the sunken ship threatened to drag it down—and drown the
walrus on it—within a day or two at most. Not that he even noticed the
walrus as his eyes gazed at the white mass.

"Minha sereia?" he called in disbelief.

Caroline waved at him. Her hair streamed in the breeze and his
heart began to beat fast as his lovespoon pulled up alongside the iceberg
and he jumped across to embrace her.

"We meet again," she said as she accepted his hugs.

"Alone together at last!" he cried.

Then he noticed the walrus and fixed the mermaid with a
questioning glance. Oblivious of his jealousy, she said:

"This is (*name of walrus*) and we have become close friends."

The Traveller sneered. "Pleased to meet him!"

"If we can't rescue him soon," she said, "he will drown. I refused
to abandon him, so I remained here."

For the sake of his mermaid, The Traveller did his best to swallow
his annoyance and made the following offer:

"Climb into the other bowl of my lovespoon. I'll cast off again
and try to steer back to the Arctic regions."

Caroline was delighted and so was the walrus. They boarded

the giant lovespoon and the currents changed direction especially for this section of the story and rushed them northwards. But The Traveller was stung by a comment made by his mermaid:

"He has a huge heart, you know."

"You mean the walrus?" he gasped.

He hid his face from her, chewing his lower lip savagely. He had heard this comment numerous times but it had always been directed *at* him. He had never heard it applied to anyone or anything else. A hollow ache filled him from top to bottom.

Being both generous and stingy, Herr I.M. Wright decided to contact the other tutors of all the other nightschools and hold a sale of the products created by their pupils. This happened every year. The money such sales brought in kept the tutors in those things that tutors seem to need, at least until the following sale the next year, such things as corduroy jackets, thermos flasks and dandruff shampoo (guaranteed to fill the cleanest hair with flakes of dry skin). The sale was held in the art college on Alexandra Road, a real college in Swansea, take it from me. Only five tutors turned up but they all brought examples of the work of their students which the students hadn't smuggled home for themselves.

Herr I.M Wright addressed them as follows:

"There aren't many of us here, certainly less than last year, but I note we all have some truly remarkable pieces to put up for sale. I'm confident we can raise more cash for ourselves than ever before, so let us open the doors to the public and see what happens!"

Monica was one of the first to enter. She quickly saw what was worth buying and what wasn't and she ended up with all the items made by The Traveller during his time in the various nightschools. In other words, she purchased: (a) one enormous wine glass, (b) one gigantic cushion, (c) one massive pie, (d) one immense knitted scarf and (e) one vast saxophone. She dragged them back to Huw's house, or maybe she had them delivered by truck, a more plausible absurdity.

As he watched her leave, Herr I.M Wright cursed himself for allowing The Traveller to keep the giant lovespoon. But she turned to look over her shoulder and announced: "The bohemians of this city are having a beach party tomorrow night. Why not come along? Just because you're tutors doesn't mean you don't deserve fun!"

Shall I start wrapping things up? Fair enough, that's what I'll do. I'll tweak the remaining plot a little and arrange for the lovespoon to drift into the path of the *other* lens from Mondaugen's missing storm glasses. The tempest that arose when this lens broke was as dreadful as the one that sunk *The Shiver Timbers* but this was only a spoon, so the terror was worse for the passengers, with the exception of Caroline, who could have just dived into the sea to save herself, but she was too loyal and bravely remained above with her companions.

The wind and rain and particularly the bolts of lightning shattered the rods, stems and struts holding the two spoons together. The vessel split apart and the spoons went off in different directions. What made this so tragic for The Traveller was that he was seated in one spoon while his mermaid sat in the other with the walrus. *They* were blown due north and *he* was blown north west. He saw this as an omen, a sign Caroline had fallen in love with the walrus. His wept until the storm abated and cursed nature for giving him such short teeth.

The long awaited beach party was in progress. Only a fire was missing. The bohemians and tutors sat on the gigantic cushion, eating slices of the massive pie, wrapped in the same immense knitted scarf and periodically helping to play the vast saxophone. They had plenty of wine to drink but not from the enormous wine glass. Oh no! That glass had been inverted and propped on the tallest turrets of very high sand castles and served as a shield from the rain, a mighty transparent dome as significant as that of a cathedral, at least in the eyes of those who enjoy exaggerations. I'm not one of those—it wasn't quite so big.

Watching the rain beyond the edge of the wine glass, Stuart pointed at the sea. "What's that?" he cried.

"A spoon surfing the waves to shore," said Huw.

"That's not bohemian. It's plain silly!"

"There's a man on the spoon... He rides the breakers with considerable aplomb... One might suspect an artistic statement of formal merit... One might equally well not... I don't."

The tutors weren't listening. "A man on the spoon? That never really happened. Almost certainly a hoax."

The Traveller jumped onto the gloomy beach and with a sigh dragged his lovespoon through the wet sand towards the party. His clothes had become rags and his chin was obscured by a long beard. With a shrug of his shoulders, he dropped the spoon next to the cushion and said, "Take this junk for a fire, if you want it."

"Great!" cried Huw. "Just what we need."

They crowded around to set it alight with matches when another shout made them swivel their heads towards the sea again. The Traveller was laughing and dancing. Out of the surf came a mermaid, swimming at an incredible speed. The Traveller realised the truth, that she was not in love with the walrus after all but had simply wanted to accompany the animal back to the Arctic Circle to ensure it got home safe. Now she was looking for *him*. He waved at her but she didn't notice. Even when she was out of the sea she kept swimming!

The problem was the rain. It was so persistent and inevitable she just didn't understand she had reached the surface. She thought she was still below the waves. This is why Wales—that particular small country in Western Europe—is considered by mermaids to be equivalent to the sky. There's no telling where ocean ends and sky begins. As he watched, she rose into the air and swam up through the downpour into the clouds, higher and higher until she was a speck.

"I've lost her again!" The Traveller wailed.

Herr I.M. Wright stepped forward with a suggestion. "My previous expertise in the field of catapults has given me an idea. Before we burn this giant spoon, let us employ it to propel you into the upper atmosphere after her. According to my calculations, we will have to shoot you at an initial velocity of a little over eleven and a quarter kilometres per second for you to catch up with her."

"Is that feasible?" The Traveller spluttered.

Herr I.M. Wright tested the spoon, running his hands along its length, and nodded. "Ja, it is springy enough!"

"Please hurry!" roared The Traveller.

The bohemians and the tutors worked together, planting the spoon into the sand and bending it back. The Traveller sat in the empty cup with his knees drawn up into his chest. On the count of three, they all relaxed their grips. The handle straightened with a mighty twang and The Traveller felt himself launched into the sky. It was chilly up there and he was grateful for his beard but he remembered that other things that fly extremely fast such as asteroids and meteors are smoothly shaven, so he reasoned that maybe it grew warmer again eventually.

Down below they started burning his spoon.

He was halfway to outer space when he caught up with Caroline. He took her hand as he passed her and that is how they continued up into the heavens, hand in hand. Neither of them had a specific destination in mind but the moon was directly ahead, and as it is closer than the other planets, not to mention the stars, that is where they made for. Her necklace of seashells didn't jangle delightfully this time, because in space there is no sound. Kisses are completely silent too.

SOMETHING FISHY
Mo Ali

It was the 19th Century nudist and explorer Isambard Thrustmore who had recounted an incident of great significance, which took place whilst studying the indigenous peoples of the Arctic shores. He had of course realised that the Arctic Walrus (*Odobenus Rosmarus*) was a vital source of food for these people—who had to endure living in such a harsh and unforgiving place—as well as finding out that the animal would also be used for other purposes.

It was this reference to 'other purposes'—a phrase slick with ambiguity—that had intrigued him when he'd first heard it and had led him, inevitably, to view these animals up close to learn more.

We now know that some of these other purposes would've been, for example, using the skin for boat covers and the intestines for clothing and material, the oil for light and heating, the tusks and bones for spears and so on and so forth; it is therefore difficult to comprehend what had intrigued Thrustmore about the phrase exactly.

It might have been something that he had gleaned from his investigations, insinuations that the walruses served not just material needs but also aided those matters of a metaphysical and spiritual nature —perhaps it will remain unknown to us now, but whatever the case it must have been intensely fascinating for him to decide to stroll, stark naked, up to the nearest walrus and ask it a question—*the* question— in a timeless and forgotten language:

"I trembled with excitement, as well as the frostbite, slowly making my way towards the nearest of the beasts. A large cumbersome looking animal that stared serenely into the distance, its watery gaze shifted from the desolate white wastes as it regarded my careful approach, bristle-like whiskers twitching ever so slightly.

My breath clouded the air before us as I bowed a fraction and then danced around with verve, following the intricate requirements of the ritual as instructed by that crazy old fool, who'd told me everything in exhaustive sweaty detail as we grappled vigorously the night before.

The words I spoke were foreign to me, parting as they did from m'lips in a flurry of choking and gagging and barking.

A moment passed, and the animal bowed slightly (in reply?) before looking skyward, as if considering my question, and then finally, finally, finally, finally, finally it spoke..."

— June 1ˢᵗ, 189?, from the writings of I. Thrustmore (Esq.)

Was he suffering from some kind of cold-induced psychosis when he wrote that the walrus had replied? Today we know that walruses have vocal cords and can communicate on a basic level through auditory means, but could we, should we, believe such a thing is possible, or do we scoff and curse Isambard Thrustmore and call him names now that he's well past his expiry date?

Is he, was he, a madman? A buffoon? An ignoramus of the highest order conceivable?

Many today think so—especially as his bizarre diary was recovered incomplete—but over the intervening years there have been many more who have sought to uncover the truth behind these words, with hilarious results.

Plenty of hairy hints and clammy clues have been dropped throughout the annals of history, for those with the eyes to spot them, when considering the allure of these 'cumbersome' beasts; whether it be walrus-themed headdresses from the Mesolithic Age, Egyptian monuments and statues, or even livery badges in England—where the walrus was a banned emblem of Richard III, whose actual symbol was officially proclaimed to be a boar (rather appropriate)—and Frisian jewellery with its distinctive curled tusk designs and on and on, reverberating through cultures and civilizations with a death-knell consistency.

The 1900's saw this search for the wisdom of the 'Odobenidae' begin to cause ominous fractures amongst old allies; disputes between Russia and Germany regarding walrus research predictably led to Kaiser 'Cutie-pie' Wilhelm deciding not to renew the treaty with Russia, paving the way for the First (attempt at a) World War.

The superpowers that knew of this hidden Walrus wisdom took their own steps to gain understanding through various means and trying to communicate with the animals in a variety of different ways. They tried: talking, shouting, screaming, bleating, bellowing, crying, pleading, begging, cursing, swearing, daring, caring, scaring as well as more subtle methods like torture and experimentation—and it wasn't until the introduction of the U.S. Marine Mammal Protection Act of 1972 that put an end to most 'research' in America.

However, whilst this research was 'all the rage daddio,' departments of the U.S. government dealing with such studies had a hard time of things.

Many walruses used in these experiments would escape their human jailors from time to time in search of watery sanctuary, resulting in specially designed flying saucers being deployed to hunt 'them rascals' down.

The public instances of this taking place are: 1947 in Washington State (the government UFO crashed into the ocean), 1960 in New York, 1961 in Wisconsin, 1966 in the North-West Pacific (involving the USS Tiru), 1967 at Shaq Harbor in Nova Scotia (they crashed another one), 1968 in Vermont (two counselors were mistaken for walruses and subsequently abducted from the vicinity of Lake Champlain before being probed energetically), 1969 in the Gulf of Mexico and 1971 in Costa Rica.

In 1962 during the side-splitting Cuban Missile Crisis, President Kennedy and his crack team of merry men the 'ExComm' (the Executive Committee of the National Security Council, for all you youngsters out there) discussed the potential of the clandestine walrus research in diffusing the tense situation between the United States and Russia via secret talks that were taped by Kennedy for post-coital enjoyment—but thanks to a 'clerical error' the offending articles have failed to surface with the rest of the (mostly mundane) tapes from these talks.

The only clue to these conversations is a scrawled list on a cocktail napkin found in Kennedy's medicine cabinet that illustrates a few highlights:

1 – In diplomatic situations a walrus should not be confused with an elephant seal. It gets mighty upset.

2 – Walrus calves tend to be chewy. So take care my friend, take care.

3 – I am not a Walrus. (Repeat x3)

4 – Walrus? Code for: Walls 'R' Us, Whales Rust, War is Lost, Wool Rusk, War or Us? Whorls Roust? Why Are Lusty Rednecks Usually Sour? And thus we should continue in this fashion until either my head or your head hurts.

5 – It has been brought to my attention that Alaskan natives call the penis bone of a Walrus male an 'oosik' and use it to make knives. This frightens me on many levels.

From the 1970's onwards it appeared that the feverish pursuit of Walruses by shadowy men-in-black had abated, with nation states turning their attention to more co-operative animals instead.

Events, however, took an exciting turn in early 1999, as the final page of Thrustmore's journal was discovered, found amongst a stash of cowboy comics and 'hentai' pornography in Downing Street.

The page was tested for authenticity and finally, after much heated debate, was declared to be the genuine article.

It was therefore with tingly groins that the historical community publicly showcased the final page of the diary of Isambard Thrustmore —and now everybody can find out what all the fuss was about:

A moment passed, and the animal bowed slightly (in reply?) before looking skyward, as if considering my question, and then finally, finally, finally, finally, finally it spoke…"

—Final page—

Its voice was at once intelligent and soothing, and flowed from beneath its wet snout like warm honey…and I listened intently and quietly like a young infant sitting before a moustachioed mage.

Warmth seeped into my body and I felt that I was at peace in the eye of a storm. Tears rolled down my face and froze in mid-excursion, but I paid them no notice; my eyes were fixed firmly on this wise majestic creature, as it looked around at the other walruses carefully and then again at me…sighing heavily it leaned forward and whispered eloquently into my ear:

"What are you asking me for? I'm just a Walrus."

AUTHOR BIOS

GREG BEATTY lives with his wife in Bellingham, Washington, where he tries, unsuccessfully, to stay dry. He writes everything from children's books to essays about his cooking debacles. Many of the creative works have won awards, including the 2005 Rhysling Award and the 2008 Dwarf Stars Award. For more information on Greg's writing, please visit his website: http://www.greg-beatty.com/

BENTLEY LITTLE is the author of over twenty novels. His first, *The Revelation*, published with St. Martin's Press in 1990, won the Bram Stoker Award for "Best First Novel" in 1990.

PAUL A. TOTH lives in Sarasota, Florida. He is the author of three novels. The majority of his short fiction and other works, as well as information on ordering his novels, can be accessed from www.netpt.tv

DAVE FISCHER is a filmmaker from Providence, RI.

JAMES CHAMBERS is the author of the short story collections *Resurrection House*, published by Dark Regions Press, and *The Midnight Hour: Saint Lawn Hill and Other Tales*. His tales of crime, horror, fantasy, and science fiction have appeared in numerous anthologies and magazines, including Allen K's *Inhuman*, *Bad Cop, No Donut*, *Bad-Ass Faeries* (volume 1-3); *Bare Bone*, *Breach the Hull*, *Cthulhu Sex*, *Dark Furies*, *The Dead Walk*, *The Domino Lady: Sex as a Weapon*, *Dragon's Lure*, *The Green Hornet Chronicles*, *New Blood*, *So It Begins*, *Warfear*, and *Weird Trails*. His collection of Lovecraftian novellas, *The Engines of Sacrifice*, was released by Dark Regions Press in 2011. His website is www.jameschambersonline.com.

JOHN SUNSERI lives in the Pacific Northwest. His work has appeared in such publications as *Barbarians at the Jumpgate, Cthulhu's Dark Cults, The Spiraling Worm: Man Versus the Cthulhu Mythos, The Undead: Headshot Quartet, Horrors Beyond—Tales of Terrifying Reality, Timelines: Stories Inspired by H.G. Wells 'The Time Machine, Bare Bone,* and *The Dream People.* He also co-edited the *Cthulhu Unbound* anthologies.

EKATERINA SEDIA resides in the Pinelands of New Jersey. Her critically acclaimed novels, *The Secret History of Moscow, The Alchemy of Stone* and *The House of Discarded Dreams* were published by Prime Books. Her short stories have sold to *Analog, Baen's Universe, Dark Wisdom* and *Clarkesworld*, as well as *Japanese Dreams* and *Magic in the Mirrorstone* anthologies. Visit her at www.ekaterinasedia.com

ANDERSEN PRUNTY is the author of several books including *The Driver's Guide to Hitting Pedestrians, My Fake War,* and *Zerostrata*. Visit him at www.andersenprunty.com or contact him at andersenprunty@gmail.com. He lives and breathes in glorious Dayton, Ohio.

VIOLET LEVOIT started her writing career as a film critic and arts journalist for various print and on-line publications in the US (including *Baltimore Magazine, City Paper, Popmatters.com* and *Urbanite*) and the UK (*The Little Black Book: Movies*). A parallel shadow career as a slash fictionista led her to penning the erotic novel *Hotel Butterfly* and the short story collection *I Am Genghis Cum* (2010). She lives in Philadelphia. www.violetlevoit.com

ALAN M. CLARK grew up in Tennessee in a house full of bones and old medical books. He has a Bachelor of Fine Arts degree from the San Francisco Art Institute. His illustrations have appeared in books of fiction, non-fiction, textbooks, young adult fiction and children's books. Awards for his illustration work include the World Fantasy Award and four Chesley Awards. His short fiction has appeared in magazines and anthologies and four of his novels have been published. Lazy Fascist Press, an imprint of Eraserhead Press, released a collection of his fiction titled *Boneyard Babies* in November, 2010. Clark's publishing company, IFD Publishing, has released six books, the most recent of which is a full color book of his artwork, *The Paint In My Blood.* He and his wife, Melody, live in Oregon. www.alanmclark.com

NICOLE CUSHING is an author of weird, dark stories (occasionally spiked with humor). Her short fiction has appeared in the mass market anthology *Werewolves & Shape Shifters: Encounters With The Beast Within*, and will also be in the forthcoming Richard Laymon tribute anthology *In Laymon's Terms* (Cemetery Dance Publications). Her first short story collection, *How To Eat Fried Furries*, was published in late 2010 by Eraserhead Press. She is currently working on her first novel, a science fiction project. Readers can connect with her via the web at Facebook, Twitter, or www.nicolecushing.com.

NICK MAMATAS is the author of several novels, including *Sensation* (PM Press), and *Bullettime* (ChiZine Publications). He's also published dozens in short stories in magazines such as *Asimov's Science Fiction, Weird Tales,* and *New Haven Review,* and in anthologies including *Long Island Noir, Lovecraft Unbound,* and John Skipp's *Psychos.* He's a five-time Bram Stoker nominee, most recently for his writing guide *Starve Better* (Apex Publications), and has also been nominated for the Hugo and World Fantasy Awards.

MITCH MARAUDE, originally spawned of the grit and glitz of New Jersey, now lives in Boulder, Colorado, where he is an MFA candidate in Prose Writing at the Jack Kerouac School of Disembodied Poetics. He is currently at work on his first full-length novel, in his trademark stoner-splatter-zombie-noir style, to be released on Swallowdown Press. He has released two limited-edition chapbooks of short stories, available from him at mitch.maraude@gmail.com.

JEFFREY A. STADT has been writing strange, short fiction for years. His work has been featured in *Bizarre Dreams* (Masquerade Books), *Into the Darkness, Terminal Fright, Cyber-Psychos AOD, Gaslight, Crossroads, Heliocentric Net, Elegia, Aberrations, The Dream People,* and *Bare Bone.* Cyber-Psychos AOD Press published his novella, *Stigma: Afterworld.*

GINA RANALLI has contributed fiction to a number of anthologies and zines, as well as being the author of many novels including *Wall of Kiss, Mother Puncher, Chemical Gardens, Praise the Dead* and *House of Fallen Trees.* She currently resides in Seattle, WA.

CARLTON MELLICK III is one of the leading authors in the bizarro fiction movement. His influences range from offbeat children's book authors such as Dr. Suess and Roald Dahl to Japanese cult directors such as Takashi Miike and Shinya Tsukamoto to trashy B-movies such as those from Troma and John Waters. He lives in Portland, OR, where the breweries, bookstores, and strip clubs are the best in the country.

R. ALLEN LEIDER began writing short stories in 4th grade. He has a BA from Queens College, 1968 and a MS from Brooklyn College, 1973. During Grad School, he worked as copy boy for CBS-TV's Cronkite News. In 1973 he left CBS to become Associate Editor for *Show Magazine*. Later, he was a features writer, interviewer and editor for many domestic and international magazines including *Glitter, Celebrity, Grooves, New Jersey Living*, and *Elite Magazine*. His first film script was *Liquid A$$ets*, followed by *Glitter, Star Angel* and *Sexcapades*. His first mainstream horror film was *The Oracle* (1985). While reviewing film for magazines and newspapers, he maintained a career in PR for 15 years as Executive VP at Donna Gould Associates publicizing best-selling books and other commercial products.

His first published book was *A Field Guide to Monsters* (2004) co-written with C.J. Henderson and Dave Elliott. His short stories appear in the anthologies; *Hear Them Roar, Bad Ass Faeries, Crypto Critters, Barbarians at the Jump Gate, Dark Furies, Walrus Tales and Hellfire Lounge 1 and 2*.

The second of his Wicca Girl quadrilogy launched on its website: www.wiccagirlmovie.com.

JOHN SKIPP is a New York Times bestselling author, editor, zombie godfather, compulsive collaborator, musical pornographer, black-humored optimist and all-around Renaissance mutant. His early novels from the 1980s and 90s pioneered the graphic, subversive, high-energy form known as splatterpunk. His anthology Book of the Dead was the beginning of modern post-Romero zombie literature. His work ranges from hardcore horror to whacked-out Bizarro to scathing social satire, all brought together with his trademark cinematic pace and intimate, unflinching, unmistakable voice. From young agitator to hilarious elder statesman, Skipp remains one of genre fiction's most colorful characters.

MYKLE HANSEN Mykle Hansen (Hansenodious Myclodipus) is found primarily in the shallow waters surrounding the rocky shoals of Portland, Oregon. A gregarious, bony mammal with numerous prehensile genitalia, he can grow to twelve feet in length and achieve a weight of over seven hundred pounds, thriving on an exclusive diet of hipsters and red wine. Once hunted to near-extinction, and with his traditional spawning grounds decimated by Californians, Hansen was recently granted protected status by Eraserhead Press, and his populations are gradually returning to their pre-gentrification levels.

BRADLEY SANDS is the author of *Sorry I Ruined Your Orgy, Rico Slade Will Fucking Kill You,* and *My Heart Said No, But the Camera Crew Said Yes*! He edits the journal, *Bust Down the Door and Eat All the Chickens.* Website: www.bradleysands.com

A D DAWSON, also known as the English Devil, writes from the heart of Sherwood Forest. Visit him at www.myspace.com/theenglishdevil

RHYS HUGHES is a master of the surreal, absurd and metafictional, and one of the most prolific and successful Welsh writers. He published his first short story in 1992 and since then has written almost six hundred items of fiction of varying lengths; he hopes eventually to combine all his fiction into a single intergrated cycle of tales. Many of these stories and novellas can be found in books such as *Worming the Harpy, The Smell of Telescopes, Stories From a Lost Anthology, Journeys Beyond Advice, The Percolated Stars, The Postmodern Mariner, The Brothel Creeper* and *Link Arms With Toads*! His work is notable for its combination of intellectual depth and inventive playfulness. When not writing, he travels as much of the world as he can, as cheaply as possible.

MO ALI was born in a haunted hospital and lives in the south-east of England. He's an artist, poet and Pushcart Prize-nominated writer.

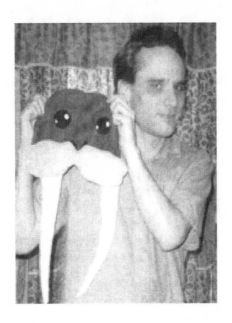

ABOUT THE EDITOR

KEVIN L. DONIHE resides in the hills of East Tennessee. He has published ten books via Eraserhead Press, including SPACE WALRUS and the Wonderland Award winning HOUSE OF HOUSES. His short fiction and poetry has appeared in *Psychos: Serial Killers, Depraved Madmen, and the Criminally Insane, The Mammoth Book of Legal Thrillers, ChiZine, The Cafe Irreal, Electric Velocipede, Dark Discoveries, Poe's Progeny, Bathtub Gin, Not One of Us, Dreams and Nightmares, Bust Down the Door and Eat All the Chickens,* and many other venues. He also edited the *Bare Bone* anthology series for Raw Dog Screaming Press, a story from which was reprinted in *The Mammoth Book of Best New Horror 13.*

He is not a walrus, but wants to thank Ashli Carte for making him a walrus hat so he might occasionally look like one. Visit Kevin, if you will, at facebook.com/kevin.l.donihe

BIZARRO BOOKS

CATALOG   SPRING 2012

ERASERHEAD PRESS

Your major resource for the bizarro fiction genre:

WWW.BIZARROCENTRAL.COM

Introduce yourselves to the bizarro fiction genre and all of its authors with the Bizarro Starter Kit series. Each volume features short novels and short stories by ten of the leading bizarro authors, designed to give you a perfect sampling of the genre for only $10.

BB-0X1
"The Bizarro Starter Kit" (Orange)
Featuring D. Harlan Wilson, Carlton Mellick III, Jeremy Robert Johnson, Kevin L Donihe, Gina Ranalli, Andre Duza, Vincent W. Sakowski, Steve Beard, John Edward Lawson, and Bruce Taylor. **236 pages $10**

BB-0X2
"The Bizarro Starter Kit" (Blue)
Featuring Ray Fracalossy, Jeremy C. Shipp, Jordan Krall, Mykle Hansen, Andersen Prunty, Eckhard Gerdes, Bradley Sands, Steve Aylett, Christian TeBordo, and Tony Rauch. **244 pages $10**

BB-0X2
"The Bizarro Starter Kit" (Purple)
Featuring Russell Edson, Athena Villaverde, David Agranoff, Matthew Revert, Andrew Goldfarb, Jeff Burk, Garrett Cook, Kris Saknussemm, Cody Goodfellow, and Cameron Pierce **264 pages $10**

BB-001 "The Kafka Effekt" D. Harlan Wilson — A collection of forty-four irreal short stories loosely written in the vein of Franz Kafka, with more than a pinch of William S. Burroughs sprinkled on top. **211 pages $14**

BB-002 "Satan Burger" Carlton Mellick III — The cult novel that put Carlton Mellick III on the map ... Six punks get jobs at a fast food restaurant owned by the devil in a city violently overpopulated by surreal alien cultures. **236 pages $14**

BB-003 "Some Things Are Better Left Unplugged" Vincent Sakwoski — Join The Man and his Nemesis, the obese tabby, for a nightmare roller coaster ride into this postmodern fantasy. **152 pages $10**

BB-004 "Shall We Gather At the Garden?" Kevin L Donihe — Donihe's Debut novel. Midgets take over the world, The Church of Lionel Richie vs. The Church of the Byrds, plant porn and more! **244 pages $14**

BB-005 "Razor Wire Pubic Hair" Carlton Mellick III — A genderless humandildo is purchased by a razor dominatrix and brought into her nightmarish world of bizarre sex and mutilation. **176 pages $11**

BB-006 "Stranger on the Loose" D. Harlan Wilson — The fiction of Wilson's 2nd collection is planted in the soil of normalcy, but what grows out of that soil is a dark, witty, otherworldly jungle... **228 pages $14**

BB-007 "The Baby Jesus Butt Plug" Carlton Mellick III — Using clones of the Baby Jesus for anal sex will be the hip sex fetish of the future. **92 pages $10**

BB-008 "Fishyfleshed" Carlton Mellick III — The world of the past is an illogical flatland lacking in dimension and color, a sick-scape of crispy squid people wandering the desert for no apparent reason. **260 pages $14**

BB-009 **"Dead Bitch Army" Andre Duza** — Step into a world filled with racist teenagers, cannibals, 100 warped Uncle Sams, automobiles with razor-sharp teeth, living graffiti, and a pissed-off zombie bitch out for revenge. **344 pages $16**

BB-010 **"The Menstruating Mall" Carlton Mellick III** — "The Breakfast Club meets Chopping Mall as directed by David Lynch." - Brian Keene **212 pages $12**

BB-011 **"Angel Dust Apocalypse" Jeremy Robert Johnson** — Meth-heads, man-made monsters, and murderous Neo-Nazis. "Seriously amazing short stories..." - Chuck Palahniuk, author of Fight Club   **184 pages $11**

BB-012 **"Ocean of Lard" Kevin L Donihe / Carlton Mellick III** — A parody of those old Choose Your Own Adventure kid's books about some very odd pirates sailing on a sea made of animal fat. **176 pages $12**

BB-015 **"Foop!" Chris Genoa** — Strange happenings are going on at Dactyl, Inc, the world's first and only time travel tourism company.
"A surreal pie in the face!" - Christopher Moore **300 pages $14**

BB-020 **"Punk Land" Carlton Mellick III** — In the punk version of Heaven, the anarchist utopia is threatened by corporate fascism and only Goblin, Mortician's sperm, and a blue-mohawked female assassin named Shark Girl can stop them. **284 pages $15**

BB-027 **"Siren Promised" Jeremy Robert Johnson & Alan M Clark** — Nominated for the Bram Stoker Award. A potent mix of bad drugs, bad dreams, brutal bad guys, and surreal/incredible art by Alan M. Clark. **190 pages $13**

BB-031**"Sea of the Patchwork Cats" Carlton Mellick III** — A quiet dreamlike tale set in the ashes of the human race. For Mellick enthusiasts who also adore The Twilight Zone. **112 pages $10**

BB-032 **"Extinction Journals" Jeremy Robert Johnson** — An uncanny voyage across a newly nuclear America where one man must confront the problems associated with loneliness, insane dieties, radiation, love, and an ever-evolving cockroach suit with a mind of its own. **104 pages $10**

BB-037 **"The Haunted Vagina" Carlton Mellick III** — It's difficult to love a woman whose vagina is a gateway to the world of the dead. **132 pages $10**

BB-043 **"War Slut" Carlton Mellick III** — Part "1984," part "Waiting for Godot," and part action horror video game adaptation of John Carpenter's "The Thing." **116 pages $10**

BB-047 **"Sausagey Santa" Carlton Mellick III** — A bizarro Christmas tale featuring Santa as a piratey mutant with a body made of sausages. 124 pages $10

BB-048 **"Misadventures in a Thumbnail Universe" Vincent Sakowski** — Dive deep into the surreal and satirical realms of neo-classical Blender Fiction, filled with television shoes and flesh-filled skies. **120 pages $10**

BB-053 **"Ballad of a Slow Poisoner" Andrew Goldfarb** — Millford Mutterwurst sat down on a Tuesday to take his afternoon tea, and made the unpleasant discovery that his elbows were becoming flatter. **128 pages $10**

BB-055 **"Help! A Bear is Eating Me" Mykle Hansen** — The bizarro, heartwarming, magical tale of poor planning, hubris and severe blood loss... **150 pages $11**

BB-056 **"Piecemeal June" Jordan Krall** — A man falls in love with a living sex doll, but with love comes danger when her creator comes after her with crab-squid assassins. **90 pages $9**

BB-058 **"The Overwhelming Urge" Andersen Prunty** — A collection of
bizarro tales by Andersen Prunty. **150 pages $11**

BB-059 **"Adolf in Wonderland" Carlton Mellick III** — A dreamlike adventure that takes a young descendant of Adolf Hitler's design and sends him down the
rabbit hole into a world of imperfection and disorder. **180 pages $11**

BB-061 **"Ultra Fuckers" Carlton Mellick III** — Absurdist suburban horror
about a couple who enter an upper middle class gated community but can't find their way
out. **108 pages $9**

BB-062 **"House of Houses" Kevin L. Donihe** — An odd man wants to marry
his house. Unfortunately, all of the houses in the world collapse at the same time in the
Great House Holocaust. Now he must travel to House Heaven to find his departed fiancee.
172 pages $11

BB-064 **"Squid Pulp Blues" Jordan Krall** — In these three bizarro-noir novellas, the reader is thrown into a world of murderers, drugs made from squid parts, deformed gun-toting veterans, and a mischievous apocalyptic donkey. **204 pages $12**

BB-065 **"Jack and Mr. Grin" Andersen Prunty** — "When Mr. Grin calls
you can hear a smile in his voice. Not a warm and friendly smile, but the kind that seizes
your spine in fear. You don't need to pay your phone bill to hear it. That smile is in every
line of Prunty's prose." - Tom Bradley. **208 pages $12**

BB-066 **"Cybernetrix" Carlton Mellick III** — What would you do if your
normal everyday world was slowly mutating into the video game world from Tron? **212
pages $12**

BB-072 **"Zerostrata" Andersen Prunty** — Hansel Nothing lives in a tree
house, suffers from memory loss, has a very eccentric family, and falls in love with a
woman who runs naked through the woods every night. **144 pages $11**

BB-073 "The Egg Man" Carlton Mellick III — It is a world where humans reproduce like insects. Children are the property of corporations, and having an enormous ten-foot brain implanted into your skull is a grotesque sexual fetish. Mellick's industrial urban dystopia is one of his darkest and grittiest to date. **184 pages $11**

BB-074 "Shark Hunting in Paradise Garden" Cameron Pierce — A group of strange humanoid religious fanatics travel back in time to the Garden of Eden to discover it is invested with hundreds of giant flying maneating sharks. **150 pages $10**

BB-075 "Apeshit" Carlton Mellick III - Friday the 13th meets Visitor Q. Six hipster teens go to a cabin in the woods inhabited by a deformed killer. An incredibly fucked-up parody of B-horror movies with a bizarro slant. **192 pages $12**

BB-076 "Fuckers of Everything on the Crazy Shitting Planet of the Vomit At smosphere" Mykle Hansen - Three bizarro satires. Monster Cocks, Journey to the Center of Agnes Cuddlebottom, and Crazy Shitting Planet. **228 pages $12**

BB-077 "The Kissing Bug" Daniel Scott Buck — In the tradition of Roald Dahl, Tim Burton, and Edward Gorey, comes this bizarro anti-war children's story about a bohemian conenose kissing bug who falls in love with a human woman. **116 pages $10**

BB-078 "MachoPoni" Lotus Rose — It's My Little Pony... *Bizarro* style! A long time ago Poniworld was split in two. On one side of the Jagged Line is the Pastel Kingdom, a magical land of music, parties, and positivity. On the other side of the Jagged Line is Dark Kingdom inhabited by an army of undead ponies. **148 pages $11**

BB-079 "The Faggiest Vampire" Carlton Mellick III — A Roald Dahl-esque children's story about two faggy vampires who partake in a mustache competition to find out which one is truly the faggiest. **104 pages $10**

BB-080 "Sky Tongues" Gina Ranalli — The autobiography of Sky Tongues, the biracial hermaphrodite actress with tongues for fingers. Follow her strange life story as she rises from freak to fame. **204 pages $12**

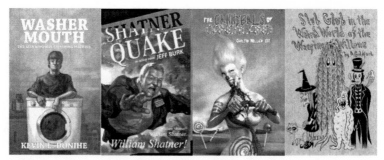

BB-081 **"Washer Mouth" Kevin L. Donihe** - A washing machine becomes human and pursues his dream of meeting his favorite soap opera star. **244 pages $11**

BB-082 **"Shatnerquake" Jeff Burk** - All of the characters ever played by William Shatner are suddenly sucked into our world. Their mission: hunt down and destroy the real William Shatner. **100 pages $10**

BB-083 **"The Cannibals of Candyland" Carlton Mellick III** - There exists a race of cannibals that are made of candy. They live in an underground world made out of candy. One man has dedicated his life to killing them all. **170 pages $11**

BB-084 **"Slub Glub in the Weird World of the Weeping Willows"**
Andrew Goldfarb - The charming tale of a blue glob named Slub Glub who helps the weeping willows whose tears are flooding the earth. There are also hyenas, ghosts, and a voodoo priest **100 pages $10**

BB-085 **"Super Fetus" Adam Pepper** - Try to abort this fetus and he'll kick your ass! **104 pages $10**

BB-086 **"Fistful of Feet" Jordan Krall** - A bizarro tribute to spaghetti westerns, featuring Cthulhu-worshipping Indians, a woman with four feet, a crazed gunman who is obsessed with sucking on candy, Syphilis-ridden mutants, sexually transmitted tattoos, and a house devoted to the freakiest fetishes. **228 pages $12**

BB-087 **"Ass Goblins of Auschwitz" Cameron Pierce** - It's Monty Python meets Nazi exploitation in a surreal nightmare as can only be imagined by Bizarro author Cameron Pierce. **104 pages $10**

BB-088 **"Silent Weapons for Quiet Wars" Cody Goodfellow** - "This is high-end psychological surrealist horror meets bottom-feeding low-life crime in a techno-thrilling science fiction world full of Lovecraft and magic..." -John Skipp **212 pages $12**

BB-089 "Warrior Wolf Women of the Wasteland" Carlton Mellick III
— Road Warrior Werewolves versus McDonaldland Mutants...post-apocalyptic fiction has never been quite like this. **316 pages $13**

BB-091 "Super Giant Monster Time" Jeff Burk — A tribute to choose your own adventures and Godzilla movies. Will you escape the giant monsters that are rampaging the fuck out of your city and shit? Or will you join the mob of alien-controlled punk rockers causing chaos in the streets? What happens next depends on you. **188 pages $12**

BB-092 "Perfect Union" Cody Goodfellow — "Cronenberg's THE FLY on a grand scale: human/insect gene-spliced body horror, where the human hive politics are as shocking as the gore." -John Skipp. **272 pages $13**

BB-093 "Sunset with a Beard" Carlton Mellick III — 14 stories of surreal science fiction. **200 pages $12**

BB-094 "My Fake War" Andersen Prunty — The absurd tale of an unlikely soldier forced to fight a war that, quite possibly, does not exist. It's Rambo meets Waiting for Godot in this subversive satire of American values and the scope of the human imagination. **128 pages $11**

BB-095 "Lost in Cat Brain Land" Cameron Pierce — Sad stories from a surreal world. A fascist mustache, the ghost of Franz Kafka, a desert inside a dead cat. Primordial entities mourn the death of their child. The desperate serve tea to mysterious creatures. A hopeless romantic falls in love with a pterodactyl. And much more. **152 pages $11**

BB-096 "The Kobold Wizard's Dildo of Enlightenment +2" Carlton Mellick III — A Dungeons and Dragons parody about a group of people who learn they are only made up characters in an AD&D campaign and must find a way to resist their nerdy teenaged players and retarded dungeon master in order to survive. **232 pages $12**

BB-098 "A Hundred Horrible Sorrows of Ogner Stump" Andrew Goldfarb — Goldfarb's acclaimed comic series. A magical and weird journey into the horrors of everyday life. **164 pages $11**

BB-099 **"Pickled Apocalypse of Pancake Island" Cameron Pierce**—A demented fairy tale about a pickle, a pancake, and the apocalypse. **102 pages $8**

BB-100 **"Slag Attack" Andersen Prunty**— Slag Attack features four visceral, noir stories about the living, crawling apocalypse.A slag is what survivors are calling the slug-like maggots raining from the sky, burrowing inside people, and hollowing out their flesh and their sanity. **148 pages $11**

BB-101 **"Slaughterhouse High" Robert Devereaux**—A place where schools are built with secret passageways, rebellious teens get zippers installed in their mouths and genitals, and once a year, on that special night, one couple is slaughtered and the bits of their bodies are kept as souvenirs. **304 pages $13**

BB-102 **"The Emerald Burrito of Oz" John Skipp & Marc Levinthal** —OZ IS REAL! Magic is real! The gate is really in Kansas! And America is finally allowing Earth tourists to visit this weird-ass, mysterious land. But when Gene of Los Angeles heads off for summer vacation in the Emerald City, little does he know that a war is brewing...a war that could destroy both worlds. **280 pages $13**

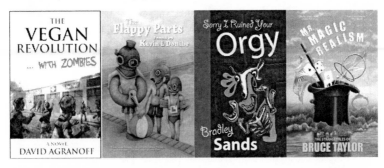

BB-103 **"The Vegan Revolution... with Zombies" David Agranoff** — When there's no more meat in hell, the vegans will walk the earth. **160 pages $11**

BB-104 **"The Flappy Parts" Kevin L Donihe**—Poems about bunnies, LSD, and police abuse. You know, things that matter. 132 **pages $11**

BB-105 **"Sorry I Ruined Your Orgy" Bradley Sands**—Bizarro humorist Bradley Sands returns with one of the strangest, most hilarious collections of the year. **130 pages $11**

BB-106 **"Mr. Magic Realism" Bruce Taylor**—Like Golden Age science fiction comics written by Freud, *Mr. Magic Realism* is a strange, insightful adventure that spans the furthest reaches of the galaxy, exploring the hidden caverns in the hearts and minds of men, women, aliens, and biomechanical cats. **152 pages $11**

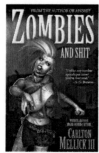   

BB-107 **"Zombies and Shit" Carlton Mellick III**—"Battle Royale" meets "Return of the Living Dead." Mellick's bizarro tribute to the zombie genre. **308 pages $13**

BB-108 **"The Cannibal's Guide to Ethical Living" Mykle Hansen**— Over a five star French meal of fine wine, organic vegetables and human flesh, a lunatic delivers a witty, chilling, disturbingly sane argument in favor of eating the rich.. **184 pages $11**

BB-109 **"Starfish Girl" Athena Villaverde**—In a post-apocalyptic underwater dome society, a girl with a starfish growing from her head and an assassin with sea anenome hair are on the run from a gang of mutant fish men. **160 pages $11**

BB-110 **"Lick Your Neighbor" Chris Genoa**—Mutant ninjas, a talking whale, kung fu masters, maniacal pilgrims, and an alcoholic clown populate Chris Genoa's surreal, darkly comical and unnerving reimagining of the first Thanksgiving. **303 pages $13**

BB-111 **"Night of the Assholes" Kevin L. Donihe**—A plague of assholes is infecting the countryside. Normal everyday people are transforming into jerks, snobs, dicks, and douchebags. And they all have only one purpose: to make your life a living hell.. **192 pages $11**

BB-112 **"Jimmy Plush, Teddy Bear Detective" Garrett Cook**—Hardboiled cases of a private detective trapped within a teddy bear body. **180 pages $11**

BB-113 **"The Deadheart Shelters" Forrest Armstrong**—The hip hop lovechild of William Burroughs and Dali... **144 pages $11**

BB-114 **"Eyeballs Growing All Over Me... Again" Tony Raugh**— Absurd, surreal, playful, dream-like, whimsical, and a lot of fun to read. **144 pages $11**

BB-115 "Whargoul" Dave Brockie — From the killing grounds of Stalingrad to the death camps of the holocaust. From torture chambers in Iraq to race riots in the United States, the Whargoul was there, killing and raping. **244 pages $12**

BB-116 **"By the Time We Leave Here, We'll Be Friends" J. David Osborne** — A David Lynchian nightmare set in a Russian gulag, where its prisoners, guards, traitors, soldiers, lovers, and demons fight for survival and their own rapidly deteriorating humanity. **168 pages $11**

BB-117 **"Christmas on Crack" edited by Carlton Mellick III** — Perverted Christmas Tales for the whole family! . . . as long as every member of your family is over the age of 18. **168 pages $11**

BB-118 **"Crab Town" Carlton Mellick III** — Radiation fetishists, balloon people, mutant crabs, sail-bike road warriors, and a love affair between a woman and an H-Bomb. This is one mean asshole of a city. Welcome to Crab Town. **100 pages $8**

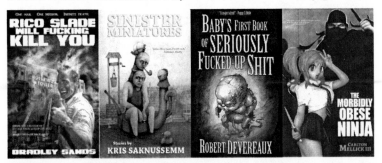

BB-119 **"Rico Slade Will Fucking Kill You" Bradley Sands** — Rico Slade is an action hero. Rico Slade can rip out a throat with his bare hands. Rico Slade's favorite food is the honey-roasted peanut. Rico Slade will fucking kill everyone. A novel. **122 pages $8**

BB-120 **"Sinister Miniatures" Kris Saknussemm** — The definitive collection of short fiction by Kris Saknussemm, confirming that he is one of the best, most daring writers of the weird to emerge in the twenty-first century. **180 pages $11**

BB-121 **"Baby's First Book of Seriously Fucked up Shit" Robert Devereaux** — Ten stories of the strange, the gross, and the just plain fucked up from one of the most original voices in horror. **176 pages $11**

BB-122 **"The Morbidly Obese Ninja" Carlton Mellick III** — These days, if you want to run a successful company . . . you're going to need a lot of ninjas. **92 pages $8**

BB-123 **"Abortion Arcade" Cameron Pierce** — An intoxicating blend of body horror and midnight movie madness, reminiscent of early David Lynch and the splatterpunks at their most sublime. **172 pages $11**

BB-124 **"Black Hole Blues" Patrick Wensink** — A hilarious double helix of country music and physics. **196 pages $11**

BB-125 **"Barbarian Beast Bitches of the Badlands" Carlton Mellick III** — Three prequels and sequels to *Warrior Wolf Women of the Wasteland*. **284 pages $13**

BB-126 **"The Traveling Dildo Salesman" Kevin L. Donihe** — A nightmare comedy about destiny, faith, and sex toys. Also featuring Donihe's most lurid and infamous short stories: *Milky Agitation, Two-Way Santa, The Helen Mower, Living Room Zombies,* and *Revenge of the Living Masturbation Rag.* **108 pages $8**

BB-127 **"Metamorphosis Blues" Bruce Taylor** — Enter a land of love beasts, intergalactic cowboys, and rock 'n roll. A land where Sears Catalogs are doorways to insanity and men keep mysterious black boxes. Welcome to the monstrous mind of Mr. Magic Realism. **136 pages $11**

BB-128 **"The Driver's Guide to Hitting Pedestrians" Andersen Prunty** — A pocket guide to the twenty-three most painful things in life, written by the most well-adjusted man in the universe. **108 pages $8**

BB-129 **"Island of the Super People" Kevin Shamel** — Four students and their anthropology professor journey to a remote island to study its indigenous population. But this is no ordinary native culture. They're super heroes and villains with flesh costumes and outlandish abilities like self-detonation, musical eyelashes, and microwave hands. **194 pages $11**

BB-130 **"Fantastic Orgy" Carlton Mellick III** — Shark Sex, mutant cats, and strange sexually transmitted diseases. Featuring the stories: *Candy-coated, Ear Cat, Fantastic Orgy, City Hobgoblins,* and *Porno in August.* **136 pages $9**

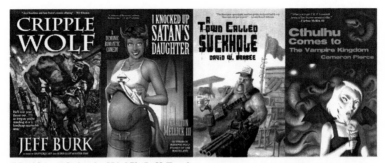

BB-131 "Cripple Wolf" Jeff Burk — Part man. Part wolf. 100% crippled. Also including *Punk Rock Nursing Home, Adrift with Space Badgers, Cook for Your Life, Just Another Day in the Park, Frosty and the Full Monty*, and *House of Cats*. **152 pages $10**

BB-132 "I Knocked Up Satan's Daughter" Carlton Mellick III — An adorable, violent, fantastical love story. A romantic comedy for the bizarro fiction reader. **152 pages $10**

BB-133 "A Town Called Suckhole" David W. Barbee — Far into the future, in the nuclear bowels of post-apocalyptic Dixie, there is a town. A town of derelict mobile homes, ancient junk, and mutant wildlife. A town of slack jawed rednecks who bask in the splendors of moonshine and mud boggin'. A town dedicated to the bloody and demented legacy of the Old South. A town called Suckhole. **144 pages $10**

BB-134 "Cthulhu Comes to the Vampire Kingdom" Cameron Pierce — What you'd get if H. P. Lovecraft wrote a Tim Burton animated film. **148 pages $11**

BB-135 "I am Genghis Cum" Violet LeVoit — From the savage Arctic tundra to post-partum mutations to your missing daughter's unmarked grave, join visionary madwoman Violet LeVoit in this non-stop eight-story onslaught of full-tilt Bizarro punk lit thrills. **124 pages $9**

BB-136 "Haunt" Laura Lee Bahr — A tripping-balls Los Angeles noir, where a mysterious dame drags you through a time-warping Bizarro hall of mirrors. **316 pages $13**

BB-137 "Amazing Stories of the Flying Spaghetti Monster" edited by Cameron Pierce — Like an all-spaghetti evening of Adult Swim, the Flying Spaghetti Monster will show you the many realms of His Noodly Appendage. Learn of those who worship him and the lives he touches in distant, mysterious ways. **228 pages $12**

BB-138 "Wave of Mutilation" Douglas Lain — A dream-pop exploration of modern architecture and the American identity, *Wave of Mutilation* is a Zen finger trap for the 21st century. **100 pages $8**

BB-139 **"Hooray for Death!" Mykle Hansen** — Famous Author Mykle Hansen draws unconventional humor from deaths tiny and large, and invites you to laugh while you can. **128 pages $10**

BB-140 **"Hypno-hog's Moonshine Monster Jamboree" Andrew Goldfarb** — Hicks, Hogs, Horror! Goldfarb is back with another strange illustrated tale of backwoods weirdness. **120 pages $9**

BB-141 **"Broken Piano For President" Patrick Wensink** — A comic masterpiece about the fast food industry, booze, and the necessity to choose happiness over work and security. **372 pages $15**

BB-142 **"Please Do Not Shoot Me in the Face" Bradley Sands** — A novel in three parts, *Please Do Not Shoot Me in the Face: A Novel*, is the story of one boy detective, the worst ninja in the world, and the great American fast food wars. It is a novel of loss, destruction, and--incredibly--genuine hope. **224 pages $12**

BB-143 **"Santa Steps Out" Robert Devereaux** — Sex, Death, and Santa Claus ... The ultimate erotic Christmas story is back. **294 pages $13**

BB-144 **"Santa Conquers the Homophobes" Robert Devereaux** — "I wish I could hope to ever attain one-thousandth the perversity of Robert Devereaux's toenail clippings." - Poppy Z. Brite **316 pages $13**

BB-145 **"We Live Inside You" Jeremy Robert Johnson** — "Jeremy Robert Johnson is dancing to a way different drummer. He loves language, he loves the edge, and he loves us people. These stories have range and style and wit. This is entertainment... and literature."- Jack Ketchum **188 pages $11**

BB-146 **"Clockwork Girl" Athena Villaverde** — Urban fairy tales for the weird girl in all of us. Like a combination of Francesca Lia Block, Charles de Lint, Kathe Koja, Tim Burton, and Hayao Miyazaki, her stories are cute, kinky, edgy, magical, provocative, and strange, full of poetic imagery and vicious sexuality. **160 pages $10**

BB-147 **"Armadillo Fists" Carlton Mellick III** — A weird-as-hell gangster story set in a world where people drive giant mechanical dinosaurs instead of cars. **168 pages $11**

BB-148 **"Gargoyle Girls of Spider Island" Cameron Pierce** — Four college seniors venture out into open waters for the tropical party weekend of a lifetime. Instead of a teenage sex fantasy, they find themselves in a nightmare of pirates, sharks, and sex-crazed monsters. **100 pages $8**

BB-149 **"The Handsome Squirm" by Carlton Mellick III** — Like Franz Kafka's *The Trial* meets an erotic body horror version of *The Blob*. **158 pages $11**

BB-150 **"Tentacle Death Trip" Jordan Krall** — It's *Death Race 2000* meets H. P. Lovecraft in bizarro author Jordan Krall's best and most suspenseful work to date. **224 pages $12**

BB-151 **"The Obese" Nick Antosca** — Like Alfred Hitchcock's *The Birds*... but with obese people. **108 pages $10**

BB-152 **"All-Monster Action!" Cody Goodfellow** — The world gave him a blank check and a demand: Create giant monsters to fight our wars. But Dr. Otaku was not satisfied with mere chaos and mass destruction.... **216 pages $12**

BB-153 **"Ugly Heaven" Carlton Mellick III** — Heaven is no longer a paradise. It was once a blissful utopia full of wonders far beyond human comprehension. But the afterlife is now in ruins. It has become an ugly, lonely wasteland populated by strange monstrous beasts, masturbating angels, and sad man-like beings wallowing in the remains of the once-great Kingdom of God. **106 pages $8**

BB-154 **"Space Walrus" Kevin L. Donihe** — Walter is supposed to go where no walrus has ever gone before, but all this astronaut walrus really wants is to take it easy on the intense training, escape the chimpanzee bullies, and win the love of his human trainer Dr. Stephanie. **160 pages $11**

CPSIA information can be obtained at www.ICGtesting.com
Printed in the USA
LVOW13s0511281213

367203LV00001B/286/P

9 781936 383542